MAGGIE SHAYNE

ANGEL'S PAIN

MIRA

MIRA®

ISBN-13: 978-0-7783-2498-0
ISBN-10:   0-7783-2498-2

ANGEL'S PAIN

MIRA and the Star Colophon are trademarks used under license and registered
in Australia, New Zealand, Philippines, United States Patent and Trademark
Office and in other countries.

www.MIRABooks.com

Printed in U.S.A.

Prologue

———

Gregor didn't need to get very close to watch his target. He was a vampire, after all, thanks to the efforts of his employers in the CIA.

They had created him, set him up in style, taught him secrets unknown even to other vamps, all to serve their own purposes. His mission, they had told him, was to become the most notorious rogue vampire imaginable. A rogue, a vampire who killed humans at will without remorse or caution, would not be long tolerated by the rest of vampire society. They would send someone after him, and Reaper would be their most likely choice. All part of the plan.

When Reaper came for him, Gregor was supposed to capture the former CIA assassin turned vampire turned vampiric hit man, and return him into the agency's tender care.

The problem was, Gregor had changed his mind, and he was pretty sure his supervisor knew it. He'd decided he liked being a rogue vampire. He liked taking whatever he wanted whenever he wanted it, without apology. He liked the wealth he was accumulating by taking everything his victims had to give. And he especially liked the power he gained when he murdered one of his own kind.

Reaper's blood would be some of the most powerful he could imagine. He had been made by Rhiannon, who had been made by Dracula himself. *Powerful*.

And now he had other reasons to want to take vengeance on the arrogant undead prick. Reaper had stolen his woman from him. He'd had no right to do that. Gregor had plucked the ungrateful little bitch from the gutters, transformed her, taken her in. And Briar had repaid him by sleeping with the enemy.

Oh, yes, the two of them had some serious pain coming.

But first things first.

If the CIA had guessed that Gregor was no longer their obedient lapdog but was, instead, working for his own gain, they would try to have him eliminated. And since the agent who'd been in charge of him, Magnarelli, had been killed during a recent scuffle with Reaper and his gang, the entire case had reverted to Derrick Dwyer, the special agent who had been Reaper's direct supervisor and who'd been running the whole operation from behind the scenes all along.

Gregor didn't trust Dwyer. But he needed to know what the bastard had in store for him. And besides, Dwyer might have a line on Reaper and Briar.

So now Gregor was lurking outside Dwyer's home in rural Connecticut. He was five hundred yards away from the small Cape Cod, concealed by shrubbery and a youngish pinon pine. From his position, he could see

Dwyer clearly as the man moved around beyond the windows. Tall, awkwardly thin, with an Ichabod Crane profile from nose to Adam's apple, Dwyer was six months from retirement. Getting Reaper back into custody and completing his work with Gregor—possibly by putting Gregor into the grave—would be his final assignment.

Gregor relaxed, surrounded by the fragrance of the pine tree's lower branches, watching by the light of a nearly full moon. He had all night, after all. Dwyer flipped on a computer, then moved out of sight. When he returned, he was carrying a coffee mug in one hand, steam spiraling from its mouth. He set it on the desk, put on a minuscule headset, and then paused, turned and stared straight at the window behind him.

Gregor ducked, even though he knew the mortal couldn't see him, much less sense him there. It was a knee-jerk reaction, and a ludicrous one. Or was it? As he watched, Dwyer got up, moved to the window and lowered the blinds.

Damn.

Rising from his position underneath the pine, Gregor lunged into rapid motion. He sped across the short distance between his vantage point and the house, stopping right beside the window. And then he peered through the slits in the blinds, and was able to see and hear everything as if he were inside looking over Dwyer's shoulder.

"Everythin's fine," Dwyer was saying softly, in his very slight Irish brogue. There was very little of it remaining, but it was clear to the perceptions of a vampire. "Nothin's goin' to hurt you. This is perfectly natural. There's nothin' to be afraid of."

Frowning, Gregor stared at the computer screen. It was dark. He could hear what sounded like rapid breaths coming through Dwyer's earpiece. Like a child getting ready to cut loose and cry its heart out.

"Open yer eyes for me. Go on. I want you to look around, see everythin' around you."

The way Dwyer spoke also suggested he was speaking to a child. Odd, Gregor thought. He'd expected Dwyer to be solely focused on one case and one case only—Reaper's. But apparently he had something entirely unrelated going on.

Or was it?

As Gregor watched, the black screen changed, as if a shade had been lifted, and he couldn't make out what it was showing at first. And then he realized what it was. It was a camera's eye view. As if the camera on the other end were walking through a long hallway, turning left and right, moving slightly up and down with the cadence of the footsteps.

"Could you go on outside, hon? Just step or two outside?"

"I'm not supposed to go out alone," a voice said, clearly and suddenly, making Gregor snap to sharper attention. It was a female voice. Adult, and yet childlike at the same time.

"You're not really *goin'* anywhere. Just step outside the door. It'll only take a minute, I promise. Then you can go right back in."

There was a bobbing motion on the screen, as if the camera were nodding. And then there was a door looming before the lens, and a slender, pale hand gripping the knob and pushing it open. The screen showed what she saw as she looked outside—a wet street, with cars rushing past now and then. Streetlights and headlights cast their glowing reflections on the slick black pavement, and no moon shone in the sky. It was not a clear warm evening, as it was here.

Dwyer watched the cars and muttered, "New York plates. Jersey. Florida. Indiana." He sighed. "Do me a favor, lass, and just turn to your left. What can you see in that direction?"

The camera's point of view changed. Something fell over the screen, and as Gregor frowned, trying to see what it was, a hand rose and brushed it away. It was a lock of hair. It had fallen over the girl's eyes, and she had moved it away. As if…as if… Gregor swore under his breath as he realized that this woman on the other end of the computer connection wasn't just *holding* the camera. Somehow, she *was* the camera.

His mind whirled with questions, possibilities, theories, but he had to bring his focus back to the matter at hand. He refocused on that computer screen and saw brick buildings, more wet roads, more streetlamps. Not a sign or a business in sight.

"Now turn the other way," Dwyer ordered.

"I don't *want* to," the girl said, but she turned. A gas station came into view. Its sign read SUNOCO. Its prices were listed. There was nothing else to help iden-tify where it might be.

"I need to go in now."

"No, no, not yet, sweetheart. You need to walk a little ways. Just to the corner, where there's a street sign or—"

"My head hurts," she whined. And then there was soft sobbing.

"It's goin' to hurt like that when you refuse to do what you're told, I'm afraid. It's just the way this works."

The girl sniffled. "What about the little boy?"

"What little boy?" Dwyer asked.

"He comes into my head, just like you do. Only I can see him. I can't see you, I can only hear you, but I can *see* him. And he needs me, and I want to help him, but I don't know who he is or where he is or *how* to help him. Is he with you?"

"No," Dwyer said. "Listen, as far as I know, that other vision, that boy, it's not real, love. It's likely comin' from a different part of your mind—your imag-ination, maybe. I'm thinkin' that's all it is. It's not real, not like me."

"He seems as real as you. He seems—he seems *more* real than you."

"Go up to the corner, Crisa, or your head's goin' to start to hurt again."

"Sometimes it hurts even when I do what you tell me."

"That can't be helped, Crisa. It's a malfunction, and one I'll fix just as soon as I see you. I promise. Go to the corner now, lass."

The camera went dark, and Gregor thought the

woman had closed her eyes. She moaned softly, and there was static and snow on the monitor, and then a shape. A human shape. A small one. It grew clearer as Gregor watched, until it took the form of a boy.

A boy he knew very, very well.

It was Matthias.

"I can't help you anymore," the girl moaned. "Briar's looking for me. Good night."

Briar!

Gregor backed away, stunned. Who the hell was this Crisa, and what kind of connection could she possibly have to Matthias? One thing was certain. She was a CIA plant. Somehow she'd been fitted with a camera and some sort of communications equipment, and inserted into Reaper's gang of do-gooders—because that was, as far as he knew, where Briar remained.

And somehow, he couldn't imagine how, she knew Matthias. She knew his *son*.

1

"There you are," Briar said, her tone flat and uninterested as she leaned against the doorjamb. The little snowflake was standing on the sidewalk, blinking in the darkness like a doe caught in a spotlight. The perpetually confused look on her face was just as irritating as it always was. "What the hell are you doing outside, Crisa?"

The girl seemed to draw her focus away from wherever the hell it had been—Neverland, probably—and pin it on Briar at long last. Her hair was in its usual style. Briar's initial opinion was that it had been combed with an eggbeater, and that was still the most accurate description. It was pale brown with blue highlights, short and unevenly cut. Her hair-care regimen seemed to be "fold in the mousse and beat until stiff peaks form." She was heavily made up tonight, which was rare. Too much eyeliner, thicker on one eye than the other, bright green eye shadow, lashes like a spider's hairy legs, straight lines of blush from her chin to her ear on each side of her face, and plum-colored lipstick. She wore a long-sleeved maroon shirt, made of the same material they made long johns from, with a lacy cream-colored camisole over the top of it—a combination that made no sense whatsoever. From the waist down, she sported a blazing orange broomstick skirt and a pair of red Converse high tops.

As she took Crisa in, Briar came damn close to laughing, and that was something she never did. Besides, even *she* wasn't heartless enough to want to kick a puppy. Okay, maybe an ordinary puppy, but not a brain-fried vampire-woman-child like Crisa.

The girl still hadn't answered her question. She was just staring, blinking those great big brown eyes as if she didn't understand Briar's language.

"Hey." Briar trotted down the three steps to the sidewalk and snapped her fingers in front of Crisa's purple lips. "Ground Control to Major Tom. You reading me?"

"Huh?"

"How come you're outside?"

"Oh. I don't know, he told me to."

Briar frowned a little harder. "*Who* told you to?"

"I don't know."

Suddenly alarmed, Briar clasped Crisa's shoulder in a grip that was as tender as it was protective, and she didn't bother to ask herself about that, or about the way her gut and fists clenched simultaneously as she sought to drop-kick whatever asshole had been messing with *her Crisa.* She sent a quick glance up and down the sidewalk, along with her senses, in search of enemies. Mortal or vampire, it could be either type. God knew their little band of white-hats had made enough of both kinds. She didn't see or sense anything, though.

"Crisa," she said, focusing again on the girl. "It's important that you tell me who told you to come outside."

"But I don't know." The girl's eyes began to dampen, and she pressed a hand to her forehead. "Please don't be mad at me, Briar."

"I'm *not*—" Briar bit her lip, realizing she'd barked the words at the girl. She softened her tone and tried to bank her frustration. "I'm not mad. Listen, you said someone told you to go outside. Was it someone in the house?"

"I don't think so. More…in here." As she said it, Crisa pressed her other hand to her head, cupping it between them. "God, it hurts."

"Your head hurts?"

Crisa nodded, eyes closed.

"So it was a voice in your head that told you to come outside?"

"Yes. A man's voice."

Someone communicating with her, mentally, Briar thought. It had to be a vampire. Few mortals could manage telepathy with any real effectiveness.

"Did he say anything else to you, Crisa? Did he ask you to *do* anything else?"

Crisa nodded, lowering her hands to her sides, opening her eyes. "He wanted me to walk to the corner and look around. But then the boy came, and I got…distracted."

"A boy came?"

Her nod was slow, her gaze turning inward. "He comes all the time," she whispered, almost to herself.

"In the real world, Crisa, or is he in your head, too?"

"In my head. But not like the man. I can see the boy.

I can feel him. He's more like a dream." She squeezed her eyes tighter. "It hurts, Briar!"

"Okay. Okay, come on, let's get you inside."

"You're not mad?"

"No, you nutcase. Why would I be mad? It's not your fault you've got a party going on in that head of yours, is it?"

"N-no."

"I'll bet Roxy can help you out with that headache, if you want. She and Ilyana are all into all that hocus-pocus shit. Healing with their hands. I imagine it makes 'em feel like a little bit more than plain old mortals."

"They're not plain. They're Chosen."

"Still, a mortal's a mortal's a mortal, right?"

Crisa nodded, the movement choppy as they moved down the hall. "Will Reaper be mad?"

"No one's mad, okay?" Briar sought to reassure her, and then decided to add a little enlightenment to boot. Hell, it couldn't hurt. "Besides," she said, "what do you care if anyone *is* mad at you? Toughen up, Crisa. If someone gives you crap, you give it right back and then some. Understand?"

Crisa looked at her and smiled just a little. "Yeah. I'll give it right back."

"Damn straight you will. You've got a little bit of my blood in your veins, after all. You go wimping out, it's going to pack up and move."

Briar opened the door at the end of the hall and, still holding Crisa's arm, led the other woman into the apartment. The building was abandoned but was still basi-

cally habitable. The bunch of them, Reaper and his misfit gang of fledgling vamps, had headed north from
Mexico, traveling cautiously, taking their time. Princess Topaz had volunteered her Emerald Isle mansion
for them to use as a temporary base while they planned
their next moves in the ongoing hunt for Gregor, the
murderous rogue, and his gang. But Reaper wanted to
take his sweet time getting there, just to be sure the
CIA bastards who'd been jonesing for him were no
longer following. Sure, the two agents who'd been on
his ass most recently were crowbait by now. But there
were others out there, watching.

This run-down hovel was in Atlanta, and it reminded
Briar, with a little jab, of times in her life she would
much rather forget. When she'd lived on the streets,
places like this had been home to her. Yeah. Home,
sweet home.

The others were just coming to life in various parts
of the apartment. Sundown had been recent. They'd
only just risen and begun gathering up their things to
continue the journey north. Most of them, anyway, Briar
saw, noticing that Jack and Topaz were nowhere in evidence. They were probably going at it like a pair of
horny rabbits. Again.

And Topaz's movie-star legend of a mother, Mirabella, was likely still lying in bed, in typical Hollywood
starlet fashion. Just because she automatically woke at
sunset, like every other vampire, didn't mean she felt
any need to get her ass up and moving.

Vixen and Seth stood close to one another, shoving

clothes into a backpack, rubbing and touching often, their eyes saying way more than Briar wanted or needed to hear from either of them. Sickening.

"Roxy," Briar said, averting her thoughts from the others to the matter at hand. "Crisa has a pretty severe headache. You think you and Ilyana can work some of that shit you do on her and fix her up?"

"That *shit* we do is Reiki," Roxy replied. She whirled to face Briar as she spoke, and it created a great effect with the scarlet patterned kaftan she wore. It swirled like a cloak, and her wild red curls moved just as effectively. "It's *sacred* to us both."

There was very little Briar enjoyed more than baiting Roxy. Unless it was scaring the hell out of Ilyana. "Yeah, yeah," she said. "To you mortals, *everything* is sacred. All that spiritual garbage must make a nice crutch for people destined for the grave."

"We're *all* destined for the grave in the end," the ageless redhead told her. "Vampires like you, the Chosen like Ilyana and me, whether we eventually choose to be transformed or not, and ordinary humans like the rest of the world. There's no such thing as immortality. Not really. And you're fooling yourself if you think there is."

"Yeah, and I'll be fooling myself long after you're dust."

"Bitch," Roxy muttered.

"Whore," Briar replied.

Ilyana followed the exchange, looking slightly nervous, while Crisa seemed downright frightened by it.

Reaper, the arrogant bastard, lounged on the wooden crate he was using as a chair, tipped back against the wall, looking mildly amused.

Roxy sent Briar one last dirty look, then took Crisa's hand and softened her expression. "Come on, Crisa. You can lie down on that old couch in the next room and we'll try some Reiki on you, okay?"

Crisa nodded, and Ilyana beat them both into the adjoining room.

Alone with Seth, Vixen and Reaper, Briar waited until the door to the next room closed. "I found Crisa outside, kind of disoriented. Told me some voice in her head told her to go out there and take a look around."

Reaper's crate came down, the front of it hitting the floor with a thud. "Gregor?"

"That wouldn't make sense," Seth said. "Gregor doesn't even know Crisa exists, much less that she's with us."

"As far as we know, that is," Vixen said softly. "He could have found out."

"It could also be some other vampire, hell-bent on destroying us," Reaper pointed out. "It's not like we haven't pissed off a few along the way." He glanced at Briar. "You know her best."

"I don't know her any better than the rest of you," she denied. It was automatic, and it was a lie.

"You shared blood with her, saved her life. You know that creates a powerful bond, a psychic link."

"I know." She averted her eyes. His were too dark, too knowing, and entirely too full of the sex they'd once had. Once. God, you'd think it had been a three-year affair the way it had affected him. It hadn't even fazed *her*.

Briar sighed and drew her attention back to the subject at hand. "But I still don't know what's going on with her. I don't even know if this is really mental communication from someone outside her. I think it might just be…you know, voices in her head." She made a twirling motion at her ear with a forefinger.

Reaper rose from his chair. "What makes you suspect that?"

She shrugged. "The fact that she's also seeing some boy she says feels more like a dream to her. The fact that she's got a headache the size of Jupiter most of the time. The fact that she was a few cookies short of a full jar from the first day we set eyes on her. She's *nuts*, Reaper. We already know that."

He was studying her. So was Vixen, far more closely than was comfortable. Her little head tipped to one side and then the other, long copper hair falling over one shoulder, and her nose crinkled up just slightly.

"What?" Briar demanded.

"You…you have a headache, too," Vixen said.

Briar rolled her eyes. "Yeah, I have a pile of headaches. Three out here asking stupid questions, one sleeping in, two banging their brains out, a pair performing hocus-pocus in the next room, and one choo-choo train whose little red caboose has gone chugging around the bend."

Vixen smiled, then laughed softly. "That's funny. I didn't know you could be funny."

"I *wasn't* being funny."

"You're feeling her pain, aren't you?" Reaper asked.

Briar shrugged. "Either that or I've got a simple headache all my own. The easiest solution is usually the right one, Reaper."

"You could let Roxy and Ilyana work on you next," Seth suggested.

"Right. I'm going to lie in a bed and let two mortal females put their hands on me. Not in this lifetime, pal."

"It was just a thought."

"Thanks. I prefer to suffer. A slight headache or untold agonies. Either way."

After she said it, she glanced toward the closed door beyond which the two women were working on Crisa. Then she noticed Reaper noticing *her,* and she averted her eyes.

"You're worried about her," he accused.

"Yeah, right. And I'm also taking up a collection to save the whales. You wanna contribute?" She rolled her eyes and left the room, heading into the empty bedroom where she'd spent the night.

Sinking to the floor and drawing up her knees, she bent her head and rubbed her temples. She closed her eyes and tried to relax away the pain in her head. But she couldn't relax it away or massage it away, or even will it away, because it wasn't her pain.

It was Crisa's. So all she could do was wait.

Fortunately for her, the two most irritating mortals on the planet were extremely gifted healers. That shit they did, they did very well, though she would die before she would acknowledge it to either of them. Roxy was already far too cocky, while Ilyana was petrified of her, and Briar preferred to keep it that way.

Still, she thanked them silently when the pain in her head began to ease and finally faded to almost nothing.

She rested only for a few moments, then got up when someone tapped on her door. She opened it to see Jack, with his dirty blond hair that was always a little too long and his slightly scruffy whiskers, making him seem like a rebel, wearing the satisfied smirk of a man who'd had far better sex than he deserved.

"We're getting ready to move out, Bri. You got your stuff together?"

"Two minutes," she told him.

He nodded, his eyes doing a quick survey of her face. "Your headache better?"

"Gone," she told him.

"I figured. Crisa's is, too."

She frowned at him.

"Reaper filled us in. I'll help you keep an eye on her. Don't worry."

"I wasn't. And I don't need your help 'keeping an eye' on Crisa, because it's not my job to keep an eye on Crisa. Jeez, who appointed me the keeper of the nuthouse?"

He shrugged. "Need help packing?"

"Go jump your freaking princess again or something, and stop pestering me, will you?"

"Okay." He winked and left the room.

Why the hell, she wondered, was everyone so determined to see things in her that didn't exist? She wasn't *worried* about Crisa. She didn't give a *shit* about Crisa—

or anyone else, for that matter. This pile of do-gooders just couldn't seem to accept that about her. They didn't understand it, sought to project their own moral bullshit onto her. But she didn't believe in it. Never had.

She was out only for herself, her own best interests and the fulfillment of her own needs. And right now those needs included only two things. The basic need to devour living blood in order to survive, and her sole purpose for wanting to.

She had to kill Gregor for what he'd done to her.

Revenge was the only reason she continued waking up each night. It was her life force. And once it was done, well, hell, she would probably be done, too, despite her tough talk to Roxy about being a true immortal.

There really wasn't, as far as she could see, much of a point to it, after all.

2

"I understand you've been looking for me," Gregor said, speaking as if he were perfectly calm. As if every cell in his body wasn't coiled tight at the notion of what he was about to do.

"Yes, that's true," Special Agent Dwyer confirmed. He kept his hands thrust into the deep pockets of his raincoat, shoulders hunched, collar turned up against the icy drizzle that pelted them both where they stood in a rest area off a major highway in the middle of nowhere.

3:00 a.m. Gregor was at the peak of his wakefulness. Dwyer was having trouble keeping his eyes open, despite the fact that he reeked of the coffee he'd been guzzling.

"So?" Gregor asked.

"Look, I appreciate you comin' in, Gregory."

"Gregor," he snapped. "Nobody calls me Gregory. Not anymore."

"Sorry." Dwyer had jerked backward a bit at the barked correction, and Gregor was glad to see it. It wouldn't do to have this man thinking of him as just another mortal operative under his command. He wasn't mortal. And he wasn't just another anything. He was a vampire.

He was a god.

"Sorry," Dwyer repeated. "Still, it's good you decided to come in for this meetin'. It'll go a long way toward convincin' the powers that be of your sincerity."

"Fuck the powers that be."

Dwyer went silent, his head coming up slowly and his eyes seeming to reflect uncertainty for the first time during their clandestine meeting.

"I know full well there's a burn order on me, Dwyer. Frankly, I'm surprised you haven't tried to take me out already."

"No one's goin' to kill you, Gregor."

"You're right about that much, at least." Gregor lifted a hand, snapped his fingers. Immediately, the drones came lumbering out of the wooded area behind the rest stop.

They were not pretty, and they couldn't even begin to pass for human. Their size, their lumbering gait, the blank, not-quite-right look in their eyes. They were a step evolved from the popular version of Frankenstein's monster, but only in that their heads were not visibly stitched onto their necks, nor did they have bolts sticking out on either side of their throats.

Aside from those minor differences, though, they were pretty close.

A woman came out of the restroom, saw the drones lumbering across the slightly sloped lawn toward her, a dozen of them, and ran shrieking for her car. Change jangled like hailstones onto the pavement as a stunned man stared, his hand seeming to lose its ability to grasp the coins. A car that had veered into the parking area suddenly accelerated, nearly running other vehicles off the road as it sped back to the highway.

The mayhem caused by the appearance of the monsters lasted only seconds. And yeah, Gregor thought, maybe the witnesses didn't really think of them as monsters. But there was no question something about them wasn't quite right, no question that there were a lot of them, no question that they were big, oversized, powerful and intent on...something. That was enough.

And he liked to think someone might have had the word *monster* whisper through their mind.

"What is this?" Dwyer asked. He was already pulling a gun from inside one of those deep pockets, no doubt the one he'd intended to shoot Gregor with, and backing toward his car. The rest of the place was now deserted.

"This is what I believe you would call an ambush, Dwyer. But don't worry. I'm not going to have them kill you." He smiled slowly. "Not right away, at least." And then he ducked behind the concrete building to watch as the drones closed in.

Dwyer lifted the gun, fired off a round, and one of the drones dropped in an oversized heap on the ground and lay there, moaning and bleeding and too damned dumb to do anything about it. Nor did any of his cohorts rush to his aid. They had one purpose. Obey their master.

They kept coming. Dwyer kept shooting. A few fell, but the rest came on faster. Dwyer grappled for his car door, yanking it open, stumbling backward into the car while still firing.

A wounded drone grabbed at his ankle. He fired

again and tugged himself free, yanking his leg inside, slamming the car door, hitting the locks.

He thought he was free as he struggled to fit the key into the ignition.

The idiot.

A drone tore the driver's door from the car and sent it sailing through the air. Another gripped Dwyer by his gun-wielding arm, squeezing his wrist until the pistol dropped uselessly to the ground. Then he picked Dwyer up easily as the terrified man struggled.

Why did he fight, Gregor wondered, when he knew he was beaten?

One paw to the side of his head and Dwyer was fighting no more. Gregor stepped out from behind the concrete bunker that housed the public toilets and tasted victory.

"Tie him up and put him in the Jeep," he commanded. "I'll take him from here."

The lug with Dwyer over his shoulder gave a mind-less nod and carried the agent to the Jeep Wrangler, tossing him into the back like so much dirty laundry, then binding his wrists and ankles.

Gregor looked around the parking lot. There were three dead drones, a handful more wounded. There was too much here to clean up. Bullets, casings, blood. "Leave the dead," he said. "Leave it all, but tend to your wounded. Stanch the bleeding the way I've shown you. Remember not to bind the wounds too tightly," he said, recalling how one injured drone had lost an arm the first time he'd tried to show them basic vampire first aid.

"Once you've stopped the bleeding, help them back to the mansion. Understood?"

They nodded dumbly, and the healthy ones began lumbering toward the bleeding ones, tearing their shirts to make tourniquets on the way.

"Be back before dawn," he added, because that was how dumb they were. You had to tell them specifically what to do. They couldn't think or reason for themselves.

It was a lot of trouble to make more, though. And getting candidates from the CIA's stockpile of potentials would be impossible now.

He climbed behind the wheel of his Jeep, started the engine and glanced back in the rearview mirror at his unconscious former employer. "You're going to tell me about this spy you've planted in Reaper's gang, my friend. You're going to show me how to communicate with her, tell me exactly how it works and what you've learned."

To his surprise, Dwyer sat up slowly, rubbing his head with his bound hands. "I'm not tellin' you anythin'."

"Oh, hell, of course you are, given time." He lifted a dart gun, loaded with a human-sized dose of his favorite tranquilizer, just in case the spook tried anything. "I've become very adept at torture, Derrick."

"So I've heard."

"And I know you were Rivera's immediate supervisor. I know you were the one who recruited him in the first place, and I know you've fought your organization every step of the way on his behalf ever since."

Dwyer averted his eyes. "You don't know shit."

"Yeah, I do. I've seen the files. You argued against

the brainwashing...excuse me—*programming*—from the start. You tried to cover up the fact that he'd become a vampire when you first found out. You tried to talk them out of trying to retake him, and you were vehemently against the plan to use me to do it. You were against all of it. On his side, all along."

The older man was shaking his head slowly from side to side, but his denials wouldn't convince Gregor of anything, and he had to know it. Gregor *knew*. This bastard had been secretly advocating on Reaper's behalf from the beginning.

"You've been biased all along. What I don't know is why."

"You're insane."

"Perhaps. But you're Reaper's friend. Whether he knows it or not, you're his only friend in the agency. Aren't you, Derrick?"

"I'm no one's friend. I'm in charge of gettin' him back, and then I retire. Period."

"Yeah. Right. You came out tonight to kill me."

"I came to talk."

"Bull. So tell me, Dwyer, what's the point of having a plant in Reaper's little gang if you don't intend to bring him in? What other reason could you possibly have for wanting to keep tabs on him?"

"None."

"You know I don't believe you."

"I know."

"And you know I'll find out."

"Not from me, you won't."

Sighing, Gregor pulled the Jeep up to the towering arched wrought-iron gates of what had once been known as the Marquand Estate. His, now.

As Gregor waited for the aging gates to open, thanks to the electronics he'd repaired, Dwyer stared at them through the rain spattered windshield, then beyond the tall leafless trees that lined the drive to the castle-like mansion beyond them and the cliffs beyond the mansion.

"For the love of God, this is—"

"Yes. The former home of Eric Marquand. He abandoned it once the DPI learned of its existence, knowing he'd never know peace here again. It fell into government hands. The CIA lost interest in surveilling it but wouldn't allow it to be sold for a long time. And then they did. I bought it for back taxes a few months ago. Thought it would be…I don't know, nostalgic to have one of the truly ancient ones' former homes. A place where vampires battled DPI agents. A place where Rhiannon and Roland de Courtemanche and Eric himself once walked. His laboratories are still in the basement, you know."

"No."

"No one would expect a new generation of the Undead to take up residence in a place the CIA knows all about. But since they've stopped paying it any attention, what place could be better?"

Dwyer said nothing. Gregor drove through the gates when they finally opened widely enough, then waited to see to it that they closed again before driving on over the bumpy, poorly tended driveway to the mansion itself. He loved the grandeur of the place. Three stories, all made of rough-hewn stone blocks, each one too large for three ordinary men to lift. The place was magnificent. More so with the modifications he'd been working on.

He stopped right in front, opened the hatch in the rear of the Jeep and gripped Derrick Dwyer by his bound wrists, tugging him out. Dwyer didn't fight much. The lump on the side of his head, and the blood on his face and neck, told Gregor why. The man was hurting, possibly dizzy as well, and no doubt weak. He was also, Gregor thought, cagey, sharp, intelligent and probably biding his time and making an escape plan.

He dragged his captive up the stairs to the front door and flung it open.

He strode inside, tugging Dwyer behind him by the dangling end of the rope that bound his hands. The older man had no choice but to follow, feet dragging, stumbling often. Perhaps it was for real, or maybe it was an act designed to lull Gregor into complacency, into taking his weakness for granted and making a fatal mistake.

As they entered the hall, the young boy got up from his spot on the floor in front of the fireplace, his toy soldiers—the only playthings he was permitted—scattering out of formation as he rose.

He stood still, staring, wide brown eyes unblinking, thickly fringed and nearly void of any innocence they might once have possessed.

"Well?" Gregor demanded.

The boy swallowed visibly, his throat swelling as he did. "Hello, Father. Welcome back. Was your evening a good one?"

"That's better. And yes, actually, my evening was quite a pleasant one. Get your ass to my office and fetch my keys. Can't you see I've brought a prisoner that needs locking up?"

"Yes, sir!"

The boy spun on his heel and raced out of the room as fast as he could manage to move. Gregor chuckled softly under his breath, careful not to let Matthias hear it. Better to keep the child afraid of him. He would obey far more easily that way.

"You have a child?" Derrick's voice was a bare whisper, and yet loud enough to convey the horror he clearly felt at the notion.

"Obviously." Gregor tugged the rope and moved through the great room, onward down a hallway to a cellar door.

"But…where is his mother?"

"Dead. To me. To the rest of the world, too, if she ever dares come near Matthias again." Then he smiled slowly, refocusing himself on the task at hand. "But that's not your concern, is it? Your attention should be solely on deciding how much torture you intend to suffer before you tell me what I need to know."

"I don't know anythin' that can help you."

"Mmm, but you do. You know how to communicate with this *Crisa*. You know how to use her to keep tabs on Reaper. You know how to bring her in, I imagine. I want to know all that. And I want to know more. I want to know *how* you managed it. Does she work for you?"

"She doesn't even know who I am. She's an innocent, Gregor."

"I really don't care." They'd moved down a flight of stairs into what had once been a basement laboratory. Much of the equipment was still in place. Scales and burners and bottles and jars, microscopes and other gadgets Gregor couldn't begin to identify. He opened a door off one side of the lab. The room might have been an office once. An aging desk stood along one wall, and empty file cabinets lined another. There was a chair, its leather upholstery split in several spots. Other than that, the place was empty. But the room was windowless, and its door had a good lock. It was the perfect place to store a captive.

Gregor shoved his prisoner into the chair, then proceeded to go through the man's pockets, tearing his clothes in the process. Eventually he located a set of keys and, smiling, pocketed them.

Dwyer's eyes widened. "There's nothin' in my house that you can use!"

"No? Well, I tend to disagree, given what I so recently observed through your windows. But I'll judge for myself once I've gone through the place. Tell me, are you expecting your wife home soon?"

"I—I don't— We're divorced."

"Convenient." He smiled slowly, then, unable to contain it, chuckled deep in his chest.

"What…what's so damn funny?"

Gregor met the frustrated, frightened man's eyes. "I was just thinking how many people would kill to be in my position. My former employer becomes my captive. And I can do anything I want to him."

"The CIA was good to you, Gregor. We never gave you any reason to—"

"The CIA *used* me. Just like you used Reaper. He was content to escape and move on. But I'm smarter than he is, Derrick. I'm turning the tables. I'm going to use *you* now, to get exactly what I want. And I'm going to enjoy the process."

"You're a bastard."

"Yes, I know. Sadly, we've wasted too much time to allow me to go visit your home tonight. Tomorrow will have to be early enough. I'll have one of the drones toss some food and water in to you to get you through the day. I want you alive and kicking for this, after all."

He turned, and stepped to the door. "See you tonight, Derrick. I can't tell you how much I'm looking forward to it."

Then, stepping into the hall, he closed and locked the door, leaving the man to his thoughts, which would do, Gregor estimated, at least half his job for him.

The caravan of vehicles arrived at Topaz's mansion-like home on Emerald Isle, North Carolina, in the dead of the night, which was, Reaper speculated, for the best. Not as many tourists out and about to get a gander at "Shirley," the bright yellow, customized conversion van that Roxy insisted was nearly human. It would draw a lot of unnecessary attention.

Topaz's home sat on a rise near the far end of the long, narrow island, surrounded by scrubby-looking bushes and trees. From the main road, no one could even see the ten-foot fence that bordered the place just within the boundary of flora.

The lead vehicle in their little vampiric parade was Jack's Carrera, sleek and black and dangerous-looking, but not terribly out of place. Topaz rode with Jack, naturally. The two rarely seemed to be more than a foot apart these days. Jack used to be a hard-ass, like her, Briar thought. Now he'd gone soft. Fallen in love. Fallen for a fairy tale was more like it, in her considered opinion.

Roxy drove the canary-yellow van, which managed to keep up, in spite of its bulk. Ilyana sat in the passenger side, Reaper and Briar in the middle set of seats. In the rear seat, Mirabella rode alongside Crisa, and she'd been gently massaging the childlike vampiress's neck for the last several miles. Bringing up the rear were Seth and Vixen, in the Shelby Mustang Seth had liberated from its former owner. He insisted it would have been presumed destroyed in the fire that had consumed the celebrity's home, and anyway, it had been covered by insurance. Though Briar doubted any amount of money could compensate for a classic like that one.

Seth had potential, she thought. Or at least a backbone. And that was worth a lot.

As the gates swung open to admit them and the van

trundled through, Mirabella caught her breath. "This is where my daughter lives?"

"Yeah," Roxy said from the driver's seat. "She's done pretty well with that money you left her, hasn't she?"

"She's done extremely well," Mirabella said. "This is stunning."

"It is," Reaper said, even as he frowned at Briar, probably due to the smirk of distaste crossing her face. She didn't think much of the rich and famous. She'd grown up hard, homeless, on the streets. There probably weren't too many like her who *could* think well of those who seemed to have it all, especially those who'd never had to work for it.

Still, she was aware that Topaz had suffered for her wealth. Not as much as Briar had suffered for her lack of it, though.

As they pulled to a stop near the doors, the gates closing slowly behind them, Briar muttered, "Why the hell does one person *need* all this? Where does she even get off having so much?"

Crisa piped up. "I think it's pretty."

"Yeah, it's pretty, all right. Pretty freaking ridiculous."

"Oh, I don't know," Roxy said. "You can't really judge a person by what they have. No more than you can judge someone for not having anything at all. It's who they are that counts, don't you think?"

"I wasn't judging her. I don't care enough to judge anyone. I just think it's stupid for one person to take up so much space, that's all."

Roxy shut off the engine, opened her door and got out. Then she stretched the kinks out of her back and shoulders, as the others disembarked and headed for the front door.

Topaz hesitated near the front door, her key ring in her hand.

"What's wrong?" Jack asked, searching her face, worry clouding his own.

Briar rolled her eyes. *Here we go again with the sappy, emotional bullshit.*

Topaz lowered her gaze. "I—I haven't been happy in this place. Not for a long time. Walking in here…it feels like walking back into heartache and tears and—"

Jack pulled her gently into his arms. "No more of those for you, princess. Not if I have anything to say about it. And I kind of think I do."

When he released her and she lifted her head again, there were tears on her cheeks, but she was smiling through them. "I'm being silly. I have everything I've ever wanted now. Right here, holding me."

He smiled back at her, but there was regret in his eyes. Jack had been a bastard to her in the past, and Briar knew that now he wished he could undo the hurt he'd caused the woman he—gag—loved. He shouldn't. He'd been being honest. He was who he was. At least, he used to be. Briar wasn't sure who the hell he was anymore.

"Everything happens for a reason," Roxy said. "You two wouldn't be as good together now if you hadn't been through what you have."

"Maybe not," Topaz whispered.

"Always the philosopher, aren't you, Roxy?" Seth asked.

Roxy sent him a wink, and everyone smiled in a sickening, whimsical way that made Briar think vomiting might be in order.

"Are we going inside or what? Castle Kissy-face has been sitting empty long enough, and I'm craving a little me time." She shot Topaz a look. "I'm assuming I get my own room."

"A whole suite, if you want," Topaz said. "The more space we put between you and the rest of us, the better." She held Briar's eyes as she said it, and there was a hint of humor in her eyes. "Grumpy bitch," she added.

Before she could stop it, a smile split Briar's face, and she wished someone would slap it off. She bit it into submission, but it was too late. They'd all seen. Damn.

"I don't want you to be by yourself, Briar," Crisa said. "I want to be with you."

Briar closed her eyes and thought, *Jeez, Topaz, I need a break from her.*

I hear you, Topaz replied, speaking mentally to her alone. *There's a two-bedroom suite in the west wing. Would that work for you, do you think?*

I don't think I could pry her any farther from me than that with a crowbar. Do you?

Doubtful. I can't figure out what the hell she sees in you, though.

Fuck you, Topaz.

You're welcome.

She damn near smiled again, but she averted her face this time, just in case it showed in her eyes.

Topaz inserted the key and opened the great big, ornate, expensive doors. A vaulted foyer spread out before them like something out of a fairy tale, and they all trooped inside.

"You all want the grand tour now or later?" Topaz asked.

"I want my room and a stein of warm blood," Briar said.

"Fine, we'll do that. The rest of you, feel free to wander around. Pick out a bedroom, if you want. They're all vampire-friendly."

"How, with all these windows?" Vixen asked. She wore an excited look as her gaze took in one thing after another. The furniture, the chandelier, the fireplace, the paintings, the sculptures, the marble floor.

"They automatically darken when the sun comes up," Topaz explained. "The tint is so dark it's opaque. Perfect for our kind."

"Every window in the place?" Vixen asked.

Topaz nodded, and Briar said, "Must have cost a bundle." Then she sent Topaz a look. "My room?"

"This way. Come on, Crisa, you can come, too."

Crisa looked at Briar as if seeking permission. Briar nodded at her. "Yeah, come on. Whatever."

The girl's smile was bright, and the three of them moved through the foyer and started up the stairs.

But on the third step, Crisa screamed. It startled Briar so much that she damn near jumped out of her skin, but then, even as she turned to the nutcase, she felt it: a tearing, ripping pain deep inside her head. She grimaced against it. Crisa pressed her hands to her head, sobbing softly as she sank to her knees.

And then Reaper was there, right beside them, followed immediately by Roxy.

"Crisa? Crisa, what's wrong?" Reaper demanded.

Briar held herself erect on the step just above them. "It's the headache again," she said, and she hoped her voice didn't sound strained. "It's hitting harder this time."

"We'd best get her into a bed, Reaper," Roxy said.

Reaper bent and scooped up the trembling, sobbing girl.

"This way," Topaz called, trotting up the stairs more quickly now. Reaper caught up to her, while Briar and Roxy followed right behind.

Roxy put her hand on Briar's arm. "You too, yes?"

"I'm fine."

"The hell you are. You're holding your jaw so tight, I'm surprised you haven't broken a tooth."

"If I did, it would grow back during the day sleep."

"You're in pain, Briar." Roxy frowned, as they made their way up the stairs, more slowly than the trio ahead of them. "It's not part of her…condition, then, is it?"

"What do you mean?" Briar asked.

"Whatever is happening to Crisa…is happening to you, too."

Briar averted her eyes. "Maybe. I don't know."

"I think it is. And I think this bond between you two is more powerful than just what would come from sharing blood. I think it's…deeper."

"Oh, hell, what are we, sisters separated at birth, then?"

"You know what I'm saying, Briar. For every vampire there's one of the Chosen with whom the natural bond is even more potent. I think Crisa is that one for you, even though she's already one of us. I think she's your...*chosen*. Chosen."

Briar grimaced. "Insightful as all hell, Roxy, but otherwise, a useless piece of speculation."

"Maybe it'll be worth something later. For now, I'm going to do some Reiki on you, see if I can get this to ease up a bit."

Briar shook her head. "Work on her first."

They'd reached the top of the endless staircase and were heading down a hallway lined with doors now, but Roxy stopped and stared at Briar.

"What?" Briar snapped.

"You care about her. You do. You *care* about her!"

"Oh, Jeez, don't go breaking out the violins there, Pollyanna. If I'm feeling her pain, then the best way to end it for me is to end it for her. I'm thinking about me. Number one. Always."

"Oh," Roxy said softly. She started walking again, but this time, she did so with one hand touching Briar's upper arm. Not holding it, just touching it. "Thank you for clearing that up. I'd hate to go thinking you had a heart."

"God forbid," Briar told her, and she sidestepped enough to break physical contact with the woman. Then she hurried the rest of the way along the hall, ignoring her own pain, and ignoring, too, the high-gleam shine of the rich hardwood on the floor, which matched that of the stairs and the curving banister. She ignored the art on the walls, probably original, in the Renaissance style she might have chosen herself. She ignored the elaborate stands, and the vases and sculptures they bore, each one echoing some image in the nearest painting, like the sculpted raven on a stand in front of *The Magic Circle,* by Waterhouse.

She grudgingly acknowledged that she approved of the princess's taste, then swept through an open door and into the lap of luxury. Not that the rest of the house was anything less than luxurious, but the idea that she would be staying right here sort of rattled Briar.

Deep carpeting lined the place; it was the color of French cream, as were the sheer curtains that hung in front of the tall, narrow windows. The room held an elegant love seat, a matching overstuffed chair and ottoman and an oak rocker. Every piece had forest-green accents: the throw pillows, the cushions lining the rocker, the tiebacks on the curtains, the throw rugs on the carpet. There was a gas fireplace, its wooden mantel sporting two oil lamps that looked like antiques, and a portrait hung on the wall above.

It was of Topaz's mother, the actress, Mirabella DuFrane. Though with her, no last name had been necessary. She'd been the stuff of legend before she'd vanished, leaving the world and her daughter to believe she'd been murdered. But she'd only become undead.

A soft, pain-filled moan drew Briar's attention to the left, where another open door showed her a bedroom. Her body jerked her into reflexive motion without warning when she spotted Crisa in the bed, hands pressed to either side of her head, tears streaming down her face. Briar was crowding up to the bedside before she could stop herself, shoulder to shoulder with Reaper, who was leaning over the girl.

"I wish I knew what the hell to do for her," he said, and he sounded apologetic. "It's not like we can take her to a doctor."

"Of course we can."

Reaper frowned at her, and from across the bed, Topaz did the same. Roxy paid no attention. She was squeezing in between Topaz and the head of the bed, bending close and laying her hands gently over Crisa's, on her temples.

"Well, come on," Briar said. "Don't tell me that out of all the vampires in the world there's not one who was a doctor in life."

Reaper held her gaze, and she sensed he hated like hell to burst her bubble. "None that I've heard of. The closest we have is the scientist Eric Marquand."

"Then get him here," she snapped.

Reaper's eyes were probing hers, and she realized she was acting way too emotionally invested in the loon.

"You're hurting, too, aren't you?" Reaper asked.

She lowered her head quickly, hiding her eyes and whatever they might reveal from his probing gaze. "If I wasn't, do you think I'd be demanding you bring vampire Einstein to me?"

He didn't answer, so she glanced upward to see that he was waiting for her to meet his eyes. When she finally did, he said, "Yes, Briar. I'm starting to think maybe you would."

"Then you're deluding yourself, Reaper."

"Am I?"

Crisa's movements—and Briar's own throbbing pain—stopped all at once, and her moaning stopped, too. Briar snapped her attention back to the girl, fearing, for one heart-jolting moment, that she'd died. But she hadn't. She was lying there with her eyes wide open, staring at some invisible spot halfway between her and the ceiling.

Not giving a shit what sort of noble motives her bleeding-heart peers would attach to the act, Briar leaned closer but didn't touch. "It's better now, isn't it?"

"I feel him. He's calling to me now," Crisa said.

Briar frowned at her, and Crisa's eyes suddenly locked on to hers. Just as quickly, her small hand closed around Briar's wrist and drew her down until she was sitting on the edge of the bed.

"He needs me."

"Who does?"

"The boy. The little boy." She frowned at Briar. "Don't you see him?"

"I don't—"

And then she stopped, because she *did* see him. Just slightly, and maybe it was her imagination, or maybe it was something else. Frowning, she tried to attune her senses to Crisa's, and she shifted until her hand met the girl's and clasped it, fingers interlacing, to help her solidify the mental link.

The vision didn't solidify, though. It was just a hazy shape. Could have been a boy. Could have been a bulldog. She was damned if she knew.

Crisa sat up. "I have to go to him."

"You're in no condition to go anywhere right now," Reaper told her.

She shot him a defiant look, then turned it into a pleading one and aimed it at Briar. "I have to."

"Not alone, though, right?" Briar said. "You're gonna want us to go, too. If this boy of yours needs you so bad, he must be in some kind of trouble, right?"

"I don't know."

Topaz patted the girl's shoulder. "I think she's right, Crisa. If this boy is in trouble, then we need to help him. But we need to make sure you're okay first. You won't be able to help him if you're in debilitating pain."

"It hurts," she whispered. "But I have to go." She brushed Roxy's hands away from her head as if they were bits of cobweb stuck in her hair and swung her legs to the side.

"Crisa, you're not going anywhere," Briar said, and if she sounded impatient, she thought, all the better. Maybe the odd squad would stop thinking she'd turned soft. "Lie the fuck down. *Now*."

Crisa didn't even look at her, which shocked Briar to hell and gone. Instead, the cracker-factory dropped her feet to the floor, sliding her backside to the very edge of the mattress; then, bracing her hands on either side of her, she started to get up, edging between Reaper and Briar.

Briar turned to face her, clapped her hands onto Crisa's shoulders and pushed until the girl's ass hit the mattress again. "I *said* lie down," Briar repeated. "You're not well."

"The headache's gone."

So what was the vague, unfocused look in her eyes? Briar wondered. And why wasn't *she* feeling Crisa's urge to run to the imaginary blur in her head, when she was feeling everything else the girl did?

"The headache will come back, and when it hits you, it hits me, too. I'd like to get it fixed, if you don't mind, before you go taking off on me, okay?"

"You can't tell me what to do!" Crisa shouted, clenching her fists and shaking them in frustration as she did.

That stunned Briar so much that she took a step backward in reaction and just stared, gaping, dumbfounded.

Reaper pressed his hand to her back as if in a show of support, right between her shoulder blades. And she resented it.

"Crisa," Roxy interrupted, probably in an effort to defuse the situation. "Did you get these headaches before?"

"Before when?"

"Before you came to us. Before Reynold died."

Crisa lowered her head, closed her eyes, but not before they welled with glistening tears. "No. Never. Rey-Rey would've known what to do. He would have made it better."

"Did he ever have to make anything else better for you, Crisa?" Roxy pressed on. "Were you ever sick or in pain or—"

"Rey-Rey says vampires don't get sick."

"I see."

"I cut myself once. I had a glass, and I was running. I fell and it cut my hand and it bled really bad. But Rey-Rey fixed it."

"Yeah. But no headaches?"

Crisa shook her head. "No."

"It's too late to go anywhere tonight," Topaz reasoned. "You know we can't be out in the daylight."

"I know."

"So you should rest until dawn, and then the day sleep will restore you, and we can talk more about this boy at sundown."

Crisa looked up sharply. "No talking." Then she swung her head to the other side, staring intently at Briar. "I'll go to him. I have to."

"You don't even know where he is," Briar said. "Hell, you don't even know *who* he is."

"I'm going to him. I have to," Crisa repeated.

Reaper's hand slid from Briar's back to her shoulder, and squeezed. *Try not to agitate her.*

Agitate her? Hell, I'm getting ready to smack *her.*

"You can't stop me, Briar," Crisa insisted.

"Why the fuck would I want to?" Briar asked. "Listen, you do whatever the hell you want, okay? Just don't get yourself into trouble in the middle of nowhere and expect me to come running to the rescue, Crisa. I'm nobody's hero."

Crisa turned her face into the pillows and buried it there as Briar shook her head in frustration and stomped out of the room.

Topaz and Reaper followed. Roxy remained, her hands moving gently to Crisa again, one on the uppermost shoulder, the other cupping the nape of her neck.

Topaz pulled the bedroom door closed gently. "Your

room is the one on the right. I didn't think she should
have the one with the balcony. Each one has its own
bath. There's a minifridge over there." She pointed to
what looked like a hardwood stand. Clearly it was a re-
frigerator, cleverly disguised to match the rest of the
décor. "You can help yourself to sustenance."

"Fine."

"Briar, she's sick. Something's wrong. She's not
turning on you, not really."

"As if I give a damn."

"Well, just in case." Topaz sighed. "Good night."

"Whatever."

Topaz left them. But Reaper remained.

It hadn't taken quite as much torture as Gregor had
expected. The beatings didn't do the trick, but once he
started skinning Derrick Dwyer alive, he talked plenty.
In fact, it only took one small strip from his forearm to
get him going.

Shame, that.

According to Dwyer, the girl, Crisa, was a mentally
tweaked vampiress with a chip in her brain. Some ex-
perimental thing that let Dwyer see through her eyes,
hear through her ears, and to some extent control her by
speaking to her inside her head. That part hadn't been
thoroughly tested yet.

There was more. Nothing that mattered, though. Something about it only being functional for a short period.
Something about it deteriorating and killing the girl once
it did, unless it was removed in time. Like he gave a shit.

All Gregor knew was that he had a way to track down Reaper, a way to watch him, to get an advantage over him. He wanted that bastard. He wanted his power, and he wanted to exact vengeance.

And as for Briar, oh, he was going to *enjoy* hurting her. She had betrayed him.

She would die slow.

But for right now, Gregor had to focus on the matter at hand. He'd left the agent hanging—quite literally, he thought with a smile—and told his son to take care of getting him down and into a bed. He'd had to hurry to get here, to Dwyer's home and his computer, while enough of the night still remained.

And now, even as dawn approached, Gregor remained, riveted to the screen, watching and seeing it all just as Dwyer had described. He saw Reaper, his face above the girl, as he apparently carried her through a house. He saw the house, as well, through the girl's eyes, though her vision seemed blurry. He saw the girl being placed in a bed and Reaper bending over her. And Briar was right beside him, damn her.

Seeing Briar's wild hair and dark, dark eyes again was like feeling a blade twist in his chest. He didn't like that feeling.

There were others there, too, and as he watched and listened, he learned their names. Roxy, a sexy redheaded mortal, and Topaz, a beautiful, classy brunette. He thought the redhead might be one of the Chosen, but he wasn't sure.

And then, as he watched, the girl started ranting

about needing to go, needing to go to him, to the boy. The *boy*. And then static filled the screen and a shape took its place, slowly taking form amid the snow.

He frowned and narrowed his eyes, leaning closer to the screen. It was…it was Matthias.

Dammit! How was that possible?

Clearly he had more questions to ask of Derrick Dwyer. But they were going to have to wait until night-fall. The sun was tugging at his senses, dulling them. He was going to have to take refuge in Dwyer's house for the day. But he had one more task to accomplish before he surrendered to the power of the day sleep.

He had drones in place in various locations around the country, ready to obey his commands, some of them to the west, where there were still a few hours of darkness left. He phoned them now, to set his plan in motion.

Briar ignored Reaper's presence and went to the fridge, opened it and removed a plastic bag with the Red Cross logo on its face. The fridge had two doors, a lower one that was larger and an upper one that was smaller. It looked just like a full-sized model with the freezer on the top, only about a quarter of the size. But when she opened the top door she was surprised to find a micro-wave instead of a freezer.

"Damn, where do people even *find* shit like this?" She tossed the bag in and hit the 30 second button. Then she looked around for glasses.

Reaper walked over from the other side of the room,

a wineglass in each hand. "They were in the cabinet over there," he said. "Here."

"Two? I don't remember inviting you to join me."

"I don't remember offering to leave."

She pursed her lips, but opened the microwave when it beeped and removed the bag. Then she filled the two glasses. There was some blood left in the bag, so she downed hers quickly, then refilled her glass, which she set on a table near the bedroom door before knocking softly. "There's a drink out here for her, Roxy, when you're ready."

"Thanks, Briar," Roxy called.

Nodding, Briar turned, crossed the room and entered the bedroom she would be calling her own for as long as she was here. As she did, it crossed her mind that maybe it shouldn't be for very long. It might be better all around if she just left.

She stood just inside the doorway, examining the bedroom. The same color scheme as the room in between: cream and pine. French doors, sheer curtains, a balcony beyond with wrought-iron patio furniture, all curlicue vines and leaves. The bed was huge and soft-looking. Two doors set side by side must lead to a closet and a bathroom.

The place was incredible.

Too bad she couldn't stay long.

"You going to be all right?" Reaper asked.

"Yeah. I always am." She waited for him to say goodnight and get the hell out. He didn't, though.

Finally she turned and faced him. "You hanging around for a reason?"

"Yeah."

He held her eyes. And he didn't need to elaborate from there, because she felt it. A slowly building flame of desire flickering inside him. He'd been keeping it banked ever since the first and only time they'd had mind-blowing sex in a car on a city street. She'd done it to distract him and delay him, on Gregor's orders.

But that didn't mean she hadn't enjoyed it. And that had shocked her. She'd never had an orgasm with a man before that night.

"I could stay," he said. "If you want me to."

3

Reaper watched the reactions cross her face one by one. There was surprise, a slight lifting of her lush, dark brows and a widening of her deep brown eyes. That reaction was brief, little more than a flash. It was followed quickly by those same eyes narrowing, the brows gathering close, a look of suspicion and perhaps even dislike.

"We're not going to start having sex on a regular basis, Reaper."

He shrugged. "I didn't say anything about a regular basis."

"The next thing you know, you'll be going cow-eyed and sappy—like Jack is over the princess. It would make me puke."

"I was offering sex, Briar, nothing more. If you're not interested, it's all the same to me. Just don't go to sleep with the idea that I'm going...what did you call it? Cow-eyed or sappy over you. You're not the type to inspire that sort of reaction in a man."

She turned away as he watched her, and he wondered if his barb had stung her just a little. But that would imply that she had feelings, and she'd gone to great lengths to make sure everyone knew she had none.

"So you're just like every other man I've ever known, then. You just want to get laid."

"If I just want to get laid, I'm a bastard. If I feel something for you, I'm a sap. I can't win with you, can I, Briar?"

"No. You can't. Why don't we leave it at that and call it good?"

"Fine." He turned and stalked back into the suite's shared living room, then paused. "The truth is, I thought you could use a little relief. Despite your denials, I can see that you're worried about Crisa, frustrated by her sudden rebellion against you, drained by sharing her pain. A little distraction from all that, a little release, would do you a world of good."

"Sounds remarkably sappy to me. As if you give a damn."

He turned to see her standing in the bedroom doorway. "Not at all. I'm just a bastard who wants to get laid."

She smiled just slightly. "That's better. Go find a pretty victim, Reaper. Take her by force, or make her submit by controlling her mind, drink her and fuck her and enjoy yourself." Then she tipped her head to one side. "No doubt you'll top it off by making her forget it happened, or telling her to remember it as a pleasant, erotic dream."

"Is that what *you* intend to do with what's left of the darkness?" he asked.

She met his eyes, and a spark of desire, unmistakable, flashed in hers. "Jealous?"

"Not in the least."

"So are you going to take my advice, then?"

"No."

"So it's *not* just sex you want. It's me." She narrowed her eyes on him, curious now, rather than suspicious. "Why?"

Lifting his gaze, Reaper met her eyes. "Not because of anything sappy or emotional, don't worry on that score. Good night, Briar."

He turned and walked to the door.

"Why, then?" she called after him.

He didn't answer, just opened the door and left the room.

Why? The question plagued him all night. Why *did* he want her? Physical contact with others tended to make him extremely uncomfortable. It had for a long time. Ever since Rebecca…

No, he wasn't going to think about that, about *her*. She was off-limits. And yet, since he'd met Briar, Rebecca had been popping into his mind on a regular basis. More and more often, with more and more insistence. And it was getting harder, night by night, to keep the memories at bay.

He had an hour to get through before the day sleep would take him. As he retired to the room Topaz had deemed his, he noted the big-screen television and the stereo system, and knew both were bad ideas. Any program, any song, might contain the single word that would send him into a murderous rage, thanks to the brainwashing techniques of his old friends at the CIA.

His misfits all knew what the trigger word was. Briar knew. They wouldn't utter it in his presence. But the television or radio might.

Gregor knew the trigger word, as well. The difference was that Gregor also knew the word that would bring him out of it again. That was information for which he could easily kill.

He undressed and sank into the bed, trusting the automatically darkening windows to keep him safe. Topaz wouldn't lie to him about something like that. He yanked out a cell phone from his pants pocket before dropping them back onto the floor beside the bed, deciding to kill the remaining time by trying to get a message to Eric Marquand.

Rhiannon answered on the first ring. "Hello, darling," she purred. "I wondered when you'd get around to thanking me for my help on that little Mexican adventure."

Reaper smiled slowly. Rhiannon wouldn't have needed caller ID to know who was calling. She was his maker. They shared a psychic bond that couldn't be stronger.

"Hello, Rhiannon. Thank you for your help on that little Mexican adventure."

"Right. That's not why you're calling, though, is it?"

"No."

"What do you need, Reaper? Has that bitch vampiress bitten you too hard?"

"If you're referring to Briar, no. She hasn't *bitten* me at all."

"You are such a liar. You're doomed, you know. You stand no chance against her."

"I'm not against her."

"But you want to be." She laughed softly, enjoying her torment of him. "I like her," she said, when her laughter died.

"You're the only one, then," he said.

"Oh, I don't think so. You like her, too."

"I *want* to like her," he admitted. "She's not making it easy."

"She wouldn't. But there's Crisa. That one seems to adore her."

"Not anymore."

Rhiannon went silent. "What's happened?"

"Crisa is having debilitating headaches, hearing voices, seeing things. Briar gets the headaches when Crisa does. We don't know what's causing them."

"Is it part of the girl's…condition?"

"I don't think so. She says not. And she's insisting there's a boy somewhere who needs her, who keeps calling out to her, and that she has to go to him. Briar forbade her, and Crisa defied her."

"Really? That must have come as quite a shock to Briar."

"Came as a shock to all of us."

"Well, it would, wouldn't it? It's the first hint of a backbone the girl has shown."

He nodded, sighed. "Do you think Eric Marquand might be able to help us figure out what's happening to Crisa?"

Rhiannon was silent for a moment. Reaper could hear her long nails rapping in steady rhythm on some surface. Finally she said, "I don't know for sure, of course. But I can't think of anyone who'd more likely be able to help. Where are you?"

"At Topaz's place, Emerald Isle, North Carolina."

"I'll pass on your request," she told him. "I'll phone you when I have his answer. Meanwhile…I have another answer for you."

Reaper frowned. "An answer to what? I haven't asked a question."

"Well, you must have, or I wouldn't have an answer screaming in my mind right now, would I? I don't know what the question is that's been plaguing you, darling, but I do know the words you need to hear right now."

Closing his eyes, Reaper lowered his head. He knew damn well what question had been plaguing him. *Why was he so drawn to Briar?* But he didn't like opening himself up, revealing his weaknesses, his feelings, to anyone. Even Rhiannon.

"Shall I tell you?" she asked him.

"Do I have a choice?"

"Of course not. The answer is, because you think you can't hurt her."

"Because I think I can't hurt her," he repeated.

"Yes. That's it. Now, sate my burning curiosity and tell me, what was the question?"

"None of your business."

"It's about that prickly bitch, isn't it?"

"It's nearly dawn, Rhiannon. I have to go. Good rest."

"Stubborn prick," she muttered. Then she hung up.

Reaper ended the call and set his cell phone on the

nightstand. Then he lay down in the bed, pulled up the covers and waited for sleep to come, all the while trying not to replay his own question—and Rhiannon's answer—in his mind. He didn't need this, not now. Besides, he could already feel the day sleep pulling at him. His body grew heavy. His eyes fell closed. In his mind, he saw Briar, straddling him in that car, bouncing up and down on him, kissing and biting at him as she drove him toward the most shattering climax he'd ever experienced.

Thank God, he thought, that vampires didn't dream during the day sleep. Otherwise, he thought the memory of that one explosive encounter would haunt him until sundown.

She probably should have taken him up on it, Briar thought, as she examined her new digs with appreciation and ridicule warring for top spot in her mind. She took a long look at the giant Jacuzzi tub, the bottles of oils, scents, lotions and soaps that filled the shelves around it, the loofah and the candles, all of them with clean white wicks. She wondered if Topaz threw them all out and bought new ones every time one of the wicks was blackened by flame. How stupid was that? And what was with the towels? she wondered, as she tugged one off the rack. It was as big as a bedsheet. Who *needed* a towel that big?

For a moment she envisioned herself soaking in the giant Jacuzzi and making use of the girlie shit that surrounded her. Then, with a roll of her eyes, she opted for the stand-alone shower instead.

It was opulent enough all by itself. Corner-shaped and huge, with not one but three showerheads—so that she could wash, rinse and masturbate all at the same time, she guessed.

Nothing too good for the princess.

Briar made her shower quick, and tried really hard not to enjoy the pulsing pressure massaging her back and shoulders, though privately, she supposed she had to admit, it was nice.

Even so, she spent the entire time judging Topaz for her spending habits—not that she gave a damn, she told herself; she was simply keeping her thoughts from heading down the alley they really wanted to explore.

But it didn't work for long. There wasn't enough overindulgence in freakin' Buckingham Palace to keep her from thinking about that. About him.

Reaper.

He wanted something from her. He was up to something. She wasn't stupid enough to think men ever did anything for any other reason. And she thought he was a little bit beyond the caveman-level mentality. It wasn't just sex, like with her stepfather. That Neanderthal hadn't had another thought in his entire head. There'd been no motive, no scheme or scam or reason. Just beady eyes that were way too close together, and a serious death wish she had yet to fulfill.

It was on her list. Gregor first, though. Then Stepdaddy-dearest. And then she would move on through the rest of them. The pimps, the dealers, the Johns. All of them. They would pay.

She wasn't a lost, weak, homeless addict anymore. She was a vampire now. Thanks to Gregor. Ironic, that.

Reaper, though…he was different. Smart. Even half-way decent. So he wanted something, he had something to gain, besides a good time, by getting into her pants again. What was it?

She didn't know. And she wasn't going to figure it out in the time between her shower and sunrise, so she toweled off, slung the giant towel over the wide rack to dry and padded into the bedroom. She snagged a fleece bathrobe from a hook on the way. The thing was as soft as down, cream-colored, knee-length. She pulled it on, and, in spite of herself, hugged it around her a little bit. Then she headed through the living room and toward Crisa's door. It was closed, but the glass of blood she'd left on the table just this side of it was gone.

She moved closer, opened the door very quietly, just a little, and peeked inside.

Crisa lay in the bed, sound asleep, but uneasy. She twitched every few seconds, and her head kept moving from side to side. Roxy was still there, but she got up when she saw Briar peering in, crossed the room on tip-toe and joined her in the living room.

As she closed the door quietly behind her, she met Briar's eyes. "I don't like it."

"No, neither do I."

"It just doesn't make any damn sense. If she didn't hear voices or see things or get these headaches before, why now? What's changed?"

"I don't know. Maybe her damn Rey-Rey had her on

some kind of medication that we don't know about. Something that kept all this shit under control."

"What kind of medication would work on a vampire, Briar?"

"Only two that we know of. The tranquilizer, and that potion of Rhiannon's that lets us stay awake by day, and makes us meaner than hell and twice as jittery. But that doesn't mean there might not be more."

"Right. Antipsychotics for the undead. Makes all kinds of sense."

She shot Roxy a look. "If it's not that, then what?"

"I don't know. Some kind of possession?"

"You don't believe it could be drugs, but demons seem like a possibility to you?" Briar rolled her eyes.

"Maybe some other vampire is messing around with her head, then?"

"Why would anyone want to?"

"I'm damned if I know!" Roxy lowered her head. "I know, I know, you're as baffled by this as I am. I just hate seeing her in pain. And so confused by it. And the way she's changing… No, I don't like it. I want to help."

Briar lowered her head, because it was becoming too heavy to hold up. The sun must be near to rising. "The Reiki helps. Both of us."

"That's something, anyway." Roxy patted Briar on the shoulder. "Go on to bed before you collapse and I have to carry you. She's out for the day. She'll be fine until sundown."

"Yeah, but what then?"

"We'll decide when it gets here."

Briar nodded and went back into the bedroom. She just managed to crawl into the lush nest of teddy-bear-soft fabrics before the sleep took her gently into its embrace.

In the basement of the mansion in Byram, Connecticut, the ten-year-old boy stood in the open doorway and stared at the man inside the room. Derrick Dwyer dangled. His hands were chained together, the chain looped over a hook in the ceiling. His toes barely reached the floor. The man's head hung low, chin touching his chest. He was barefoot. His shirt was gone, and so was a strip of his skin, on his forearm. It looked as if someone had peeled him there, like peeling a potato.

He wasn't dead. Matt could tell, because he was still breathing. It was raspy enough to hear without listening too hard.

His father must have gotten whatever he wanted from the man, because he'd told Matt to get him down and tend to his wounds, as he'd gone running from the house. That had been an hour ago, and it had been pretty close to sunrise, so Matt thought wherever his father was going, it must have been pretty important.

He knew what his father was. A vampire. They were mean, evil creatures, but he didn't suppose they could help it. And besides, now that his mom had died, his dad was all he had left.

So he tried to obey and not be too afraid, though he sure did see a lot of things to be afraid of.

He grabbed a wooden chair and dragged it closer to the

man. Then he climbed up on it, but he couldn't reach the hook in the ceiling. As he stood there, contemplating what to do, the man moaned and lifted his head just slightly.

"Hey, are you awake?" Matt asked him.

The man lifted his head higher and stared straight into Matt's eyes.

"Father said I should get you down now. Only I can't reach."

The man kept staring, as if not understanding him, so Matt pointed upward until the guy looked up, too, and saw the hook beyond the boy's reach.

"If you can get up on this chair, though, you could probably get it off yourself. You think you can?"

The man nodded weakly, so Matt hopped down from the chair and then steadied the older guy so he could get up onto it. It took some doing. The man was weak, and his wrists were bleeding. But he finally got up onto the chair and got the chain off the hook. He lowered his arms with a groan, gripped the back of the chair and climbed down again.

"Here, give me your hands." Matt tugged the key from his jeans pocket and waited. When the man lifted his hands, Matt slid the key into the little lock, wincing at the blood that was all over it, and popped the wrist shackles open.

They were not handcuffs. Handcuffs would have been worse. These things had wide metal bands that had cut into his skin as he'd hung there, but Matt was pretty sure handcuffs would have cut him clean to the bone.

The guy peeled off one manacle, then the other, grating his teeth and baring them in a grimace of pain.

"Can you walk, do you think?"

"Not very far. Why? Where are you takin' me?"

"Well, I wasn't supposed to take you anywhere. Just patch you up and leave you locked in here. But it's daylight, and my father didn't come back, so he won't be home until dark. And I'm all alone, 'cause the drones are all sleeping, too. Not that they're any fun, anyway." He knew he was talking a mile a minute. His father would have cuffed him upside the head and told him to slow down, be quiet, say only what needed saying and then shut the hell up. But this old man seemed to be listening with interest, and maybe even a little amusement.

"So you can come upstairs if you want. I can bandage you up way better up there. And you can take a shower or a bath—if you think it won't hurt too much. And then we can eat—I never have anyone to eat with. 'Cause, you know, *they* don't eat."

"I know."

Matt took the man's hand and led the way out of the room, through the basement and to the stairway that led up to the rest of the mansion.

"Why do you think your father didn't come home before sunrise?" the prisoner asked.

"Prob'ly just got too busy. I'm sure he found shelter in time."

"Would you be terribly upset if he didn't?"

Matt paused on the stairs and stared up at the man.

"Well, I'd be an orphan then, and I don't really want to be an orphan."

"He told you your mother is dead, then?"

"Yeah." They reached the top of the stairs and entered the main level of the mansion. "What should I call you?"

"You can call me Derry, if you want."

"Derry. I like that. You can call me Matt. It's what Mom used to call me."

"All right, Matt. I don't want you to get into trouble for this, you know. Are you sure you won't?"

"He'll never know."

Derry nodded. "Well, first things first, Matt. I think we'd better tend to these wounds. Some ointment, some bandages, a nice washup, and maybe some pain relievers, if you have any in the house."

"We have all that. I'm in charge of making the shopping lists. Father never lets me go out to the grocery store, but I make the lists. It's one of my jobs. The downstairs bathroom will be easier for you. It's this way."

The man was smiling at him as they made their way into the bathroom. "Does your father ever let you go anywhere, Matt?"

"Oh, he takes me out sometimes. But only at night, of course, and never around other people."

"It must get pretty borin' and lonely."

"Yeah. Well, you know, I have tons of stuff. An Xbox and a PS3 and a Wii, and every game they ever invented for any of them. So not so much boring, but yeah on the lonely, and I get crazy being in this house all the time."

"Hmm." They entered the bathroom, and Derry took

a seat on the toilet—lid closed, of course. Matt got all the first-aid supplies from the cabinet and laid them out on the sink counter for him. He soaked a gauze pad in peroxide and handed it to Derry, then soaked another and kept it for himself. "You work on those wrists. I'll get started on your back."

"Okay." Derry turned, then winced as Matt began cleaning the welts and cuts with the soaked pad. Matt tried to be careful, but he knew it had to hurt like mad.

"I...wonder," Derry said, in between sucking air through his teeth in pain.

"What?"

"Well, if you're sure your father won't be back until nightfall..."

Leaning around to face him, Matt said, "He *can't* come back before nightfall. Vampire, remember?" He grinned and was happy when Derry grinned back. Then he tossed the gauze pad in the garbage pail and grabbed the tube of triple antibiotic ointment. "This won't hurt as much," he promised. He tried to dollop it onto the hurt places without too much contact, then handed it to Derry.

"You know, we could sneak out for a while. Maybe go to the zoo, a fast food joint for burgers and fries, a game arcade, a park. We could have fun, Matt."

"Are you sure you feel up to it, Derry?" Matt laid the strips of gauze over the wounds, then stuck them in place with adhesive tape. "I don't know why you didn't just tell him whatever he wanted to know to begin with." He shook his head sadly. "It's always best to do what he says." Then he finished and came around in front. "You really feel good enough to go out, Derry?"

"Well, I don't of course, but…you helped me. I owe you one. And this might be our only chance."

"Yeah, that's for sure."

"If only there were a car…oh, wait, there's my car. Your father brought me here in his, but I heard him tell the drones to bring mine. I wonder if he still has it?"

"Sure he does," Matt said. He was wrapping gauze around Derry's ointment-covered left wrist now. "It's around back."

"Really? That's great. I love that car." Then Derry frowned. "Still, I don't imagine you know where he keeps the keys."

"Of course I do," Matt said. He finished the first wrist, taped the gauze in place, then began wrapping the other.

"So what do you think? Should we do it? Should we get out of here for the day?" Derry asked.

Matt frowned hard, taped off the gauze, then turned to the counter to shake three tablets out of a pain reliever bottle. He handed them to Derry and spoke sternly, making his eyes very serious. "All right, but if you start feeling weak or sick or anything, we'll just chuck it and come home, okay?"

"Of course that's okay," Derry said, and patted Matt on the head.

"And my father can never know."

"Absolutely," Derry promised. "You have my word on that."

So Matthias carefully gathered up all the items he'd

used and put them away, and then he took Derry's hand and led him through the house in search of some clean clothes.

Derrick Dwyer admired the boy. He was mature for his age, probably because he'd been forced to learn to fend for himself. He was smart as well.

Not smart enough to realize, though, that he was about to become a hostage.

Derrick had been pushed beyond the edge of his endurance, and while he liked the kid, he wouldn't hesitate to use him.

Or even kill him, if necessary.

4

When she woke at sundown, Briar rose instantly. She'd never been one to linger in bed. When the sun sank and the power of the day sleep vanished, it happened, for her, all at once. Her eyes opened wide, her mind came sharply alert and her senses automatically scanned her immediate surroundings for any hint of a threat.

She found none and sat up, flipped back the covers, got out of the bed and listened. But the house remained quiet. The others were likely a bit slower to rouse than she was. And as for the mortals, Roxy and Ilyana, they must be napping or in some other part of the mansion.

There was no reason to hurry, but Briar always felt as if there was, always felt in a rush to do whatever there was to be done, always felt a vague sense that if she slowed down or relaxed at all, something would catch up with her. Something bad. She never bothered to analyze that feeling. It was just the way she was.

Besides, there *were* things to be done. Important things. Roxy and Ilyana had planned to spend some time on the Internet during the daylight hours, scanning the news for any signs of where Gregor might be. Locating him was her only goal right now, and she was entirely focused on it.

The sooner she knew where he was, the sooner she would be able to go after him. Alone, without this gang of white-hats weighing her down, probing her psyche, trying to find some kind of redeeming quality in her soul.

They never would. She didn't even *have* a soul.

Briar chose clothes from the duffel bag she hadn't bothered to unpack, seeing as she didn't intend to be here that long. Then she headed into the bathroom to clean up and dress and run a brush through her hair. By the time she finished, she sensed that the others were up and active. They were gathering now in one of the rooms below. She could feel their energy there. There was a sense of excitement that perked her attention. Roxy must have found something, then.

Briar hurried from her bedroom, then stopped in the living area of the suite, her attention drawn to the closed door. She wasn't sensing Crisa. Could she be sleeping? The thought that she might have expired during her rest niggled at the back of Briar's brain like claws scratching at her mind, drawing blood. Swallowing hard, she faced the door, lifted her chin and strode forward to fling it open.

Crisa's bed was empty, the covers rumpled and tossed. Her backpack was open, clothes strewn everywhere around it on the floor, including the ones she'd been wearing when she'd gone to sleep.

A breeze touched Briar's face, and she turned toward the window. It stood wide open, sheer white curtains dancing like ghosts.

An unfamiliar rush of panic drove her across the room to the windowsill, and she leaned out, staring down, half expecting to see Crisa's broken body lying below.

But there was no sign of the troubled girl.

"Dammit. Where the hell are you, Crisa?"

As she honed her senses, Briar felt something. Something dark and compelling. And then it overwhelmed her completely as she somehow melded with Crisa's mind, felt what she felt, saw what she saw.

When she opened her eyes, Briar saw trees and bushes all around her, and sensed the steady, powerful but uneven movement of her legs, plodding, setting her feet down one after the other as she moved through the brush. Branches smacked her face, stinging her, but she ignored those, driven forward. Ever forward.

Crisa! Briar cried out to her mentally. *Crisa, where are you? Where are you going? Why didn't you wait for me?*

The reply came in a rush, in a mental voice that was nothing like the girl Briar had known. There was no innocent adoration; this was no naive child who didn't understand the ways of the Undead or of the world in general. Instead, this response was dark, deep, angry and determined.

Leave me alone!

Crisa, listen to me!

No!

And just like that, the door to Crisa's mind slammed

and Briar landed back in her own body with such a jolt
that she nearly fell over. She had to grip the nearby bedpost to keep her balance. She wouldn't have believed
Crisa even knew how to block her thoughts that way.
And yet, she just had.

Something unfamiliar twisted in Briar's gut. And
then she released the bedpost and turned for the door,
running, not walking, intent on reaching the group
below, Reaper in particular.

And she kept on running, her mind racing, until she was
downstairs and bursting into the room where they all stood.

And then she paused and took stock. Since when
was her first instinct in times of trouble to run to them?
To run to *him?*

Reaper looked up when Briar burst into the den
where they had all gathered upon waking. Roxy had
called them there, and was, even at that moment, leaning over a laptop computer, punching up news stories.
Ilyana was at her side, a good six inches taller and painfully lean where Roxy was lush and curvy.

"There were four incidents, all the same, each in a
different state, and all apparently took place overnight," Roxy said.

"It had to be Gregor," Ilyana added. "Somehow, he's
responsible for every one of them."

"Even a vampire couldn't have been in four states at
once," Seth was saying.

Reaper ignored them, his eyes focused on Briar's
face, and a second later he was beside her, putting a hand

on her shoulder to snap her out of wherever she'd gone inside her mind.

"What is it, Briar? What's happened? Is Crisa all right?"

Her eyes shifted into focus again, met his. "She's gone."

"Gone?" He was blank for a moment, before the meaning grew clear to his mind. "Crisa's *gone?*"

Briar nodded hard. Her eyes seemed strained with worry, and her jaw was tight. "Her bedroom window's open. She changed clothes before she left." Blinking twice, looking down but clearly not seeing, he thought, she went on. "We have to find her."

"We will." Reaper turned to face the others, who had fallen silent one by one at Briar's entrance. "We'll split up into teams and head out in different directions. Everyone try to home in on her and—"

"I don't think so, Reaper." The declaration came quietly, but in a firm, determined tone, from the mortal Ilyana. She'd straightened away from the computer and squared her shoulders. When he shot her a look of disbelief, she pushed a hand through her short platinum hair, a slightly nervous gesture. And yet she went on firmly, saying, "We just got our first solid leads on Gregor. Finding him is our mission, or am I mistaken about that?"

Reaper held her gaze and he didn't bother making his voice gentle. "*My* mission is to find him."

"It may be your *mission,*" she said, her tone softer now, "but it's *my* goal in life. There's nothing more important to me right now."

She was afraid of them, he thought. All of them, and

Briar in particular. That she was showing enough courage now to disagree with him instigated a surge of admiration for her guts, in spite of the irritation that came with it. "And yet you've never told us why," he said.

"I don't freaking give a damn why!" Briar let the words burst from her in a rush, fueled by emotion he'd rarely seen in her. "Look, mortal, it was my goal in life, too. But now Crisa's missing, and you know she can't take care of herself. Finding her takes precedence."

"This from someone who pretends not to care about her," Roxy muttered. "I knew better the whole time, of course, but—"

"Can it, Roxy." Briar swung her gaze around the room, letting it land on the others. Seth and Vixen, Jack and Topaz, Mirabella. "No one among you wants to get Gregor more than I do, believe me. But this is Crisa we're talking about."

"She's one of us," Vixen said. "She's more important than any mission."

"She's not more important than mine," Ilyana said softly. She shared a look with Roxy, who nodded her agreement.

"Why?" Reaper demanded.

Ilyana looked at him, then lowered her head and shook it slowly.

"Oh, for the love of God, Ilyana, just tell them, will you, so we can get on with this?" Briar snapped. When Ilyana turned her wide eyes toward her, Briar rolled her own in return, then turned and paced away. "I don't have time to fuck with you and your secrets while

Crisa's out there in danger." She turned again, facing them. "She had a kid with him. With Gregor."

Reaper hadn't thought much could surprise him, but this certainly did. He looked from Briar to Ilyana in disbelief.

"She and Gregor were together and had a son, then Gregor took the kid. He still has him, as far as she knows," Briar explained. "That's why she wants to find him so bad. To get her kid back."

"How do you—" Reaper began.

"I overheard her telling Roxy. And for what it's worth, Ilyana, I totally get it. And I've got no problem with you going after him, and I'll probably even help you by fulfilling my own need to slit the bastard's throat and watch him bleed out. Slowly, I hope. But nobody is going anywhere until we find Crisa."

"You have a child?" Topaz whispered, staring at Ilyana and ignoring Briar now. "Gregor has your son?"

"Oh, my God," Vixen whispered. "Oh, my God, you poor thing. That poor child."

"Look, Ilyana," Seth told her, moving to stand beside her. "I know you don't like vamps, and we all get that. But you're with us now. And you'd better believe we'll help you get your kid back safe and sound."

"Absolutely," Topaz agreed.

Jack was frowning, his gaze jumping from the white-hats to Briar, and finally he shook his head in frustration. "The kid is fine. Crisa isn't. I think it's pretty easy to figure out where our first priority has to be."

"But we just got our first real clue as to where Gregor is—" Ilyana stopped herself, blinked, and started over. "How do you know he's fine?"

Jack held her eyes. "I saw him from time to time when I was with Gregor. You must have, too, Briar," he added with a look her way.

"I didn't know who the hell he was. Gregor kept him pretty much away from the rest of us."

"He's treated well, Ilyana. He's cared for, fed, kept healthy, never physically abused." Jack nodded. "He'll be fine. Crisa might not be, if we don't find her soon."

"We have a lead on Gregor's whereabouts," Ilyana argued. "If we wait, he'll move on. We may lose our only chance." She shook her head firmly. "No, you all go after Crisa if you want. I'm going to find my son."

"What she said," Briar snapped. "You can go after her kid if you want, but I'm going after Crisa. And unlike the mortal here, I don't fucking need anybody's help."

"Wait, wait, just calm down for a minute, both of you." Reaper looked from one to the other, shaking his head. "Roxy, tell us what you found on the Internet. The short version."

"A houseful of bodies, drained of blood, every item of value taken, no effort made to conceal the crime."

In spite of herself, Briar asked, "Where?"

"Fresno, Salt Lake City, Dallas and Oklahoma City."

Briar frowned. "I don't—"

"The same crime, committed in all four places, overnight. Bodies found this morning. The ones in Dallas were found before sunrise, and the initial reports include puncture wounds in the throats of the corpses, though later medical exams say there were no such wounds."

"They would vanish with the first touch of sunlight," Seth muttered.

"All right. All right." Reaper paced away, then back again. "We can't let Gregor slip away with an innocent child. Nor can we ignore the fact that Crisa, who's our charge, for all intents and purposes, and every bit as much an innocent child as...as..." He sent Ilyana a questioning look.

"Matthias. I call him Matt," she said.

"As innocent as Matt, is in danger." He narrowed his eyes. "Gregor couldn't have done all those raids at once. There's something off here."

"We need to split up," Seth said. "Much as I hate to say it, I think it's the only way."

Jack nodded at the younger man. "I agree. We need to check out all four crime scenes *and* search for Crisa. And there's no earthly reason to argue about what to do first, when there are enough of us to do it all at once."

Reaper nodded and looked at the others. "Everyone agree on that?"

They all nodded. Ilyana said, "Great. Roxy and I will—"

"You two make a great team, Ilyana, but I don't like your chances against Gregor on your own. You're mortals, both of you. I want vampires on every team, just to be safe."

"I'll go with them," Mirabella said.

"Good. You three will be the back-up team, in case

anyone gets into trouble." When he sensed that Ilyana was about to object, he added, "You'll also be ready to go once we *do* find Gregor. Seth and Vixen, head to Oklahoma City. Topaz and Jack, you take Dallas. Once you check out those two crime scenes, you can decide where to go from there. Report in as you go. Don't take too much time, and don't be seen. This is not an assault on Gregor. If you find him, you stay low, do some recon and call it in. No one moves on him until we're all together. I don't want your bodies to be the next ones found lying bloodless in some death house."

He eyed them, and saw and sensed that they all agreed—except for Ilyana. There was defiance in her eyes. Roxy met his gaze, though, and said, "I'll see to it."

"Good. Go then, get on it. While you're doing that, Briar and I will track Crisa down." He turned to Briar, took her arm and led her from the room, ignoring the stunned way she stared at him.

When they reached the stairs and he started up them, she whispered, "Why?"

"We need to put on some more practical clothes, toss a few supplies in a bag in case we're gone longer than we anticipate, pack up some first-aid gear in case she's hurt. It'll only take a few minutes, and then we're out of here, I promise."

She shook her head. "No. I meant, why are you coming with me instead of going after Gregor? *He's* your mission. Not Crisa. Not me."

He glanced at her, then shook his head. "I'd do the same if any one of the others had gone missing."

"I'm not so sure about that."

"Well, you should be, because I would. I never asked to feel responsible for this band of misfits, but I feel it anyway. I have to think there's a reason I ended up with a litter of pups to ride herd on, but I'm damned if I can figure out what it is." He stopped outside her bedroom. "Grab what you think you'll need. And don't forget to bring a tranq gun and plenty of darts in case…" He didn't finish, but he didn't have to. Briar had to know damn well what he meant: In case someone uttered his trigger word and sent him into a frenzy of violence.

"You were hired to find Gregor," she said.

"And I will. Hell, it's not like I'm going to run out of time, Briar. He and I are both immortal." He tried to inject a little lightness into his tone, because she seemed more tense and more worried than he'd ever seen her.

More vulnerable, too. He'd never thought of her that way, not once since he'd known her. But he saw it now. It was clear to him that if anything happened to Crisa, a girl she pretended to tolerate, and that only barely, she would be devastated. It was a weakness she would hate like hell to admit, but he was pretty sure she knew he could see it. And undoubtedly resented him for it.

"I'll meet you out back in ten minutes," he told her.

She nodded, stared at him for one more moment, then shook herself and went into her room, closing the door behind her.

He was an idiot, Reaper told himself as he walked down the hall to his own room. She wouldn't appreciate his help. He was a little bit shocked she was even accepting it, but he knew that was more about Crisa than about herself. She cared about that kid.

The knowledge made him feel a bit lighter, though he had no idea why.

Crisa just walked. Her head hurt, but she ignored it. Her belly was painfully empty, and that made the pain in her head seem worse, but she didn't have time to eat. She just kept on walking. She had to find him. She had to find the boy.

And there was something else. That voice in her head.

It had changed, that voice. This evening, when it had woken her from her deep, deep sleep, it hadn't been the same as the voice she'd been hearing before. This voice was deeper, with a gruffness to it, and a coldness she hadn't felt before. But it seemed to come from the very same spot inside her head, and it reverberated and seemed to echo, just as the other voice had. It hurt, when the voice came. But it hurt a lot more when she tried to ignore it.

"I want you to come to me," the voice said. "I want you to come to me, and I want you to bring Reaper and Briar with you. No one else. Just those two. That's your job, Crisa, and I will not let you rest until you've done it. So get busy."

"Who are you?" she whispered. "You're different. I don't know you."

"I'm your lord and master, Crisa. You do what I say, or I'll punish you."

"I can't." The words came weakly. It was exhausting, hearing this voice, trying to communicate with it when speaking aloud didn't really work. She had to *think* her replies, and really focus when she did so. But she couldn't do that in silence, so she spoke them aloud, as well.

"You can and you will," he said.

"No. You can punish me if you want, but I can't, I have to go to him."

"You dare defy me? Do you have any idea how much I can make you suffer? How efficiently I could take your life, Crisa?"

"I have to go to him," she repeated. Because nothing else mattered.

"To *whom?*" the voice demanded. It was filled with impatience and anger, and those emotions shook Crisa. They scared her.

"The boy. He—he needs me."

"The boy. Ah, yes, I've seen the boy. Do you know his name?"

"No."

"Well, I do. His name is Matthias."

She blinked, feeling with everything in her that this was true. Matthias. No. Matt. "His name is Matt," she corrected.

"I think I know his name a bit better than you do, Crisa. But fine, call him Matt, if you want to. It makes no difference. Do you know where he is?"

She blinked and tried to translate her feelings, the compass inside her that kept turning her toward him as she trudged through forests and over roads and across fields. "North," she said. "He's north."

"He's with me," the voice said.

And for the first time since she'd leapt from her bedroom window, Crisa stopped walking. She stood very still. "You...you're real?"

"Of course I'm real. What did you think I was, part of your imagination?"

She breathed. In. Out. In. Out. Inout, inout, inout. She was agitated. It hurt more now. Her head pulsed in time with her increasing respirations. "So many things are," she said. "That's what Rey-Rey used to tell me. That so many things were just my imagination. That he had to tell me what was real and what wasn't. But now he's not here to tell me. There's only Briar, but she's kind of mean to me, and—"

"Yes, yes, that's all very interesting. But let's get back to the subject at hand, Crisa. You want the boy. You are determined to get to the boy. I have the boy. And unless you do as I tell you, I'll hurt the boy. Do you understand me?"

"No! No, don't hurt him. Don't hurt him. Don't—"
"Shut up!"

Crisa's hands flew to her ears, as she dropped to her knees on the forest floor. She screamed aloud, tears springing to her eyes at the power of the shout inside her mind. It was deafening and painful.

And as the echoes slowly died and she pried her eyes open again, she sought the source, carefully, like poking at a sore spot. She found it, inside her, and she whispered, "Please don't shout anymore. I'll do whatever you say. Just don't hurt the boy."

"Good. Now get Briar and Reaper, and bring them to me."

"I will," she promised.

And then he withdrew. She sensed him pulling out of her mind, and she wished she knew how to close the door tightly enough to keep him out. She knew how to block her thoughts. Roxy had taught her. But for some reason, those techniques didn't work against this invader.

She believed him when he said he had the boy.

She also knew he would hurt her, or hurt Matt, if he said he would.

She knew more than that now, though. She knew he was evil. His energy reeked of it. And she knew he was a vampire. Not the more-or-less gentle soul who'd spoken to her in this same unusual way before. That man had been mortal. She hadn't been afraid of him.

This man was dark, powerful and dangerous. And Crisa was *very* afraid of *him*.

But she wasn't going to do what he told her. She would pretend to. She would promise to. But she wouldn't do it. She wouldn't bring Reaper and Briar with her. And there were several reasons for that dancing around in her brain.

First and foremost, going back for them would mean losing time, and she was compelled to keep moving forward, ever forward, ever closer to the boy. She couldn't go back. Literally. She was convinced that even if she tried to turn and walk in the other direction, her feet would not obey. They insisted, as did her entire body and her mind, on moving north. She was having trouble even getting her limbs to cooperate when she came to a barrier in her path and had to veer around it. And that made no sense. It was as if her body had a mind of its own. As if she were being steered by some outside force.

Her second reason for not going back to get Briar and Reaper was because she knew they would try to keep her from leaving again. They might try to stop her from going to the boy. To Matt.

And her third reason was that she had sensed something in the evil vampire's voice and in his essence when he'd said their names inside her head. He wanted to hurt them. He wanted it so badly he couldn't even keep her from sensing it. He wanted to kill them. Make them go away forever, like Rey-Rey.

"I can't let him do that," she whispered as she continued lumbering onward. "I love them. So I can't let him do that."

And so she walked on to the north, and she kept her mind blocked to keep her friends from finding her, wondering why she could keep Briar out but not this intruder.

When she came to a river and decided to turn east in search of a bridge, every step got harder. It felt as if there were a giant rubber band wrapped around her, pulling her toward the boy, and every step away stretched it farther. Every step made it pull back harder, until she couldn't bear to put one foot in front of the other again. She turned, and the moment she faced north again, the resistance vanished.

So she walked into the river, and it got deeper and deeper. And she kept walking. Water rose up to her waist, then to her breasts, then to her neck, and still she moved on. The current tried to sweep her westward, but she felt that resistance again, holding her to her course in spite of the current. And she began to swim when she could no longer walk, and the power that pulled her helped her make it across

Soon her tired feet dragged the bottom, and she planted them and walked, and the water level dropped as she moved, to her breasts, to her hips, to her knees. She sloshed out of the water, up onto the shore and onward.

Ever onward, toward the boy.

5

When Gregor returned to his Byram castle, leaving all Dwyer's computer equipment and files in the Jeep, he sensed trouble immediately.

His brow furrowed as he felt the absence of his prisoner. The elation of knowing his enemies were on their way to being delivered to him vanished. Slamming the door and bellowing for the drones, he surged through the mansion, down the basement stairs and into the room where the prisoner had been kept.

Nothing. The manacles lay on the floor, the key still in their lock. And that was all. Dammit!

"Matthias!" he shouted, stomping out of the room and up the basement stairs. "I told you to unchain him, not let him go. Matthias, where the hell are you, boy?"

No answer.

And suddenly he was aware of the *other* absence he sensed: that of his son.

As he entered the hallway from the basement stairwell, one of his drones, one he called Brutus, though they all pretty much looked alike, stood there looking at his own feet. "Master, the prisoner and the boy were gone when we awoke from the day sleep. We didn't know what to do."

In his hand, the drone held a sheet of paper with handwriting covering one side.

"What the hell is that?" Gregor demanded.

"It was in the boy's room."

Gregor snatched the sheet from the drone's hand, and read it rapidly.

> *I have your son.*
> *I won't harm him as long as you do*
> *exactly as I say.*
> *Turn yourself in at CIA headquarters*
> *in White Plains. I'll tell them to be*
> *ready for you. You have forty-eight*
> *hours. If you fail, the boy dies.*
> *I can play hardball, too.*
> *D.D.*

"You promised I'd be home before dark!"

When they stepped out of the arcade and onto the sidewalk, Matt was shocked to see that it was dark outside. The sun was long gone. His father had to be home by now, and he was going to be in big trouble.

Still, it had been the best day he'd spent in a long time—since before his mom had died. Even though Derry had been hurting pretty badly most of the day, he had been fun. Once they got the car, he'd found some medicine in the glove compartment, and that had seemed to make him feel better. He still had to be sore, though.

Their first stop had been lunch. Derry let Matt pick the place, and Matt picked his favorite fast-food chain, one he used to visit with his mom sometimes. Then they'd gone to the zoo. Derry rented a golf cart to drive around the place, probably 'cause he was too sore to walk all that way. He stayed in the cart most of the time, just rested, and he took some more of his pills while Matt was busy looking at the tigers.

Then they sat on a bench in the shade for a long time, sipping lemonade and resting some more. And finally Derry had driven him to the arcade, handed him a whole role of quarters and then sat where he could watch over him and let him play until he could barely move his thumbs.

It had been great. But Derry had been looking more and more worn out as the day went on. And now it was dark.

"I am in *so much* trouble."

"I guess we lost track of the time," Derry said. He patted Matt's shoulder. "I don't want you to worry about it, though. You're not goin' to get into any hot water over this."

"You don't know my father," Matt told him.

"Actually, I do, Matt. I know him better than you do, I think."

Matt frowned up at the man. "I know he's not a very nice person. And that he hurt you. Pretty bad."

Derry nodded.

"I'd have let you go sooner if I could."

"That wasn't your job, Matt. Don't waste any time feelin' guilty about that, okay?"

"It's just…my father's different. And special. Too special to have to follow the same rules as everyone else."

"Did he tell you that, Matthias?"

Matt nodded. "He said I'm special, too. Not as special as him. Not yet, but I will be someday."

"And is that what you want? To be like him?"

Matt pursed his lips in thought. "Not…*mean* like him."

"What if you could have anythin' in the whole world, any kind of life you wanted, Matt? What would you want for yourself?"

"That's easy." Matt lowered his head. "I'd want my mom back."

"I don't blame you."

"She wasn't like him. She wasn't mean like him, and she wasn't…you know."

"Yeah, I know what you mean. She didn't sleep durin' the day and have superhuman strength and all that kind of stuff, right?"

"Right."

"And your father told you she was dead, right?"

"Yeah."

"Did he tell you how she died?"

"Car accident," he said.

"Hmm."

Matt tipped his head to one side, looking at Derry and thinking the way he'd said "hmm" was odd. "I never really believed him, though. Not, you know, all the way."

"Why not?"

"Well, we didn't have a funeral. Don't you usually have a funeral when someone dies?"

"Yeah, usually."

"And I saw her car. After. It was in the garage, just like always. Not banged up or anything. I saw it right before Father and I left."

"Where did you go?"

"I don't know. One place after another. Always a great big house someplace I'd never been before. I'm not allowed to go outside or go to school or leave at all, so the house is pretty much all I see."

"How long has it been like that for you?"

"A year. Before that I lived with Mom. Dad left us. I barely even remembered him until he came back. And then they fought, and then she died, and he took me and we left. But one night, I swore I heard her voice, yelling at him."

Derry was silent for a long moment. He said, "You know, I'm sort of like a cop."

"You are?"

"Yeah. And keepin' track of your father has been a big part of my job for the past ten years. We didn't know he was goin' to go back to you and your mom, and end up takin' you away with him. Heck, I didn't even know he *had* a son. But we knew about your mom, and if there had been a car accident, we would have known about that, too."

Matt's head came up slowly, his eyes widening as he searched Derry's face. "You mean there wasn't one?"

"No, Matt. When your father left with you, your mom was still alive. She disappeared a while later, but I'm fairly certain she went lookin' for you. And I've got no reason to believe she's dead."

Matt felt something huge filling up his chest, something so big he thought he might bust right open. "My mom's alive?"

"Yeah, as far as I know."

Matt's eyes were burning, and he blinked fast to keep tears from spilling over. "You wouldn't lie to me, would you, Derry? Not about my mom."

Matt didn't think the man was lying. The talent he had—the one his mom had called a gift and warned him not to tell anyone about—was telling him that Derry wasn't lying. But he was afraid to trust it about something this big.

"No, Matt. I wouldn't lie about that. Your father lied to you, not me. So here's the thing. I'd like you to stay with me, until I can find your mom for you and get you two back together."

Matt's eyes widened. "But if Dad finds out—"

"We can keep him from findin' us. We'll just have to be careful, and you'll have pay attention to what I tell you and do what I say. But we can do it."

"He'd *kill* me if he caught us!"

"If he should catch us—and he won't—but if he does, I'll say I kidnapped you. You know, to pay him back for hurtin' me like he did."

"K-kidnapped me?"

"Sure. That way he can't be mad at you. Only at me. Okay?"

Matthias stared hard at Derry; then he narrowed his eyes. "That's what you really *are* doing, though, isn't it, Derry?" And when Derry looked at him in surprise, Matt went on, telling him what he knew, but not entirely how he knew it. Felt it. "I saw you writing the note, leaving it in my room. I kind of figured that's what was happening."

"You knew I was kidnappin' you? And yet you came with me anyway?"

Lowering his head, Matt sighed. "I guess I figured I'd be better off with a kidnapper than staying with my father. And I think it will be easier to run away from you than it would be to run away from him. You know?"

"You don't have to run away from me, Matthias. You're goin' to be safe with me. I promise."

Matt thinned his lips and slowly nodded his head. But he wasn't nodding because he believed Derry. Because he didn't.

That gift of his, the one that Derry didn't know about, let him hear people's thoughts. It hadn't always been as sharp as it was now. Maybe it had gotten better from living in a house full of vampires and drones who spoke more to each other with their minds than with their mouths. But whatever the reason, it had become stronger and stronger, until now, it happened without him even trying. He heard a lot of what people were thinking.

And just now, he'd heard Derry's thoughts.

He's a good kid. I sure as hell hope I don't have to kill him.

Matt hoped so, too. But he wouldn't count on it. If he wanted to survive, he was going to have to be smart, and not trust anybody besides himself. Because everyone else in the world would always put themselves first. His father had been right about that.

Matt wondered if his mom really was still alive, or if Derry had just been lying to him to get what he wanted. It had felt like the truth, when Derry said it. He hoped his gift was being honest with him.

It didn't matter. He would find out. And even though Derry was thinking about killing him, Matt thought, he was better off with him than he'd been before. One step closer to being free. Just like he'd planned from the day he'd seen his father drag Derrick Dwyer through the house and down to the basement. One look into the man's eyes and he'd known: this man would be his way out.

Briar knelt on the back lawn, just beneath Crisa's bedroom window, palms to the ground, feeling.

"Anything?" Reaper asked.

Rising slowly, Briar stared off toward the thick brush at the lawn's edge. "This way," she said, and she started walking. Not running, because it would be far too easy to get off course, lose track of the signal in favor of speed, and that would do more harm than good.

Reaper caught up in short order, and they made their way into the brush and weeds, pushing through branches, limbs and undergrowth. Crisa hadn't left a physical trail, only a mental one, and that was what Briar followed as she moved through the tangled limbs.

"Does she feel close?" Reaper asked.

"You can't sense her for yourself?"

"I can, slightly. But my connection with Crisa is no-where near as powerful as the one she has with you."

She rolled her eyes. "Yeah, and who's to blame for

that?" She shot a look over her shoulder at him as she asked the question and saw an amused look in his eyes, one he hid quickly.

"*Someone* had to give her blood to save her life, Briar. You were the closest."

"I didn't want to do it. I didn't want—this."

"What? To care about her?"

"It's not caring, it's a compulsion. I don't have a choice but to help her. The damn fact that *my* blood is running through *her* veins is what's driving me, nothing more."

"Right. And there's no…feeling behind it."

"None whatsoever."

"So if she died, the bond would be broken, and you'd feel…?"

"Nothing," she said, pushing limbs aside, pausing to look around, to try to sense where Crisa had gone.

"I don't believe that," Reaper said softly.

She spun around to face him. "You're right. I *would* feel something. Relief to be rid of her. She's like a weight around my neck. I don't *like* feeling responsible for anyone besides myself."

She turned forward again, putting her back to him and her nose to the wind; picking up Crisa's essence, she once again began moving toward her.

"That much I understand," he said as they pressed on. "I didn't like it, either, when I started accumulating this…this gang of ours. I've always worked alone."

"So why didn't you walk away?"

"Same reason you haven't, I guess. I had a bond with Seth, once I shared the gift with him. Then, when we came upon Topaz, she didn't give us a choice but to take her along. We had no option but to rescue Vixen and Ilyana. And Roxy—well, hell, saying no to Roxy isn't really something anyone can do."

She paused and turned to look him in the eye. "And what about me? You can't say you had no choice with me. You kidnapped me, held me by force."

"We were planning to burn Gregor's headquarters and everyone in it. The alternative to taking you was to let you die."

"You ever think I might have preferred it?"

He searched her eyes, her soul, until she had to look away. "Would you?" he asked.

She shrugged and started walking again. "Anyway, you're wrong about us being the same. You may be unable to walk away from your little dysfunctional family, but I'm not. As soon as Crisa is safe, I'm leaving."

"By yourself?"

"Yes, by myself. What do you think I'm going to do, adopt her?"

He sighed but said nothing.

"You don't think I'll do it, do you?"

"I think it's something that's far easier said than done. That's been my experience, at least."

She picked up the pace, feeling Crisa closer than before, and she called out mentally, *Crisa! Wait for me. I'm coming to help you. Just stop running, right now, and wait for me.*

No! You'll make me go back!

And then she felt the girl's flight take on a new urgency. "Dammit, that was a mistake. Come on." Reaching behind her without forethought, she clasped Reaper's hand and began running through the forest. "I never should have told her I was coming. She's running even faster than before."

"We're stronger," Reaper told her. "We'll catch up."

They raced for several hundred yards, before emerging from the brush onto a barren slope that descended to pavement, a parking lot that surrounded a cluster of buildings: gift shops, a diner—a haven for tourists. There were several vehicles taking up spaces. And Crisa was nowhere in sight.

"Briar?"

"She's here. I know she is." She felt Reaper's hand tighten on hers, a gesture meant to reassure her. All it did was remind her that she was holding on to him and make her wonder why. She immediately released her grip. He didn't try to stop her.

And then she spotted Crisa. She was climbing into the passenger side of a pickup truck with a male driver, and before Briar could shout that she absolutely forbade her to go, the truck pulled out of the parking lot and sped away.

"Dammit!" She lunged as if to run after the truck, but Reaper caught her arm, holding her back.

"You'll be seen. Besides, they'll be off the island in minutes, and if you can't catch them on foot in time— which you can't—they'll be even farther ahead. We're going to have to go back and get a vehicle."

She lowered her head, sighing in frustration.

"We'll find her. She'll be okay."

Raising her head, she met his eyes and narrowed her own. "Why are you *really* with me, instead of chasing down leads on Gregor?"

His lips thinned, and he shook his head very slightly. "Why are *you* chasing after Crisa instead of Gregor? I thought finding him was your top priority."

"I told you, it's the blood bond. I don't have a choice."

"Maybe I don't, either," he said softly.

Briar rolled her eyes. "Don't be ridiculous. There's no bond between us."

He was still staring at her, staring deeply into her eyes, and she didn't need to probe his mind to know what he was thinking. He was thinking that there *was* a bond between the two of them. He was thinking about that night when they'd had sex in a car on the street, and how explosive it had been, how intense. He was thinking *that* had bonded them, and he was wishing it could happen again.

Her throat went dry. She swallowed against it. "Let's go find a car."

Crisa sat next to the man in the pickup and let her mind, blissfully silent for a moment, float back only a few minutes, to when she'd been stumbling through the forest, almost blinded by the pain in her head. She was being pursued. She knew it. Arms out ahead of her, she moved faster, even while trying to avoid the scratching branches and pummeling limbs in her path. It wasn't easy, with the boy's image in her mind's eye and the voice in her head that kept urging her on.

Come to me, Crisa. Come here. You must come here. Byram, Connecticut. Just come here. You know you have to do this. For the boy's sake, if not your own.

"Yes."

Her face hurt. She was certain there were scratches on her cheeks and arms, and yet she barely noticed the pain, intent only on moving north. Always north.

And then, suddenly, the image and the voice in her mind vanished utterly, replaced by the certainty that someone was closing in on her from behind. No, not just someone. *Briar.* She realized it even before Briar spoke to her, told her to wait, that she was coming.

She couldn't wait. Briar would try to stop her from doing what she was compelled to do. She ran faster, bursting into preternatural speed, moving more rapidly than any human eye could detect. She stopped only when she burst from the trees into openness, and then stood still for a moment, fighting to get her bearings.

She was on a hill, the woods behind her. Below and in front of her there were buildings and people and... vehicles.

As a man emerged from one of the buildings, heading toward a blue pickup truck while fumbling with a set of keys, she jogged down the small hill toward him, smoothing her still wet hair as she went. "Hey!" she called. "Hey, mister."

He turned in her direction, smiling, but his smile froze in place when he saw her. A frown came instead, and he glanced beyond her, then back again. "Are you all right? Do you need help?"

He was a sturdy young man, with thick dark hair and a whisper of shadow on his cheeks and jaw. He wore faded jeans and a red button-down shirt.

She stopped just two feet from him and nodded. "I need a ride. Do you have room?"

"Yeah. Sure. Here, hop in." He opened the passenger door of his truck and looked, once again, beyond her.

She climbed into the truck and settled herself on the seat, as he stood there holding the door. He said, "You're soaked, and all scratched up. Are you sure you're okay? Did you have an accident or something?"

"I'm fine…but I'm, um, kind of in a hurry."

He nodded. "Okay, then." He closed the door, trotted around to his side of the truck and got in. Within another heartbeat, the vehicle was in motion. "You heading anywhere in particular?"

"North," she told him.

He pulled onto the road, and soon they were picking up speed. "That's not very specific."

"Connecticut."

He smiled a little, then reached past her to flip open the glove compartment. He took a box of tissues from it and dropped it in her lap. "That's definitely more specific. I'm only going as far as Maryland, though."

"Is that the right way?"

He looked at her a little oddly. "Yeah. Maryland is lots closer to Connecticut than you are now."

She nodded, then frowned. "Will we get there before sunrise?"

"Oh, for sure."

"Good. Then I'll go with you to Maryland." She plucked a tissue from the box and dabbed at the sore spots on her face.

"There's a mirror there, above the visor," he said, flipping the visor down as he spoke to show her.

She flipped it back up again, a knee-jerk reaction so fast it made him jump. Vampires cast no reflection. And mortals must never know them for what they were. Rey-Rey had told her that countless times. It was ingrained in her, she guessed. It certainly hadn't come from practice. She'd had very little interaction with mortals since she'd been made over. Other than Roxy and Ilyana, and she'd only known them for the past several days.

The man was looking at her, then the road, then her again.

She covered her momentary panic with a false smile. "I must look a mess right now. I don't want to see how bad."

His frown faded. "Actually, aside from a few scratches on your face and a twig in your hair—" he reached up to plug the offending bit of foliage from her bangs "—you look really pretty."

Her fake smile turned into a real one. "That's nice of you to say."

"Nothing but the truth. What's your name, anyway?"

"Crisa," she told him. "Yours?"

"Bobby."

"It's a nice name." She settled back in her seat, feeling confident that Bobby posed no threat to her.

"Do you like music, Crisa?"

She nodded hard. "Yes, I do. I like all kinds of music."

He reached over and pressed a button. A country song filled the pickup truck, and Crisa tapped her foot in time, leaned her aching head back against the seat and closed her eyes.

But the boy was right there waiting when she did. He looked lost and frightened, and she knew that he needed her, though she wasn't sure how she knew that. She also knew that if she followed that voice, the one telling her to come to Connecticut, she would find the boy.

So that was what she had to do.

6

Topaz had a Benz and a Land Rover in her extensive garage. Roxy's van, Shirley, had joined them, as had Seth's Shelby and Jack's Carrera. The van was gone now. The note Roxy had left said that she and her team had decided to drive west to join the others in case the van with all its special features and equipment was needed. The other two teams had flown to their respective destinations.

Reaper missed his car, which had been annihilated by fire when one of Gregor's drones drove a tanker truck full of gasoline into it. That had only been a few weeks ago, though it seemed much longer.

He had no vehicle now. Shopping for one would be the first thing on his list, once Gregor was destroyed. It seemed as if this job was taking forever.

The Mercedes was a bloodred SL500, a hot car, but Reaper tempered his testosterone with a hefty dose of practicality and chose the Land Rover. It would be a lot more efficient if the terrain turned rough. God only knew how wild a chase Crisa would lead them on, though he couldn't imagine it would be very difficult or take very long to track her down.

Then again, he'd expected killing Gregor to be a fairly simple mission, too, and look how that had turned out.

"We'll take this one," he said, opening the Land Rover's rear door and tossing his bag inside. He'd packed clothes, flashlights, a pair of tranquilizer guns with a few darts and not much else.

Briar's bag looked even lighter than his own. She slung it into the back without a word, then yanked open the passenger door and got in.

Reaper took his place behind the wheel and backed the vehicle out of the garage.

"You're going to have to guide me," he told her as he turned the car so its nose pointed toward the road, then headed down the drive and through the gates at the end. The headlights were bright and cut through the darkness, though he didn't need them to see, even on the blackest of nights.

"North," Briar said softly. "She went north."

He turned right. "She must have talked that mortal into giving her a ride off the island. They'll have to take the bridge."

Briar scanned the roadside as they passed. Shops, diners, one or two places to get gas and basics, lined the island's main road. The ocean was visible on either side, and there were several thickly wooded areas along the way.

"I wonder what they do when there's a hurricane here?" she mused as she sensed the night for signs of Crisa.

"Evacuate, I think."

"I wouldn't like that."

"*You* wouldn't leave."

She looked at him sharply. "What makes you think so?"

"You're stubborn. You're tough. You're mean. You don't like to be inconvenienced. You'd take it personally, as if the storm threatening your home were a deliberate and pre-meditated attack against you, and you'd want to fight back." Reaper shrugged. "Since you don't particularly care if you live or die, you'd have no reason not to."

She blinked at his words. "You think you know me pretty well, don't you?"

"I was describing what I would do," he said. "I have a feeling you'd react the same way."

He waited, and when she didn't answer, he pressed, "Am I right?"

"No, because I'd never live here. It's not my style."

"What *is* your style, Briar?"

She shrugged. "An alley. A park bench. Gregor's dungeon."

"Those aren't real answers."

"Whatever." She sighed, and sat up straighter in her seat. "She's moving faster now."

Reaper shot her a look, read the panic on her face, saw the way her eyes focused on nothing. Her gaze seemed to turn inward, and he knew her sense of Crisa was more powerful than his own could ever be.

"What, Briar? What are you getting?"

She blinked rapidly, seeming to draw herself back all

at once, and then she shot him a desperate look. "She's getting farther and farther away."

"They must be off the island. Probably on the highway, without the speed limits there are here."

"Fuck the speed limits, Reaper. Can't this thing go any faster?"

He pressed down harder on the accelerator, passed a slow-moving hatchback. "I don't want some cop pulling us over."

"Then don't stop if one tries."

Yeah, that would be just brilliant, he thought, imagining a high-speed chase with a barricade of flashing lights and sirens eventually blocking their path. Helicopters and news crews. "We need to stay under the radar," he told her. "Not draw attention to ourselves."

Staring ahead, she lifted her chin. "They're still heading north."

"Then that's where we'll go."

Briar's gaze seemed to sharpen, her attention coming more fully back to the present. She stared at him. "Tell me again why you came with me instead of going out to follow up on one of those leads on Gregor?"

"I already told you. Twice, if we're keeping count. Crisa's more important to me than catching Gregor."

"Crisa's only been with us a few days."

He tipped his head to one side. "You saying she's not more important to you, as well?"

She didn't answer, just crossed her arms over her chest and ignored his question.

"She's an innocent," he said. "She would be more important even if she'd only been with us for a few minutes, Briar."

"Pssh."

It was a sound loaded with sarcasm. "What?" he asked.

"Oh, come on, Reaper. Tell the truth. The whole truth, for once."

He slid his gaze her way, but only briefly. They were hitting the bridge now, and he had to pay attention to his driving. "That *is* the truth. But you're right, it's not the entire truth." He swallowed hard, turned to look at her once again. "There's you."

"Me?"

"Yeah. Crisa's important to you, whether you'll admit it or not. She's managed to touch a part of you that none of us could. And you're important to me, even though I don't have a clue why. I think she's good for you. I think you two need each other. So I want her back for your sake."

She nodded slowly and didn't ridicule his confession, as he'd half expected she would. Maybe she appreciated the honesty. Hell, he didn't know.

"Why am I important to you?"

"If I knew, I'd tell you. Although, when I spoke to Rhiannon last night—"

"You spoke to Rhiannon?" She was clearly surprised. "Why?"

He frowned. "You asked me to try to contact Eric Marquand, to ask for his help. Rhiannon knows how to reach him."

Again her gaze turned intense, focused inwardly as she digested that.

"Are you surprised that I did what you asked me to?"

Turning toward him just slightly, she said, "I guess I am."

"It was a good idea, Briar. A really good idea."

She nodded, not thanking him for the compliment. "So what did she say?"

"She said she had a message for me. She didn't know what it meant, but she knew it was the answer to a question I had. And that answer was, 'Because you think you can't hurt her.'"

Her heavy lids flew upward. "And what was the question?"

"The only one I'd asked recently was the same one you asked me before we went to bed this morning. Why did I want you?" He shrugged.

"So you think you're attracted to me because you think you can't hurt me?"

"Maybe."

"Were you ever attracted to someone you...*did* hurt, then?"

He was silent for a long moment, battling the tide of memories that tried to rise within his mind. When he thought he had it dammed, he said, "Yeah. I did."

She turned to face him fully, one leg drawn up on the seat between them, knee bent. "Will you tell me about her?"

He slanted her a sideways glance and spoke without hesitation or forethought. He said the words to her that he'd never said to another person, confessed what had never been confessed.

"Her name was Rebecca," he said. "I loved her. And then I killed her."

"You comfortable, kid?"

Derry asked the question even as he tossed Matt an extra pillow. Matt took it, tucked it on top of the one beneath his head, and relaxed on the bed in the skeevy motel where Derry had booked them a room.

"Sure. But I'll never sleep."

"Why not? You still hungry?"

"How could I be, after the tacos and the pizza and the shakes?" Matt rolled his eyes. "I'm just not used to sleeping at night, is all."

"Oh." Derry sighed, nodding as if he understood, though Matt wasn't sure he could. For a whole year now, Matt had been living on his father's schedule. Sleeping days, living only by night. Today was the first day he'd been out in the sunshine for what seemed like ages. He'd enjoyed it, even once he'd figured out that he was more or less Derry's hostage. The guy was good to him. And it wasn't like he'd ever have much of a chance to hurt him. His father was going to tear this guy apart when he caught him. And he would. Matt just hoped to be long gone by then.

It was a shame. Derry seemed like a decent guy, except for being willing to kill him and all. After all, he hadn't liked the idea, when it crept into his mind. He really hoped he wouldn't have to do it. Matt knew that for sure.

"You've been up all day," the soon-to-be-dead man said. "Maybe you'll sleep better than you think."

"Maybe. Can I leave the TV on?"

"Sure. Listen, um…don't try to run off on me while I'm asleep, okay?"

"Shoot, where would I go?"

"Back to your father, I imagine. Just…just don't. Promise me, okay?"

Matt took a deep breath and sighed. Then shook his head.

"Why not?" Derry asked.

"'Cause I'm wondering if you're thinking about killing me unless my father does what you say. I'd be pretty stupid to stick around here, wouldn't I?"

Looking stunned, Derry sank onto the mattress. "What makes you think I'd kill you, Matt? Have I done anythin' to even hurt you up to now?"

"No."

"And I'm not *gonna* hurt you, kid. I want to get you back to your mother."

"Yeah, so you said. That would be a really good way to keep me from running off, though, wouldn't it? Telling me my mom's alive, and that you can help me find her?"

"I didn't lie about that."

"Yeah. Sure." Matt drew a breath, because his senses told him it was the truth. But he wanted to believe it so badly, maybe his senses were off. "If I learned anything from my father, it's that you just don't trust anyone. Not *anyone.* Not when you're like us."

"Us?" Derry was puzzled, Matt could feel it in him. "You're not like your father, Matt. You're not a vampire."

Matt decided it wouldn't be smart to tell Derry that he *would* be one someday. His father had told him it was inevitable; that when he got older, it would be either that or death, and his father had no intention of letting him die. He'd said he would change Matt himself, just as soon as Matt was a grown man, just as soon as he was at his strongest, at his peak. That was how his father had put it. He said he wouldn't wait for Matt to get sick and weak. He would change him while he was young and strong. But not until he was a man.

Matt decided it wouldn't be smart to tell Derry any of that. So instead he just told him, "It doesn't matter. My father's gonna kill you for taking me. If you were smart, you'd ditch me somewhere and run as far and as fast as you can. 'Cause he's not gonna be happy when he finds you."

"Her name was Rebecca," Reaper said softly as Briar noted the shift in his tone. The intensity in his voice. The torture in his eyes. "I loved her. And then I killed her."

She stared at him for a long moment, part of her dying to ask him more—who was this Rebecca? How had he killed her? But she didn't. Because that would suggest she was interested, when, in fact, she really didn't care. Besides, his face had taken on a closed-off expression, as if he regretted saying as much as he had.

"You want to tell me about it?" she asked, unable to stop herself.

"I just did."

Message received, she thought.

Briar turned on the radio, found a driving rock song and cranked it up loud, partly to irritate Reaper and partly to distract herself. She wasn't the type to worry about anyone else. But she kept imagining the sorts of trouble Crisa could get into all on her own. And even with the music, those images wouldn't leave her alone.

Reaper reached out and turned the volume down. "I may not be tuned in to Crisa. But I am tuned in to you."

"Oh, this ought to be good."

"You're worried about her."

She rolled her eyes, shook her head, thought about turning the music up again. Then she said, "Who the hell knows what kind of a guy that was, anyway? The one she's riding with, I mean."

Reaper tilted his head and studied her for a second. "I prefer to think he's the kind of guy who sees a girl in trouble and wants to help."

"More likely the kind who sees a girl in trouble and thinks he can take advantage of the situation. Maybe get laid. And maybe he's not too particular about whether she wants it or not."

"Most men aren't like that, Briar."

"A lot you know."

He frowned, so she turned away, gazing out the window at the passing night. "Where the hell are we, anyway?"

"Virginia. We'll be in Maryland soon, though."

"Fucking Maryland. Where the hell is she *going?*"

He ignored her question and asked, "Most of the men you've known have been…like that, haven't they, Briar?"

"Don't start analyzing me, Reaper. Don't even *think* I'll put up with that crap."

"Okay." He sighed, turning his attention back to the road. But he thought he knew something. He thought he'd glimpsed one of her inner demons, and it pissed her off to no end.

"She's going after that boy she keeps seeing in her head," Briar said, to distract him as well as herself. "What the hell do you suppose that's all about, anyway?"

"Damned if I know." He thought about it as he continued driving. "You think he could be real? Not just some kind of delusion or part of whatever's… wrong with her?"

She lifted her brows. "She seems to think so."

"What if she's right?"

"That's not very likely, is it? She's freaking batshit, Reaper."

"Yeah, but she's also a vampire. So let's just say he's real, for the sake of argument. If that's the case, he's almost certainly one of the Chosen. And probably *the* one, for Crisa."

"*The* one?" Briar asked.

"We all feel compelled to protect mortals with the Belladonna antigen. Those rare few who can become what we are. You know that," he told her. "But for each of us there is one with whom that connection is more powerful than with any other. You know *that*, as well."

She nodded slowly.

"So what if this boy is that one for Crisa? What if he really is in some kind of trouble, and she really is needed?"

"What good could *she* possibly do?" Briar asked. "She can barely take care of herself."

"And yet if we stop her from going to him, we could be interfering in something we have no right to interfere with. We could be costing this kid his life."

Briar blinked, not liking where this conversation was going.

"Maybe we shouldn't try to take her back once we catch up to her," Reaper suggested. "Maybe we should go with her, instead. See if this kid is for real, back her up in case she needs us."

She glanced at him. "You really think this could be some real person and not just a figment of her imagination?"

"I think there's a chance, yeah."

She sat still, looking at her hands in her lap and not wanting him to be right. "If one of the Chosen really was in trouble, wouldn't we both be sensing it, as well?" she asked.

"We would, when we were close enough. But this kid is apparently several states away."

She frowned suddenly, and smacked her palm hard against Reaper's shoulder. "Stop! Pull over! Something's happening." Her eyes were dimming, her vision closing in from the sides as the brutal throbbing deep inside her head began all over again. Not her pain. Not hers at all, but Crisa's; she knew that now.

Reaper did as she asked, pulling onto the shoulder

near an exit ramp. As soon as the vehicle came to a stop, Briar opened the door and got out, wandering, hands out in front of her, nearly blind now, because the little boy's face was in her mind. His thoughts wove clearly through her psyche, just as they did through Crisa's.

I think this guy might decide to kill me. It's a shame, too, 'cause he seems nice. But he'll do whatever it takes.

And then she felt panic, and she knew that it, too, belonged to Crisa. The boy was calm. Thinking about his own murder as coolly as if he were thinking about the chance it might rain.

Briar was moving, walking, feeling for Crisa.

In the distance, she could hear Reaper calling her name, his voice urgent. And then she could feel him gripping her shoulders, holding her as she tried to pull free.

"Briar!" Has hand came across her face, the sting just sharp enough to pull her back into herself. The voices faded, and the feeling of panic along with them, but she still felt Crisa's pain.

Blinking her eyes clear, she lifted her head to see that Reaper was standing in front of her, hands on her shoulders, eyes staring into hers. On the highway just beyond him, traffic blew past. Vehicles in every one of the three lanes, speeding along at eighty miles per hour and raising a breeze that whipped her hair.

"Are you all right?" Reaper asked, and from his tone she gathered that he'd repeated the question more than once already.

Staring at him through wide eyes, she shook her head. "No. Wh-what…?"

"You jumped out of the car and started wandering. I thought you were going to walk right out into traffic. What the hell happened?"

She looked at where the Land Rover was parked near the exit ramp, then saw that she was standing in the small triangle of grass between the exit lane curving off to the right and where the main highway stretched ever forward.

"This is where they turned off," she said, pressing a hand to the top of her head, as if she could soothe the throbbing pain that way, then moved toward the sign until she could read it. Baltimore. Then she turned back again, and bent down, hands to the grass. "She got out for a minute. She thought the ride was over, but then she got back in and went with him again."

"So she's going to Baltimore, then? That must be where the boy is," Reaper mused. "But if so, I wonder why we aren't sensing him yet?"

"No." Briar shook her head. "No, that's not where she's going. North, she keeps thinking. Farther north." She looked at the sky. "How long before sunrise?"

Reaper looked at his watch. "About an hour."

Briar nodded firmly. The motion hurt, and she stopped, wincing, and rubbed her aching temples. "She's more capable than I gave her credit for, then. She stayed with him so she could find a place to rest for the day. She'd intended to let him go on his way—to Baltimore. Yes. And she was going to try to find another ride to take her farther. Closer to…Byram."

"Byram?" Reaper asked.

Briar shrugged and massaged the back of her neck

in an effort to relieve the pulsing pain in her head. "Must be the boy's name. Anyway, she realized it was too close to dawn, so she decided to ride into the nearest city with the redneck and find a place to rest."

"And you know all that…how?" Reaper asked.

She shifted her gaze to meet and hold his. "My blood is in her veins. Part of me is traveling with her. Part of me has *become* her. I feel everything she feels right now."

"Including her pain."

"*Especially* her pain."

Reaper slid his hand to the back of her neck, alternately squeezing and then relaxing his grip, and she would have shaken him off, except that it felt so good. She was in pain. She would take any relief she could get.

"We should find a place to rest ourselves," he said. "Might as well take the same exit, stay as close to her as we can."

He opened the passenger door and held it as Briar climbed back in. In a minute they were moving again, taking the same exit Crisa had.

He drove until he saw series of chain hotels, then pulled into the parking lot of the first one they came to.

"She's not here," Briar said.

"No, but we are."

"We still have time," she argued. "We could follow my sense of her a little farther and—"

"She's going to head right back to the highway in the morning, Briar. You said yourself, she wants to keep going north."

Sighing, she lowered her head in defeat.

"Let's get settled in. We'll use the extra time to check in with the others, see if any of those leads on Gregor have panned out, and get the room secured against sunlight. Okay?"

She wasn't having an easy time being patient. But then again, when had she? "Okay. And then…maybe you can tell me the rest of that story you started earlier."

"What story would that be, Briar?"

"The one about the woman you say you loved and killed. Rebecca, wasn't it?"

He averted his eyes, getting out of the car. She got out, too, and they walked toward the entrance. Every click of her shoes on the sidewalk was like a tiny nail spiking into her brain.

"I don't talk about that," he said.

"Oh, come on. You know you want to. I'll tell you about one of my kills, if you want."

He slanted her a sideways look. "I really don't want to hear about you murdering the innocent, Briar."

"Oh, hell, none of them are innocent." She sighed and shrugged, and as they entered the hotel lobby, she went on, speaking mentally now instead of aloud. *Fine, we won't exchange kill stories, then. I'll give you something else in exchange for you telling me about Rebecca.*

What?

Sex.

He swung his head toward her so fast the motion drew notice from the desk clerks and a couple relaxing in one of the overstuffed chairs in the lobby seating area. It had been almost unnatural, that movement. Especially since none of the onlookers had heard a word of the exchange.

She smiled slowly, in spite of her throbbing headache. *You want it, don't you?*

He just held her gaze, then turned, stepped up to the desk and said, "We need a room."

"Check in time isn't until—"

"We'll pay extra. Just check us in now."

"All right, sir. Would you like a king or two doubles?"

"King," he said, glancing at Briar once more. "One bed."

"Two beds," she corrected, then added silently to Reaper alone, *I said I'd fuck you, not sleep with you.* She sent him a sexy wink, then looked away and tried not to feel her stomach tightening in need and delicious anticipation.

But she felt it anyway.

7

— ▸ —

Seth and Vixen flew to Dallas, rented a car and went straight from the airport to the address mentioned in the news report. It was one of many dormitory buildings at a private college, and it was completely surrounded by yellow police tape.

Vixen touched Seth's arm, then met his eyes. "I don't think I can go in there."

"Yeah. The death energy is pretty overwhelming, isn't it?"

"It was brutal, what happened there." She closed her eyes and felt the panic, the pain, the fear, that had swept through the building such a short time ago. She felt the blows, saw the blood that even now stained the walls and floors. "They didn't die in the ecstasy of a vampire's embrace," she whispered. "They were brutalized, savaged. And yet…"

"And yet there were vampires here. But the energy is off." Seth dragged his gaze from the building, focusing on his beloved mate instead. "Stay here, out of sight. I'll go in, take a quick look around and come right back."

She shook her head. "I'll go with you."

"You don't have to."

"I want to." She slid her hand into his, and they exploded from the sheltering trees in a burst of vampiric speed, to keep from being seen by anyone who might be watching. And it was quite apparent to both of them that someone was. Even though it was the middle of the night, this place was a crime scene and probably the talk of the campus. The door burst open as if caught by a freak gust of wind, or at least that was how it would appear to human eyes, and then they were inside.

Seth pushed the door closed, and the two of them moved through the entryway, up the stairs and along the halls. None of the doors were closed tightly, much less locked. It was, Vixen thought, probably too much trouble for the investigators to have to unlock them every time they returned, and they were no doubt far from finished processing this crime scene.

"Three girls died in this one," she whispered, standing in the hallway outside the slightly open door, head down, eyes closed.

Seth peered inside, but she didn't have to look to know what he saw. Flashes she tried not to see snapped through her mind. The blood spatter on the far wall. The thickened puddle of it that had dried on the floor. The stains on the bed.

"Two more there," she said, pointing. "There was more than one attacker. Not humans, but not vampires, either—or not exactly."

"I know exactly what they were," Seth said. "I've

fought those bastards before." He met Vixen's eyes, his own filled with anger.

"Drones," Topaz said. "A half dozen of them, and maybe more."

She and Jack were at the house in Oklahoma City where the mass murder had taken place. The scene had been cleaned up, but thirteen victims had been killed there, and the energy their passing had left behind was laced with panic, pain and horror.

"I don't get any sense of Gregor, though," Jack said, as they moved through the house. "I don't think he was even here."

Topaz turned to face him, staring into his eyes while seeking inwardly for an answer. "But we know he commands an army of them. Do you think these drones acted of their own accord?"

"I don't know what reason they'd have," Jack said. "Besides, they don't have brains enough to do *anything* of their own accord." He stepped over a broken vase. "They didn't drain the victims. There's blood everywhere. Like they were in a rage, but we both know those lummoxes don't feel enough to work up a good anger over anything. They only do what they're told to do."

"So Gregor told them to come here and kill those people." Topaz gazed around the room. There were still half-full glasses on the table, trays filled with finger foods, bowls of already stale chips and souring dip. The sound system on the far wall had a red light flashing on and off incessantly. Someone had apparently hit the pause button, instead of Stop.

She could look at the floor and see where and how each and every body had fallen. And she could have sensed that even without the bloodstains and chalk outlines that marked the spots.

"Why would Gregor send his drones out to commit apparently random mass murders?"

Her cell phone rang. Swearing and looking around quickly, as if in fear of being overheard, Topaz tugged it from her bag and flipped it open, then glanced at Jack. "It's Roxy. What's up, Rox?" she said into the phone.

"It's a diversion," Roxy said. "It has to be. Wait, I've got Seth on the other line. I'll bring him in." She clicked a button, activating her phone's three-way calling feature. "Listen to me. You're finding the same messes at both crime scenes. I can't sense things the way you can, but I don't think this was a vampire."

"It was the drones," Seth said.

"What we can't figure out is why," Vixen added.

"You can't?" Roxy asked. "Listen, think about it. Who commands an army of drones?" She answered her own question before either of them could get a word in. "Gregor does."

"But none of us are sensing Gregor's presence," Jack said. "I'd know if he'd been here."

"Maybe not. Maybe he's found some way to conceal his presence," Seth offered. "He *has* to be behind this. Lurking somewhere, pulling the strings."

"I agree," Roxy said. "Look, find shelter for the

day. Ilyana and I will keep driving straight through—
we'll head to Oklahoma City first, because it's closer.
We should be there before the day's out. We'll pick
up Jack and Topaz then head down to meet you and
Vixen in Dallas. From there we'll plan our next move.
All right?"

They all disconnected, and Topaz turned to Jack. "I
don't have a good feeling about this," she said.

He slid his arms around her waist, pulled her close.
"It'll be okay. Roxy's right, we need to find shelter before sunrise."

She nodded her agreement, but tipped her head up for
his kiss before pulling from his arms and turning to
look at their surroundings. "This house isn't exactly
isolated," she said softly. "And we can't very well hole
up in the basement, not with the police likely to return,"
she added with a look through a window at the yellow
tape that surrounded the place.

"Wouldn't want to take shelter too close, anyway.
Those lumbering bastards could be lurking."

"Wouldn't we sense them?"

"Not if Gregor the Great taught them to shield." Jack
clasped her hand as they started back toward their rental car, and she caught him wrinkling his nose as he
reached for the door of the ordinary-looking compact.

"Missing your Carrera?" she asked.

He met her eyes, smiled a little sheepishly. "I'm not
a snob. But this is a major step down."

"You're not a snob," she agreed, as she opened her
door and got in. "But you're *such* a guy."

* * *

In his mansion, Gregor sat at a horseshoe-shaped desk in what had once been Eric Marquand's basement laboratory, computers all around him. He'd taken all the equipment from Dwyer's office, the stuff he used to monitor Crisa, and set it up here, right beside his own systems.

But it wasn't Crisa he was focusing on just now as he watched the blips move along the screen. Two separate maps filled his monitor, each one with a tiny light blinking as it inched along the spiderweb of lines that represented roads. His subjects were on the move, in search of shelter. His drones had done well, surprisingly well, in planting the GPS tracking devices on the vehicles without being seen or sensed. When the members of Reaper's misfit gang stopped to rest, he would know exactly where they were.

And if all went as it should, they wouldn't be leaving any time soon.

The abduction of his only son hadn't interfered with the elaborate plan he'd spent endless hours concocting. He couldn't allow it to interfere. He would deal with Dwyer and bring Matthias back all in good time. But nothing would delay him in his quest to lure Reaper and Briar to him—alone—to receive their well-deserved punishment.

And it wouldn't be long.

Reaper watched as Briar came out of the hotel bathroom. She wore a hotel-issue white terry robe that came only to mid-thigh, and was toweling her riotous curls as she moved. It was dark and wild, her hair. And he thought, as he watched her move across the room, that *she* was dark and wild, as well.

She sat on the first bed she reached. He was standing near the window, which faced due north, out of reach of the sun's direct rays. There were three layers of protection, besides. Vertical blinds, sheer curtains and heavy damask draperies. They would be safe here.

"So?" she asked.

"So…what?"

She stopped rubbing her hair, tossed the damp towel onto the floor and leaned back against the headboard. "You going to tell me about Rebecca?"

He nodded slowly. "I've never talked to anyone about her, you know. But for some reason, I think I want to tell *you*."

She lifted her brows, eyeing him in a way that suggested she thought that was strange but said only, "Why?"

"I think it's because I want to make sure you know just how dangerous I truly am, before this…this thing between us goes any further."

Rolling her eyes, she said, "There's no *thing* between us." Then she let her gaze slide down him and looked directly at his zipper. "Not yet, anyway."

"You do that a lot," he said.

"Do what?" She was looking him in the eye again.

"When the conversation veers toward anything deep, anything real, you shift it to something sexual."

"And sex isn't *real?*"

He said nothing. She sighed, reached over and

grabbed a hairbrush from the nightstand. Then she folded her legs on the bed and began brushing her hair, not looking at him again as she spoke. "You're the one changing the subject, Reaper. Who was Rebecca?"

He drew a breath, because he hadn't lied when he'd said that she should be warned. Because despite her denials, there *was* something between them. And there was going to be a lot more, if he could ever break through the barriers she'd spent a lifetime building up. Maybe by telling her this story, he would make her more likely to share something about her own deepest pain with him.

Because he knew she was in pain. A lot of it. He'd never seen anyone in as much pain as Briar, or more in denial of it.

She sent him a look.

She was waiting. All right, then.

"Rebecca was my wife."

Her brush hovered in the air near her head. He thought it shook a little. Was her hand trembling in reaction to his revelation?

"I married her before I knew what the Agency had in mind for me. We both knew there would be months of separation as I went through my training. But neither of us knew that I wouldn't be the same person when I returned."

"What was she like?"

"She was…you'd call her soft, I think. She was sensitive, emotional, cried all the time. When she was happy, when she was sad, when she got nervous. There was a vulnerability about her."

"She was wearing a kick-me sign, huh?"

He glanced at her. "I guess you'd see it that way."

"If you're vulnerable, you're just asking to get hurt," she said. She finished brushing her hair and tossed the brush onto the nightstand, then took a pack of cigarettes from it and shook one free. "What did she look like?" Then she held up a hand. "Wait, wait, let me guess."

"Okay, guess."

She lit her smoke, dropped her lighter, took a long drag and leaned back again, stretching her legs out on the bed. "Probably could have been a model. Tallish. Not too tall, though. Probably stick-thin. Small tits. But perky, I'll bet."

She took another puff. "Blond?"

Reaper stared at her. "That's very good."

"She probably never smoked, rarely drank, and when she did, one or two would do her in. And she considered swearing to be a sign of a lousy upbringing, a lack of class or intelligence or just bad manners."

Now he narrowed his eyes. "How are you getting all this?"

"Easy. Just imagining my polar opposite." Shaking her head, she said, "I hate women like that. Weak, needy, always playing the victim. She must have driven you crazy."

"I loved her."

"Sure you did. So then why'd you kill her?"

He averted his eyes, maybe a little too quickly. She'd hit him where it hurt.

"Let me guess. You said you came home from your training a different man from the one you'd been before. And from then on, every time you went out on a mission, went out to assassinate some dictator, killing for a living, you came back a little colder. A little harder. A little more distant."

He nodded. "I couldn't tell her what I did for the Agency. The lying, the hiding it from her, the constant fear she'd find out…it really drove a wedge between us."

"She would have left you if she'd known."

"I wish she had," he said.

"So she found out and couldn't handle it. Took a header off a roof somewhere or OD'd on tranquilizers. Some easy suicide like that, 'cause she wouldn't have been strong enough to do anything messy. And you've been blaming yourself for it ever since, right?"

He turned and looked her squarely in the eyes. "No."

Briar blew smoke rings, shrugged. "No? What do you know, I got one wrong. So how did she die?"

He held her eyes. She lowered the cigarette from her lips and stubbed it out in the ashtray on the nightstand, all without looking away.

"I was going to quit for her," he said. "I was going to walk away. But before I got the chance to tell her, she said my trigger word. I killed her with my bare hands."

He watched her reaction, the way her eyes widened in shock and disbelief. The way she blinked three times in quick succession. The way her face softened just the slightest bit.

"I raged until I passed out. When I came to, she was on the floor a few yards away. Her neck was broken."

"Shit," Briar whispered. "What did you do?"

"What I was trained to do when I got into trouble.

Called Dwyer—started to, anyway. He was there before
I even got my ass up off the floor."

She lifted her brows in question.

"Derrick Dwyer was my supervisor at the Agency.
Apparently Rebecca had called for help, but it was too
late. By the time he got there, it was over." He paused,
took a breath. "He brought in a team to clean up. They
took her body away, removed every trace of evidence,
yanked me out of circulation and told me not to speak
to anyone or ask any questions. A week later, her family were notified that she'd been killed in a car accident.
There were no questions, no investigation, no suspicion. I played the grieving widower until she was in the
ground. And that was the end of it."

Briar swung her legs off the bed and sat on the
edge of the mattress, leaning forward. "How was that
the end of it?"

"Because it just was. That was it. Done. Over."

"You ever wonder why she said that trigger word,
Reaper?"

He shook his head. "It was an accident. Probably
came up in conversation."

"Uh-uh. It's not that kind of a word. I can't even remember the last time I had a conversation where that
particular word came up. You might hear it on a TV
show, or in a song. Definitely in a song. But not in casual small talk."

He sighed. "It doesn't matter. It happened. I can't
undo it."

"Seth didn't think you would kill him. Remember

back when Gregor had you over a barrel? When he was going to kill me unless you slit your wrists and let him watch you bleed out? And I said your trigger word, because I didn't see any other way out, and you went off on all of us?"

"Seth's young and idealistic. I'd have killed him."

"You didn't, though. You banged everyone around, but you didn't kill any of us."

"You're vampires. A vampire can take a lot more than a mortal female."

"Roxy's not a vampire. You didn't kill her, either."

"Somehow I think Roxy would be tougher to kill than any of us. Mortal or otherwise."

She was shaking her head slowly. "No, there's something wrong with this story. There's something off about the whole damn thing, I'm telling you." She frowned at him, as if looking for something in his face that she wasn't seeing. "You worked for the C-I fucking A. You're telling me this whole thing doesn't stink to you?"

He shrugged. "Dead is dead, Briar. The details don't matter all that much, and to be honest, I don't think I can talk about it anymore."

She was silent for a long moment, and then, with a sigh, she said, "Okay." Then she got off the bed. "Okay."

He looked up, drained from sharing his past with her, wondering if he'd managed to make even a chink in the armor she wore day and night. She had been right about one thing: Rebecca *had* been her polar opposite. In every possible way.

She moved closer to him now, lifted one hand, and

tugged the sash that held her robe together and let it fall open. She let him take in what she had revealed. The inner swell of her breasts. The smooth skin of her belly. The dark triangle of curls between her legs.

She came to him where he sat in the chair, waiting. And then she straddled him and lowered herself onto his lap. Gripping a handful of his hair, she tipped his head back, covered his mouth with hers and kissed him. She tasted smoky and sexy and good.

He let his hands slide up underneath her robe to cup her bare ass, and squeezed. She lifted her head, and when she stared down into his eyes, hers were blazing.

"You ready for your reward, big guy? Hmm?"

He stared back at her, every bit as aroused as she was. He was hard, and he wanted nothing more than to take her right then and there. But instead, he shook his head.

"No."

Her eyes flared wider just briefly and she went still. "What the hell do you mean, 'no'?"

"I didn't tell you that so you'd screw me, Briar. I told you so you'd know. And I think maybe it's time for you to stop using sex as currency. You're not a street kid anymore, and you're not a whore."

"You don't want me?" she asked, her eyes narrow, angry.

"Not like this."

She shoved her hand between them, stroked the bulge in his jeans and said, "You're a liar."

He clasped her hand at the wrist and pushed it away. "You're right. I want you. And I'll have you. But when

I do, it will be because you want it, too. Not because you're trading it for something. Okay?"

She got up and turned to move away, but he was still grasping her wrist, so she couldn't go far. So she faced him again, head swinging around. "What the hell are you trying to do, Reaper? What do you want from me? You want me to come to you all needy like your freaking dead wife or something? You want me to beg for it?"

"No. No, that's not what… I want you to want it. That's all."

"Wanting makes you weak. I don't want, much less need, anything or anyone. Ever."

He nodded, and released her hand as he got to his feet and headed for the bathroom to take a cold shower. Pausing at the door, he said, "Do you think I'm weak or needy, Briar?"

She lifted her head, met his eyes.

"I want to have sex with you," he said when she didn't answer. "No strings. No reason. No deal. Just sex, not because it's owed but for the sole purpose of mutual pleasure. When you want that, too, you let me know."

Without waiting for a reply, he went into the bathroom, closed the door behind him, leaned back against it and thumped his head into the wood three times, not caring if she heard.

Hell, why didn't he just screw her? He'd intended to. He didn't know what the hell had happened to change his mind.

Yes, he did. He knew. He didn't want to be just another trick. He wanted her to want him. The way he was pretty sure she had once wanted that bastard Gregor, though he couldn't imagine why.

He cranked on the tap and stepped into the cold spray of the shower, knowing he had to kill the man. And not because he'd been well paid to do so. Hell, at this point, he'd do it gratis.

Maybe that would finally get Gregor and the pain he'd inflicted out of Briar's system.

Roxy sat in the passenger seat, and looked out at the passing scenery. The sun had risen. Her vampiric friends would all be resting by now, as Mirabella was in one of the van's hidden beds concealed in the back. Ilyana sat behind the wheel, taking a turn with the driving. The console between them held two paper bags that Roxy had put there, holding snacks she'd grabbed at the last rest stop. She reached into the largest of them now and tugged out a foam box, then offered it to the blonde, who looked as if she would blow away in a strong wind.

"Breakfast sandwich?" Roxy asked.

Ilyana wrinkled her nose, but at least her eyes reacted. She emerged from her self-imposed cocoon long enough to meet Roxy's gaze. "I couldn't eat."

"You really should. You're too skinny as it is." As she said it, she placed the box that held the ham, egg and cheese croissant onto her lap, and reached into the second bag. "I got us a box-o-Joe from DD. Have a cup? Best coffee there is."

"That I'll take," Ilyana said. So Roxy got the cardboard coffee dispenser into position and poured two cups. It wasn't easy on this particular expanse of highway, which was ridiculously bumpy, but she managed it, then capped the box and tucked it back into its bag.

Her expression troubled, she sipped her coffee and watched Ilyana do the same.

"You wish we were already in Oklahoma City, don't you?" she asked Ilyana.

The other woman nodded, pushed one hand through her close-cropped platinum hair, and nodded again. "Yes, I do. Gregor's behind those murders. There's no doubt about it, is there?"

Roxy shrugged. "Maybe a little doubt."

Ilyana sighed.

"Okay, precious little. But realistically, what good is our being there going to do? We have four crime scenes, two of which have already been checked out by our… colleagues—and no hard evidence Gregor ever set foot in any of them. Clearly his drones were th—"

"If those lummoxes were there, Gregor was there," Ilyana snapped.

"Where? The murders took place in four different states, Ilyana."

She lowered her head all at once. "I know. I just—"

"You just want to be going after him, wherever he is. You want your son back."

Ilyana didn't confirm that. She didn't need to. Roxy had never had kids of her own, but she thought she had a pretty good idea what the blonde was feeling right now. Helpless. Furious. Desperate.

Ilyana was thumbing the silver charm she wore around her neck, rubbing it absently as she drove.

Roxy eyed the thing. She'd never seen Ilyana without it. "Is that a locket?"

Looking up sharply, Ilyana met her eyes, then nodded.

"Do you have his picture in there?"

"Yes." Ilyana adjusted her grasp, then flipped the locket face open and held it out toward Roxy.

Roxy leaned closer, took it in her fingertips and stared at the intelligent-beyond their-years eyes of a young boy.

"That's my Matthias," Ilyana said. "He's ten, now. It was taken on his last birthday."

Roxy smiled as she eyed the boy, with his thick head of butterscotch hair in a bowl cut, and his big brown eyes, and the handful of freckles across the bridge of his nose.

"He's a looker, all right," she said. "You must miss him terribly."

Ilyana nodded. "His father can't take care of him the way I can. Gregor doesn't understand him. He never did."

"How is it that all three of you have the belladonna antigen?" Roxy asked. "It's an incredible coincidence, that."

"It's no coincidence at all. Gregor knew he was one of the Chosen, and he knew what it meant. He worked for the CIA—they'd drafted him partly because of the antigen, after all. So he knew. He deliberately sought out a woman who had it, as well. He pretended to fall in love with me, played a role, lied about everything until he got me pregnant. A child born to two parents with the antigen is almost certain to have it himself."

"But...why?" Roxy frowned as she gently closed

the locket over young Matthias's face and released it. "Why would he want to raise a child with the antigen?"

"He saw Matthias as the beginning of his dynasty. Gregor worked out almost non-stop before the CIA made him over in their monster lab or whatever the hell they have over there. He wanted to be in peak condition when he was changed. I have no doubt he intends to see to it that Matthias is even better than he was. Young, strong, not even getting close to weakening yet." She lowered her head. "He won't give Matt a chance to live out his mortal life before he makes him into one of them. And God only knows what he's doing to my son's mind in the meantime. He's so bright, so sensitive...."

"He's got intelligence in his eyes," Roxy said softly, wishing she could offer more than words in comfort.

"He's got more than that." Ilyana lowered her head. "He's special, my boy. And I'd much rather be in one of the four locations where he might be, even not knowing which one is right, than to be somewhere else where I know he isn't."

"Just hang on, Ilyana. We're on our way. And I promise you, the instant we get a lead on Gregor, we'll go after him. You and me. I promise."

Ilyana sighed. "I know."

"We might know something even before we get there. It'll be sundown by the time we get to Oklahoma City."

"That's true."

It *was* true. And it was just after dark by the time they found a diner and settled in to await contact from the others. They were still pacing and worrying when

Roxy's phone rang, and as she picked up, she heard Vixen's voice speaking very softly.

"We're completely surrounded," Vixen said. She sounded as if she were on the verge of tears. "There's no way out."

8

Topaz came awake quickly, just as she always did. She and Jack had taken refuge in an abandoned house about forty miles south of the crime scene in Oklahoma City. It was in the middle of nowhere, and in good enough repair that the locks would keep any ordinary intruders at bay.

She rolled onto her side, and smiled sleepily as Jack stretched his arms over his head, eyes still closed, then snapped one arm around her and hugged her tight. It felt good to be with him this way. Secure. Not doubting. Just knowing.

They made slow, delicious love, relishing the feelings they'd finally admitted having for each other. She hadn't thought life could ever be this good.

She kissed his chin, then eased out of his arms and out of their bed—a well-worn sofa that had been left behind. Feet bare, clad in her tank top and panties, Topaz walked to the front door and unfastened the deadbolt. The thing was so old and rusty, she'd been surprised it still worked. It took a little effort to unlock it. But she did.

"Running out on me already?"

"I just want to see what kind of night it is."

"Moon's a waning crescent. It's chilly and clear. Almost no wind. And it's dark outside. Now come back to bed."

She sent him a smile. "Patience, caveman. I'll be there before you know it." Then she twisted the knob and pulled the door open, taking a half step out into the fresh, cool night before she saw them and froze in place.

Men. Lumberjack-sized men. No. Not men. Her eyes scanned them, realizing they formed a living boundary around the place, even as she jerked back into the house, slammed the door and slid the lock. "I think we're in trouble, Jack."

Her tone, and the energy behind it, must have been pretty clear to him, because he was beside her almost before she finished the sentence, wearing his boxer-briefs and reaching for the door.

"Don't," she said. "Don't unlock it."

He frowned at her, then moved to the window, parted the layers of "curtains" they'd hung and glanced outside. He blinked long and slow, and then looked again.

"Drones." He said it like a curse word.

"Yeah. And it looks like they've surrounded the place."

"Hell." He moved to the other side of the room and took a look from another window, confirming her guess with a nod in her direction.

"Shit, Jack, what are we going to do?"

He met her eyes, then crossed the room to where she stood and folded her into his arms. "We'll think of something."

"What? Did you see how many are out there? Dozens!"

"Twenty-two," he said. "I only counted twenty-two."

"*Only* twenty-two?"

He held her harder and even laughed a little, but she knew it was fake. "Look, we'll just hang tight, see what they have in mind."

"What they have in mind is tearing us into bite-sized bits, Jack."

"I don't think so." He backed up a little, still holding her, but staring down into her eyes. "If they wanted to kill us, they'd be storming the place by now, wouldn't they? Why take up formation out there? Surrounding the place as if…"

"As if they don't want us to be able to leave," she said slowly. "Jack, what the hell is Gregor up to this time?"

"I don't know." He pulled out his cell phone. "We have to let the others know the situation, see where things stand with them."

He flipped his cell phone open, dialed Roxy's number and waited.

Baltimore.

It had been a lifetime since Briar had left this city with nothing more than a backpack stuffed as full as she could stuff it and the bruises her stepfather had left on her body. She'd been fifteen, bound for New York, determined to make it on her own.

She hadn't. She would have been dead if Gregor hadn't found her the night he had. She'd been drunk on cheap wine when her latest john had tossed her out of his car after she threw up on him. Hadn't even paid her. Called her a filthy whore and left, his tires spitting gravel as he spun away. That was where Gregor had found her. That was where he had changed her.

That was where he'd told her you couldn't trust anyone but yourself, a lesson she'd already learned the hard way. But she'd been a fool, because she'd begun to trust *him*. And in return, he'd damn near killed her. Would have, if it hadn't been for Reaper and his band of merry men. And women.

She would have vengeance on Gregor. She would.

But the list of men she intended to murder was a long one. And the man whose name was second from the top was still living right here in Baltimore. It was too good an opportunity to pass up. And it would distract her from the storm roiling deep down inside her. The one Reaper stirred up every time he tried to see something good in her. He was so wrong. Maybe this would prove that to him once and for all, and he would see her for who she really was.

Evil. She was evil personified. He'd killed because he couldn't help himself. He'd taken lives because that was what he'd been programmed to do by those who'd gained access to his mind. He regretted the blood on his hands.

She wouldn't. She would relish this.

She rose before he did, went into the bathroom and cranked on the shower taps. Then she closed the bathroom door and crept out of the hotel, into the newborn darkness.

The city was coming to life. She hailed a taxi and

gave the man the address of the house where she'd grown up, every nerve tight and tingling as they drove.

And when the taxi stopped outside the house, at the outer edge of the city, she sat there, staring at it for a long moment.

"This the place?" the driver asked.

She shifted her focus from the yard behind the chain-link fence, where she used to play, to the driver, who was frowning into the rearview mirror and reaching up to adjust it, no doubt wondering why the hell he couldn't see her face in the glass.

She opened the door and got out, then leaned back in long enough to hand him a ten-dollar bill. The fare was $8.50. Close enough. Then she turned to stare at the house while the driver pulled away.

So many memories. Dammit.

"Who lives here, Briar?"

She spun around, first startled and then furious. Reaper was standing a few feet away, hands thrust into the pockets of his coat, wind blowing his dark hair.

"This is my business, Reaper. You shouldn't be here."

"Anger is coming off you in waves."

"I get that way when people poke around in my business. Or when I'm followed."

He shook his head slowly. "You were angry before you knew I was here, and too focused on that house to even sense my approach. Who lives here, Briar?" he asked again.

She lifted her brows, tipped her head to one side. "I did. Once."

"And now?"

She shook her head and started for the door. "Go away, Reaper."

"I'm not going anywhere."

"Then you can watch." She never broke her stride again, just went up to the front door, twisted the knob until the lock snapped and then walked right inside.

A woman Briar had never seen before rose from an easy chair, where she'd been reading a magazine and smoking a cigarette. She was middle-aged, with dirty blond hair, a bad perm that had gone out of style twenty years ago, and worry lines around her eyes and mouth.

"What…who— I thought that door was locked. What is this?"

"I'm looking for Martin Rose. Does he still live here?"

"Well, yes, but—"

"Yeah, he's here. I smell the bastard." Briar started forward, crossing the living room toward the hallway that led to the den.

The woman sidestepped, blocking her path. "He's asleep."

Briar stared at the woman. "You might want to be careful, lady. This isn't your business."

"I'm going to call the police if you don't leave right now," the woman said, her voice rising with fear.

Before Briar could react, Reaper's hands were on her shoulders, firm, holding her. She wanted to turn around and punch him in the jaw, but instead she drew a calming breath.

"I'm his stepdaughter," Briar said, her words clipped.

"Why don't you just tell him I'm here and see what he says before you call out the National Guard?"

The woman blinked, staring at her. "No one could find you."

"I didn't want to be found. Who are you, my mother's latest replacement?"

The woman swallowed before speaking, clearly upset, though now she seemed to be fighting to remain calm. "I'm his nurse. One of them, at least. Your father—"

"*Step*father."

"Your stepfather is a very sick man."

And about to get a lot sicker, Briar thought. "Either tell him I'm here or get out of my way, lady. I'm not going to ask again."

The woman sent a pleading look beyond her, no doubt silently asking Reaper to control her. As if. Apparently he didn't give any sign that he was going to help her cause, because the blonde sighed and stepped aside.

Briar stared down the hallway at the den's closed door and without looking at the woman said, "It would probably be a good idea for you to get the hell out of here now."

Nurse Nancy nodded jerkily, and, snatching a jacket from the back of a chair as she passed, she hurried to the door and through it.

Reaper said, "She's going to call the police the second she's a safe distance from us."

"Yeah, I can read thoughts, too." She was still staring at the door. "I'm asking you to leave."

"I'm not going to. You don't want to do this, Briar."

"No?" She turned to glare at him. "Let me tell you

something, Reaper. If you try to stop me, I'll use your trigger word and let you do the job for me."

The threat stunned him. It was clear in the way he drew back slightly, as if she'd struck him with a fist and knocked him off balance. But she ignored that, along with the look of pain that flashed into his eyes and the wish that she could suck the words back. Too late.

She turned to the den door, twisted the knob and flung it open, stepping into the room in one long stride.

But it wasn't a den anymore. It was a bedroom, identical in every way to a hospital room, except that it was located in a house. There was an IV pump standing to one side of the standard-issue hospital bed, with three bags hanging from the hooks above it, dripping steadily into tubes that wound and merged and joined one larger tube that was stuck into Martin's arm.

That was the first thing she noticed about him. His arm. It was white, whiter than her own, and the skin was like paper. Between skin and bone, there wasn't much else. And as her gaze moved higher, she saw that the upper arm was just as thin as the forearm, before it disappeared beneath the short sleeve of a hospital gown. A blanket covered him from the chest down, his arms resting atop it.

It took her a while to force her gaze upward, to his neck, where the skin hung loose, as if the man beneath had vanished when it wasn't looking. Then, finally, she looked at his face. Sunken. Hollow. Gray. He didn't seem to be breathing. But after a moment he sucked in one long, stuttering gasp. Then nothing again.

"Good thing you got here when you did," Reaper said. "He'll be dead in a day or two, if not by morning."

She couldn't move, couldn't reply. There was a tremor working through her from somewhere down deep, making its way slowly to the surface. Her hands began to shake, her stomach, to clench.

"Well, what are you waiting for?" Reaper asked. "Do it. Kill him."

She closed her eyes, blocking out the view of the monster who'd haunted her dreams for the past seven years.

"You'll probably want to wake him up first," Reaper went on. "Though I don't know if that's even possible. So just do it. Do you want to strangle him, or just bash his head in with something heavy?"

"Shut up."

"Say the word and I'll do it for you. You know the word I mean, right, Briar?"

"Shut the fuck up!"

He shut up. She opened her eyes again, all the useless rage pooling inside her turning into something else, something heavy and dense.

In the distance, a siren sounded.

"We have to get out of here, Briar." His tone had changed. It was oddly tender now. Soft. His hand went to her shoulder.

She shook it off, knuckled a hot tear from her cheek and stepped closer to the bed. Standing right beside the man who'd taken her virginity at the tender age of eleven, she lifted her hands and bent closer, lowering them. Her left hand closed around his neck. She didn't need the right. One was enough to almost fully encircle it. Grating her teeth against the bile that rose in her throat at the physical contact, she tightened her grip. Do it, she told herself. Choke the life out of the vile bastard. It's long overdue.

Her hand trembled. Why was it taking her so long? She was a vampire; she could crush his larynx in the blink of an eye. Just squeeze, dammit.

And yet she didn't. She couldn't. Her hand shook harder, and then she relaxed her grip, jerking her flesh away from the disgusting contact with his and turning her back on the broken old man lying in the bed.

"You can't do it, can you?" Reaper asked.

She couldn't look at him. "Only because I'd be doing him a favor."

She brushed past him and walked out of the room, then out of the house.

An hour later they were back in the Land Rover, heading northeast. Briar had asked Reaper to let her drive this time, and he'd had no objections. She probably needed the distraction, he thought. She had reverted to the quiet, morose, almost clinically depressed state in which she'd been living during those first couple of weeks after Gregor had tortured and tried to kill her. Once Crisa had joined their ranks, she'd begun a slow emergence from the darkness. But this episode with her stepfather seemed to have plunged her back into the depths once more. Briefly, he hoped.

"I'm sorry, for what it's worth."

"Sorry for what?" she asked, not looking at him. The headlights of passing vehicles painted her face in streaks of pale blue and luminous white. He watched her in the changing hues, but her expression never changed. It gave him no clue to what was going on within.

"For all of it. Whatever he did to y—"

"He raped me. Repeatedly."

"And you never told?"

"Who would I tell?"

"Your mother?" he asked, watching, probing, sensing the spike of emotion that didn't show in that brief moment before she squelched it.

"He told me he'd kill me if I ever told my mother. Told me she would never believe me, anyway. Told me she would hate me for it. Told me it would kill her. That was the main thing. When he told me it would kill her. 'Cause in the end, I was pretty sure it had."

He tipped his head to one side. "She died, your mother?"

She nodded, bit her lip as if to keep herself from saying anything more.

"How old were you?"

"Fourteen. She had pancreatic cancer. But I didn't know from shit, you know? I figured she must have found out my secret. And that it killed her, just like that bastard said it would."

He nodded slowly. "That would make sense, I guess, to a fourteen-year-old." He looked at her face, watching its every nuance. "You know it wasn't your fault, right?"

"Sure." She shrugged. "And the fact that every man

I've ever known has treated me in exactly the same way really doesn't mean a damn thing."

He frowned hard, sensing she was finished with the topic, but he wanted to know more. "What happened to you after she died?"

"I lived with her mother, my gram, until she died, too, a year later. Then I was sent back to Stepdaddy Dearest. Or that was the plan. I had other ideas, though. I took off on my own, and I've been on my own ever since."

He nodded slowly and was preparing his next probing question in his mind when she said, "I would have done it, you know."

"Done what? Killed him?"

"Or forced you to, if you'd tried to stop me. I wouldn't have hesitated to use that trigger word on you to take him out."

"That would be about the worst thing you could do to me."

She lifted her brows, turned her head toward him momentarily. It was the first time her expression had altered in any way. "The worst thing I could do to you? Come on."

"No, it's true. If you racked your brain for years, even if you knew everything there was to know about me, my history, my secrets—"

"You have *more* secrets?"

"Even then, you couldn't come up with a single action that would be more of a betrayal, or that would ensure I never forgive you, than to use that trigger word to force me to kill someone."

"Why? You hate killing that much?"

He shifted in his seat, slanting her a sideways glance and wondering how the tables had turned so thoroughly. He'd been probing her psyche, and now she was poking around at his.

"I don't hate killing. I won't mind killing Gregor a bit. What I hate is having control of my own mind, my own body, my own actions, taken from me. It's like…" He searched his mind for something to compare it to, something she could understand. And then he hit on it. "It's like rape."

He thought she winced a little.

"I did it once already," she said, after a long moment of introspection. "I used the trigger word."

"You used it to save my life. And your own. You had no choice."

She nodded and refocused on the road, but not before he thought he glimpsed a shadow of relief in her eyes.

"If you'd used it this time, to make me kill that old man, that would have been different. Especially when all you had to do was ask."

Her brows crinkled, and she turned her head toward him, her eyes searching. "What do you mean? You'd have killed him for me if I'd simply asked you to?"

He nodded.

"*I* couldn't even kill him. He's in a coma, helpless, sick and in pain."

Reaper shrugged. "He hurt you. He deserves to be sick and in pain, and he deserves to die violently. I do think he's suffering more by being alive, though. Lingering like that."

She nodded, but her eyes were stunned as she aimed them back at the road. "So why would you have killed him for me?"

"It's what I do. Doesn't bother me all that much when it's someone who needs killing."

She frowned. "I can't believe it. You seem like such a… I don't know, a white hat. You don't have any ethical problem with taking someone out like that? With playing God?"

"Why would I?" He drew a breath, sighed deeply. "I'm an extremely moral man, Briar. But I don't see things the way other people do. Never have, not as a mortal and not now. I look at it like this. If a person has a cancerous tumor growing inside them, they cut it out. Mankind is one body, and the individuals make up its parts. Bastards like Gregor, like your stepfather, they're malignancies. They need to be removed for the greater good."

She narrowed her eyes. "'The needs of the many outweigh the needs of the few,' to quote Mr. Spock."

"Or to quote the Bible. 'If thy right eye offend thee, pluck it out.'"

"A principled murderer." She shook her head slowly. "Who'd have thought it?"

"I don't murder. I execute. There's a difference."

She nodded, then said, "So what happened to Rebecca was what you'd consider murder, then?"

"Yes."

"And who would you condemn for that crime?"

"Myself. And I have."

"But you weren't in control. It's like you said, someone took charge of your mind and your body without your permission."

"Doesn't matter. I was the weapon."

"Yeah. Well, when I see a shotgun get the electric chair, I'll agree with you." She drove for about a mile without a word, and then, out of the blue, she turned toward him and said, "What did her body look like?"

"Whose body?" He gaped at her. "Are you talking about *Rebecca?*"

She rolled her eyes. "Yes, Rebecca. When you came out of your rage and found her dead, what did she look like?"

"I'm not going to talk about this."

"Oh, come on. I'm interested, I really am. And you've been trying to draw me out for hours now, so here I am. Coming out. Death fascinates me. So tell me what she looked like."

He lowered his head, closed his eyes. "She was lying on the floor."

"Face up or down?"

"On her side."

She nodded. "What was she wearing?"

"A skirt. A long white skirt with flowers embroidered around the hemline. A white tank top. A pair of flip-flops." He closed his eyes.

"Flip-flops? Still on her feet?"

"Yeah."

"And this skirt, was it torn? Bloodstained?"

He shook his head while she rushed on. "How was her hair when you found her?"

"God, don't do this. I can't—"

"How was her hair?" she demanded.

He took a steadying breath. "In a ponytail." Then he lowered his forehead into his palm and whispered, "No more, okay?"

"Okay. But all this death talk has made me hungry. Can we hunt?"

He closed his eyes very slowly, then opened them again and focused on her. Could she truly be as cold and bloodthirsty as she was pretending to be? "We've still got stores in the cooler in back," he told her.

"I was hoping to sink my fangs into something warm and wiggling, though."

"You want to kill someone tonight, Briar? Is that what you're saying? Because you had your perfect chance back there with your stepfather, and you blew it."

She shrugged. "I want to kill something worth drinking. I'd have puked if I'd tried to swallow his filthy blood."

"Or maybe you know that I'm starting to see through the mask you wear, and you're trying really hard to put it back into place."

"Is that what you think? That I'm really good, deep down? That I'm just pretending to be a bad girl?"

"That's what I think."

"Bullshit," she said.

He shot her a look. Without warning, she jerked the wheel and drove the Land Rover right off the road, onto the shoulder, then jumped it across the ditch and sent it bounding up the slight rise on the far side, until she reached a flat point a hundred yards from the road, where she finally stopped. She yanked off her seat belt, then turned in her seat and undid his, as well. And then, gripping the hair at the back of his head, she swung a leg over him, straddling him, knees on the seat on either side of him. She used the handful of hair to drag his head up to hers. Her mouth took his, open wide and hungry. And her hips arched, pressing her hollows to his bulges, and making him ache for her the way a drowning man would ache for a breath of air.

Jerking her head up, she stared down into his eyes, and hers were blazing. "You don't really want to believe I'm good, deep down, do you, Reaper? Come on, admit it. It's the bad girl you're hot for, and you know it."

"Bad, yeah. Not inherently evil, though."

"No?"

"And you're not. You're not, Briar."

"Oh, I am. And since you won't let me go hunting tonight, I'm just going to have to prove it."

And with one quick motion, she tipped his head back, and then she lowered hers. Her mouth closed on his neck, wet and seeking, opening and closing, sucking and caressing. He didn't fight it. God, it was too good for him to want to fight it. No man alive would have fought it. She wouldn't hurt him. She wouldn't. She could threaten all she wanted, but he knew her. He'd glimpsed her. She was no different than he was, deep down.

He lifted his chin up a little more. "Do it," he challenged. "Go on, do it." And as he said it, he reached between them and undid his pants. The sound of the zipper seemed to excite her even more, because the next thing he knew, she had scrambled off him, kicked off her

jeans, and then returned to her former position. She
sank over him without even a second's hesitation, already wet, and he knew, as much as she might deny it,
that she wanted him.

He also knew that she felt the same things he did. The
mysterious attraction, the longing to know more, to get
closer. But he wanted more from her. He wanted to see
some hint of emotion in her eyes.

She rode him, and he drove upward into her, over and
over, as she kissed his jaw and his neck. Lips near his
ear, she said, "Be sure to let me know when you get
there, cowboy. I'm gonna make it good for you."

He wanted to tell her it was about her, that *he* wanted
to make it good for *her*, but she was driving him beyond the ability to speak, and then, when his breath
started coming more quickly, and she bounced up and
down harder and faster, she felt it. He didn't even need
to tell her.

She bent her head to his throat and sank her fangs in
deep, so deep he felt them scrape bone. And she continued to thrash him with her body as she sucked the
blood from his jugular. She drank and drank, and fucked
and fucked, and he started to get dizzy, started to get
weak. He'd already exploded inside her, and now his vision was getting blurry and darkness was starting to
close in around the edges.

Drawing a ragged breath, he whispered, "Enough,
Briar."

She lifted her head. Thank God. For a second there
he'd thought she might have been about to drain him

completely. Eyes glowing red, she stared down at him and whispered, "It's enough when I say it's enough."

And then she lowered her head and resumed feasting.

Briar lifted her head from Reaper's throat when he stopped moving. He was still hard inside her, but he was out cold. Not dead. Not yet. But she'd taken far too much from him. Enough to debilitate him. Enough to render him unconscious.

"Enough to shut you the fuck up," she muttered. And then she climbed off him, righted her clothes and settled herself back behind the wheel. "Maybe I can drive in peace for a while now, without you picking at my psyche."

She glanced sideways at him as she drove the car over the uneven terrain and back toward the highway once more, and in spite of herself, a kernel of worry niggled at her. She would have to keep careful track of him, make sure he didn't wind up dead. If he got close, she would have to give him a few drops of her own blood to make up for some of what she'd taken.

She hit the highway and drove north, attuning her mind to his every so often, just to be sure he hadn't expired. He hadn't. He was dreaming about screwing her, probably thought they were still going at it.

She rolled her eyes and told herself that he was ridiculous, even as she shifted in her seat, aroused by the visions had she glimpsed in his mind. Dammit. She slid him a look and pursed her lips. "Fine. I admit it. I want you. I never felt this much attraction for anyone before, and to tell you the truth, I never thought I'd ever actually *want* sex. It was either forced on me, or it was a necessity for survival. A means to an end. I never got off in my *life*…until that time in the car with you." Her lips pulled into a small smile. "Hey, that makes twice we've done it, and both times in a vehicle. I wonder if that means anything? That esoteric bitch Roxy would probably have all kinds of interpretations for it."

She drove a little faster, passing traffic smoothly as she came to it. She flipped on the radio but kept the volume low and soothing. "This is kind of nice," she said. "Talking to you when you're too out of it to hear a word I'm saying, or to try to analyze or dig into my mind or prove to me or to yourself that I'm really some kind of sweet thing, deep down 'Cause I'm not, you know. I'm a cold bitch, Reaper. You get too close to me, I'll take you down with the rest of them."

She stared at him for a moment, and a whisper of doubt moved through her mind like a warm breeze. She wouldn't take him down. She knew it. She wouldn't hurt him the way she intended to hurt all the others. He'd done nothing to deserve it. Nothing besides try to find something worth caring about in her. It was a futile search, but she couldn't hate him for trying. Dark and dangerous as he was, he was still one of the good guys. And the good guys tended to think there was good in everyone.

But there wasn't, not in her. Never had been.

Suddenly, out of the blue-black night sky, there came a blinding flash of pain hitting right in the center of her forehead and exploding outward. She shrieked in agony, her muscles clenching tight, hand jerking hard on the wheel in a reflexive response to the excruciating pain. She felt the tires leaving the pavement, felt the car going airborne, but even when the impact came, with its crunching metal and shattering glass, she felt the pain in her head above everything else.

9

— ◆ —

Reaper, happily faking his state of unconsciousness, hadn't realized anything was wrong until Briar's anguished shriek split his eardrums. And by the time he reacted, the car was already airborne and his grab for the wheel to try to right it was completely useless.

He glimpsed Briar as the car sailed through the night, her head bent forward, her eyes squeezed tight against her tears, her teeth bared in a grimace of pain, hands in a white-knuckled grip on the wheel. She'd opened her eyes briefly, glowing red and meeting his, insane with agony, just before the car hit a tree halfway down the side of an embankment, nose first.

His body snapped forward so hard that it felt as if the seat belt had torn his shoulder from its socket. And then…sudden stillness. Grimacing, Reaper lifted his head and reached down to undo the seat belt, even while blinking his vision into focus and looking for Briar.

Panic set in when he realized she wasn't there. She wasn't behind the wheel. She wasn't in her seat.

Shit, she hadn't put her seat belt back on!

"Briar!" Reaper wrenched his door open and got out

of the car. He was hurting but not bleeding. And he was only slightly weakened from her earlier attack. He'd pretended to pass out, knowing she wouldn't stop until he did. And he'd thought himself pretty damn clever, too, when she'd begun talking to him, revealing secrets as if he couldn't hear, when he was listening the entire time.

But if he hadn't been faking her out, he might have seen this coming.

He noted with a wince that the windshield was blown out and realized that Briar had likely sailed through it. He climbed over some brush and finally spotted her. She was lying in a shallow stream just beyond the tree they'd hit. Running forward, he slid his hands beneath her body and lifted her.

"Briar. Hey, come on. Wake up."

She didn't. Just lay there, limp in his arms. He trudged out of the water, searching in vain for someplace to go, someplace to take her. She was soaking wet, though he didn't smell blood or sense her life force ebbing.

"Dammit, Briar, wake up and talk to me."

He found a dry spot on the grassy hillside littered in fallen leaves and dandelions, and laid her down, then bent over her, examining her more closely. Her face was bruised and scratched. Her hands and arms, as well, but there were no deep cuts, no injuries that looked serious enough to threaten a vampire's life.

He cupped her cheeks in his palms. "Briar!"

Her lashes fluttered, and then, slowly, her eyes opened, but she quickly squeezed them tight again. "I can't. It hurts."

"What hurts?" he demanded.

"My head. God, my head." She lifted trembling hands and pressed them to either side of her eyes.

"Did you hit it in the crash?"

Eyes still squeezed tight, she shook her head very slightly from side to side. "It was before. It's what caused the crash. It's Crisa. Dammit, it's Crisa."

She furrowed her brows as her eyes parted to tear-filled slits. "What's happening to her, Reaper? What's hurting her this way?"

"I don't know. But we're damn well going to find out." He smoothed her hair away from her forehead. "Can you see anything about where she is?"

She closed her eyes again, tried to focus, but he could see that the effort intensified the pain. "She's riding with someone. I can see the headlights, the road… wait…they're stopping."

"Is there anything around them? Any landmarks that might tell us where she is?"

"She's going north."

"I know, but—"

"She's getting out. The car's driving away, leaving her there. It has Connecticut plates."

"Good. Good, that's helpful."

She nodded. "She's walking now. Her head hurts, too, and her vision is blurring from the pain. She's crying, Reaper. And she's weak. God, we have to help her."

"We will. We will. Just try to stay with her a little bit longer. What do you see?"

"It's a highway. It looks just like every other highway in the freaking—" She broke off there, and her brows drew together in a tight frown. "There's a sign."

"What does it say?"

"Byram," she whispered. "It says Byram." Her face relaxed, and she released a long, staggering breath. When her eyes opened, they seemed clearer. "What's Byram?"

"Not the boy's name, apparently. I didn't put it together before. It's a town in Connecticut." He helped her as she tried to sit up. "Is the pain easing?"

"Yeah. Mine is, anyway. The connection is broken. It's getting harder and harder to maintain it." She rubbed her temples, took a few breaths. "Why is she going there, Reaper? What do you know about the place? What the hell is in Byram that could be exerting this kind of pull over her?"

He shook his head slowly. "I only know two things about Byram. One is that it's the former home of Eric Marquand, though he abandoned his house there years ago, once the government learned of its existence."

"That could be no more than coincidence," she said. "What's the other?"

"It's where my former boss lives."

She lifted her head, brows raised, staring at him. "Your former boss…in the CIA?"

"Yeah. And that seems a little bit too coincidental." He lowered his head. "I'm sorry, Briar. But I think there's a pretty good chance Derrick Dwyer is using Crisa to get to me. Somehow, he's done something to lure her there, knowing I'll follow."

"How?"

"I'm about to find out." He pulled a cell phone from his pocket, flipped it open and scrolled through a list until he found the number he sought. It was saved under the initials DD.

Derry's cell phone woke Matt up with its ringing. He glanced at the clock on the nightstand. One-thirty in the morning. He opened his eyes wide, his heart jumping into his chest, as he bounded from his bed, ran to Derry's which was completely blocking the bedroom door, and shook the man hard.

Derry opened his eyes. He was still hurting, Matt could tell. They'd met up with some woman earlier, and she'd done a pretty good job of patching him up, even giving him some pain pills, all without asking any questions. But she'd been looking at Matt oddly the whole time. After they'd left her apartment, Matt had asked Derry who she was, and he'd said, "A colleague. One I trust. That's all you need to know."

Bleary-eyed now, Derry blinked Matt into focus.

"Your phone's ringing. Be careful, it's probably my dad. If he finds out where we are…"

Derry came fully awake and reached for the cell phone, which was on the bed beside him. He made a shushing motion, finger to his lips, glanced at the screen and read the words there. *Private Caller*.

He frowned, flipped it open and said, "Dwyer."

Matt sat down on the floor close to him, closed his eyes and opened his mind. He had to be careful not to let on what he was doing. It would be better if he never

let Derry find out about his gift. But he sighed in relief
when he heard the voice on the other end and knew immediately that it was not his father.

"It's been a long time," the voice said.

Matt opened his eyes to glance at Derry, and saw the
surprise in his face.

"Reaper? Dammit, I've been turning over every rock
in the country trying to find you. Where are you?"

"I'm tracking a friend of mine who's in trouble. But
you know that, don't you?"

"I don't have a clue what you're talkin' about."

Even without his skills, Matt would have been able
to tell Derry was lying.

The man on the phone could tell, too. He said, "Then
I've got no reason to talk to you. 'Bye, Derrick."

"Wait! Wait. Okay, I know. You're talkin' about the
girl. Crisa, right?"

"What the hell have you bastards done to her?"

Derry sighed. "Have the headaches started yet?"

"If you can call them headaches, you could call a hurricane a stiff breeze. She's in hell. What did you do to
her, Dwyer?"

"Nothin' I can't undo, if I can get to her in time."

"And what do you want in return?"

"I'll tell you that when you get here. Where are you?"

"I-95, border of Maryland and Jersey."

"You can make it tonight, then."

"Not without a car, I can't, and ours is embracing a
tree at the moment."

"I'll take care of that. I'll make a call and have a car

waitin' for you at the rental agency in town. I'm assumin' you can make it that far."

The man Derry called Reaper was quiet for a long moment. Then, finally, he said, "All right. Okay. I'll come in. But if this some kind of a trick, Dwyer, I swear,. "

"I've always been on your side, Reaper. I've never pulled a fast one on you, you know that."

"You never used to be the kind of man who would abuse an innocent to get what he wanted, either. I don't trust you anymore."

"Then trust this," Derry said. "I've got a much bigger priority here than bringin' you back into the fold for deprogrammin'. I've got a rogue on my hands, Reaper."

"One you created and turned loose on the world. This is all your doing."

"The agency's. Not mine. I was against this project from the beginnin'. But I have to put an end to it before any more people die. And I need your help to do it."

"I've been hunting Gregor anyway, for reasons of my own."

"Trust me, that's all I want from you right now. You have my word, I won't try to take you in. You can trust me on that."

"You want my trust?"

"I know it's askin' a lot."

"Tell me where he is, then. Where is Gregor?"

Derry shifted his glance toward Matt, so Matt pretended not to be paying attention. "He's here, in Byram."

There was a sigh. Matt thought the guy didn't believe Derry. Then he said, "You don't need to use Crisa to get me there, Dwyer. I'm coming in. Whatever it is you're doing to her head, stop it."

"I can't do that until she gets here. But when she does, I promise, I'll take care of it." He sighed. "That's the best I can do, Reaper."

"We'll be there by dawn. But we'll be holing up for the day."

"I can offer you shelter."

"I'll feel safer resting where you can't find me, so don't bother trying. I'll meet you after sunset."

"All right. Call me then and I'll give you the address. Are you, um…are you comin' alone?"

"Yes. I'm coming alone." But Matt got the clear feeling that he wasn't.

Reaper hung up the phone, got to his feet and reached a hand down for Briar. She ignored it and got up on her own. "Did you get all that?" he asked.

She nodded. "All except why you're trusting this jerk. And why you told him you were coming alone."

"I'm trusting him because I don't have a choice. We have to get to Crisa."

"And Gregor," she said, lowering her eyes. "He's there, too."

"If Dwyer's telling the truth, yes."

She nodded.

"I'm going to kill him, you know. Whether you end up hating me for it or not, it's what needs to be done."

She met his eyes, held them for a long moment and decided not to tell him that her only objection to that plan was that she would prefer to do the killing herself. And she intended to. But if believing she still had some twisted up feelings for Gregor would keep Reaper at arm's length for the remainder of their time together, it was for the best that he keep on believing it.

"You were faking before," she said. "In the car, you pretended to lose consciousness when I took your blood."

"If I hadn't, you'd have kept drinking until I lost it for real. I thought it would be best."

She nodded.

"That wasn't very nice of you, Briar. Trying to knock me out."

"I'm not a very nice person. Or haven't you figured that out yet?"

They began walking, heading for the nearby town where Dwyer had promised a car would be waiting. He didn't reach for her hand again. She told herself she was glad.

"You wanted to stop me from trying to see through the mask you wear. From probing your mind with mine."

"I wanted to shut you up."

"You screwed yourself over, though. You know that, right?"

She frowned and sent him a disgusted look. "I don't know any such thing."

"No? Stop walking for a minute."

She stopped walking, unsure where he was going with this. "We don't have time for another round, cowboy."

"Just stand still for a minute," he said. So she did. And there was silence, aside from the breeze and the passing traffic every now and then. "Now close your eyes and open your senses."

She closed her eyes, opened her senses. And she felt a heartbeat. It was strong and steady, and it wasn't her own, yet it seemed to beat in synch with her pulse.

"I live inside you now, Briar. You drank me into you. Do you feel me there?"

She did. And it suffused her with a mixture of warmth, sexual desire and panic. She popped her eyes open. "I don't feel a damn thing."

"Liar." His cell phone rang, and she started walking again, thanking the fates for the distraction and picking up the pace. The lights of town were in sight now. They were nearly there.

"Hey, Roxy," he said, as he flipped it open. "You can call the others. I have it on good authority that Gregor is in Connecticut."

"Well his drones aren't," Roxy said.

"What do you mean?"

"Seth and Vixen are surrounded by the bastards. They're gathered around the place where they took shelter for the night. Same story with Jack and Topaz."

"Are they all right?"

"Yeah, so far. The drones are just standing there, watching, so they can't leave. So far they haven't made a move to attack or anything else. They're just… lurking."

He lowered his head, sighing in frustration. "Crisa's condition is getting worse, and Briar's along with it. I talked to Dwyer, and the CIA is involved, too. They know something about this—are behind it, I think. I have to keep going, Roxy."

"I think that's what Gregor wants you to do. And he wants you to do it alone. Raphael, is there any chance this Dwyer character is working with Gregor to get you back into CIA hands? I mean, that was the original plan, wasn't it?"

"It's possible. It's even probable. I don't have a choice here, Roxy. Crisa's condition, whatever the hell is causing it, is getting worse."

Roxy sighed. "I'm assuming you know that because Briar's symptoms are worsening, as well."

"Yeah. It's getting bad."

"Do what you need to do, then. We can come up with a plan to deal with the drones ourselves. If Gregor's only goal is to keep the others from rushing to your side, then he has no reason to order the drones to attack. If he just wants to keep the rest of the gang where they are until this is finished, they should be fine."

"I don't like them being surrounded by night, knowing those thugs could move in on them at any time, but if you're going to get them out, it needs to be covert, Roxy. Don't engage. You're outnumbered. I'll get to all of you as soon as I can. And call me if there's any change."

"All right."

He hung up. And then he was moving faster than Briar was. "We need to get on with this. The gang's in trouble."

"So I heard."

He shot her a look. "Listening in?"

"Not on purpose," she said, "though I would have. I just...I didn't have to."

"We're bound now. The blood is the bond. Do you understand what that means?" he asked.

"It means the sex is going to be even better next time. Aside from that, not a damn thing."

He shook his head, but she felt the rush of desire that shot through him at her words. Yeah. She was still in control here. She could handle him.

She just wasn't certain she could handle what was happening to *her*. It was bad enough that she'd become sick with worry about Crisa, the crazy little pain in the ass. Now she was feeling an odd and unfamiliar rush of emotion regarding the others. The too-rich-for-her-own-good princess, Topaz; the cocky young fledgling, Seth; the odd little shape-shifter, Vixen. And Jack. Jack had been the closest thing she'd had to a friend in her entire life.

She'd tried to chalk up her worry for Crisa to the bond formed between them from sharing blood when Crisa's life had been ebbing away. But that didn't explain why she was worried about the rest of the white-hats. There was a fire forming in her blood, urging her to rush to them, to vent her rage on the hordes of drones, to get the gang out of harm's way. And that made no sense whatsoever. Since when did she risk herself for anyone *but* herself?

She was honestly torn. As they walked in the open, along the road that led into the nearest town, and veered off toward the car rental agency, she turned to Reaper. "Let's get two cars. I'll take one and keep searching for

Crisa. You take the other and head to the nearest airport, then fly out to help your band of do-gooders before they get themselves dead."

He stopped walking in the middle of the parking lot. "You care about them."

"I'm just trying to be practical."

He shook his head. "Look, whatever Dwyer is up to, it's about me. He's not going to give up whatever hold he has over Crisa until he gets what he wants, and it's not you, Briar."

She lifted one brow, tipping her head to one side. "Hell, all men want me. He just hasn't seen me yet."

Reaper smiled just a little. "And once you get Crisa?"

"I'll bring her with me and join you to help the others. Unless you've already rescued them by then."

He pursed his lips, nodded slowly. "Aren't you forgetting something?"

"What?"

"Gregor," he said. "Interesting."

They went inside, spoke to a man who asked no questions whatsoever, just acknowledged that yes, their car was waiting, handed them the keys and pointed them to a cherry-red Jeep Cherokee in the parking lot.

They got in, and drove onward, crossing into Connecticut with an hour to go before dawn.

Roxy waited until just before sunrise to phone Jack. He picked up on the first ring.

"Good," she said. "You're still alive."

"Yeah. The drones are still just standing out there, watching us. It's creepy, Rox. Topaz is a nervous wreck. Her fight-or-flight instinct has her jumping at every shadow. I don't know how much more of this we can take."

"Yeah, well, help's on the way."

"Reaper?"

"No. Ilyana, Mirabella and me. Reaper can't get away, and I don't have time to explain, because you'll be dead to the world in a few minutes. Just tell me where you're sleeping and how to get in."

"Where are you?"

"Five miles from Oklahoma City."

"Roxy, this is dangerous. You don't know what the hell you're up against, whether the drones are alone, or whether Gregor has managed to give them talents we don't know about."

"I'm armed and dangerous, pal. Don't waste your breath. Tell me where you're sleeping and leave the place unlocked so I can get inside. Okay?"

"Be careful, Roxy."

"Better tell that to the drones, kid."

Twenty minutes after sunrise, Roxy and Ilyana were driving very slowly over the rutted dirt track that led to the house Jack had described. Mirabella was once again sleeping in the hidden compartment beneath the van's customized rear section, safe from the sun. They didn't speak, were almost holding their breath as they got closer. Ilyana stared, wide-eyed, out the side window, scanning every tree and bush they passed. Roxy did the same, her vision straining so hard she was giving herself a headache. The sun had crested the horizon, and she was banking on the fact that vampires, even Gregor's drones, couldn't withstand sunlight. They had to have taken shelter. Somewhere.

As far as she knew.

"I don't see any of them," Ilyana said.

"They'd be toast if they tried to stop us."

"You hope. Roxy, you know what Gregor is capable of." Roxy glanced at her companion, saw the fear in her eyes. "If he's somehow made nice with the agency, if they're helping him again, there's no telling what he might have done. We already know he can seal off a room or an entire building to prevent mental communication between vampires. We know he seems to have an endless supply of drones to fight his battles for him, and that they obey without question."

"But even drones can't go out by day."

"As far as we know. We learned in Mexico that there's a drug that can enable vampires to remain awake by day. What if Gregor got hold of it?"

"Awake by day is one thing. Even awake, the sun kills them, Ilyana. They can't hurt us."

"Unless he—or the CIA's science lab—found a way to solve *that* problem, as well."

Roxy swallowed hard. As much as she'd been trying to reassure Ilyana, she knew the beanpole platinum-blonde was right. Anything was possible.

"Let's try to think positive, okay? Hey, at least we kept

those sunproof body bags from the last skirmish in Mexico. I knew those damned things would come in handy."

The house was in front of them now. It was a ramshackle building, listing badly to one side, old worn clapboards free of any hint of paint. "That Jack. He really knows how to pick accommodations, doesn't he?"

Ilyana smiled just a bit. "I think he could care less about his surroundings, as long as he's with Topaz. And she feels the same way about him, so.... "

"Yeah." Roxy swung the van around in a loop, then backed up to the front door. "All right, here's the plan. I'll take the first body bag inside, zip Topaz into it, haul her butt back out here and toss her into the back, then take the second bag back for Jack. You sit behind the wheel and keep the engine running."

Ilyana met her eyes and shook her head slowly. "You can't carry either of them alone. You might be able to drag Topaz, but it'll be faster if we work together."

Ilyana made sense. "I was thinking at least one of us could get away, if the drones somehow manage to attack."

"I know what you were thinking." Then Ilyana shrugged. "Look, these…people have been good to me. I know I've been ungrateful, fearful of them, never trusted them, but I owe them. I need to do this."

"No one blames you for being afraid of vampires. Not after what Gregor put you through."

Ilyana lowered her eyes, clearly unwilling to discuss what had happened during her time as her former husband's captive and slave. "Let's get on with this."

With a nod, Roxy climbed from the front seat into

the back, making her way all the way to the rear. She grabbed a body bag on the way, then waited for Ilyana to join her, carrying the second one.

After peering out the windows and seeing nothing and no one, Roxy opened the van's rear doors, and got out. She'd parked so close that the open doors nearly touched the house on either side of the front door, forming a sort of hallway. Roxy tried the doorknob, and it opened with only a bit of protest. The hinges creaked, making her wince and look around, in fear of having been heard.

There was no movement. She met Ilyana's eyes. The other woman nodded, and the two of them went inside.

It took very little effort to find Jack and Topaz, lying close together in a side room, its windows covered in broken shutters, nailed-up boards, and scraps of ratty fabric. They were lying on the dirty floor, and they looked like a pair of corpses. Pale, still, cold to the touch.

"I'll never get over how dead they seem when they rest," Roxy said, spreading her body bag beside Jack and unzipping it.

"How would we even know if they were?" Ilyana asked. "I mean, if they had been murdered, then laid out here like this, how would we know?"

"When they didn't wake up at sundown, I guess." Roxy rolled Jack's body into the bag, then maneuvered his long legs into place, while Ilyana was doing the same, with far less effort, to Topaz. Once they had the vampires secured, they zipped the bags tight.

Ilyana rose. "Okay, let's do this, then."

"Here goes nothing," Roxy said. She got on one end of Jack's bag, Ilyana on the other, and they lifted it. Between them, they managed to carry his body to the door and heft it into the van. Roxy quickly rolled him to one side and gave a look around, and then they rushed back inside for Topaz.

There was a sound, something moving through the nearby forest, as they shoved Topaz into the van. Roxy stiffened, then clambered in quickly, nearly stepping on the body bags. She clasped Ilyana's hand and pulled her inside, then dove for the front seat.

"Close the doors—fast. We're out of here!" She jerked the van into gear even as she heard the rear doors slam, and they bounded over the drive. Roxy kept her eyes shifting in search of attack. But all she saw was a buck, leaping a pile of deadfall and vanishing into the brush.

And then they hit a paved road, and she breathed again.

"We did it!" Ilyana reached forward to clap Roxy on the shoulder. "We pulled it off. We're like superheroes or something."

"Yeah, two down, two to go. I'm going to put up the sun shields on those rear windows, Ilyana. If you can manage it, unzip the bags and get them out. We're going to need the bags empty to rescue Seth and Vixen."

"Can we make it to them before sunset?"

"It's only a couple of hours south. We've got plenty of time."

She hoped.

10

—▸ ◂—

Just before sunrise, Reaper pulled the Jeep into the parking lot of a small motel on the outskirts of Byram.

"I wish we could catch up to Crisa before we rest," Briar said. "I hate that we have to wait."

"I know. I hate it, too, but we can't risk getting caught by the sun." Reaper opened the car door, got out and pocketed the keys. "We'll find her tonight. I promise."

"I hope so."

"How's your head?" he asked.

"Okay at the moment. Just a dull ache. I'm not sure what's better, being able to know where she is, what she's doing, feeling, with the pain raging, or feeling cut off from her entirely, but without the pain."

"Come on." He took her arm, and led her away from the motel.

She glanced up at him with a frown. "We're not getting a room?"

"I'm not comfortable staying here. Dwyer arranged for the car, so he likely knows exactly what we're driving, right down to the plate number. He can move freely by day, and he has the connections to be informed when the vehicle is spotted." He shook his head. "We'll leave the Jeep here. Find a safe place to rest elsewhere."

She nodded. "And at sundown, when we rise and come back for it? Who's to say he won't be right here waiting?"

Reaper lifted his brows. "You're right." Then he turned, walked back to the Jeep and tossed the keys inside just in case they had to abandon it for good. When he returned to her side, he said, "You think like a cop, you know that?"

"I think like a criminal," she told him. "Big difference."

They walked until they found a likely resting place, a warehouse, closed for the night, with an open window on the second story and only one lone security guard lurking outside.

"Ready?" Reaper asked, looking up at the window.

Briar was looking at the guard. "I could use a snack."

"It'll have to wait. Come on." He pushed off with his powerful legs, launching himself into the air and unerringly right through the window, somersaulting onto the floor on the other side. Then he rose and looked back down at her.

She gave one last longing glance at the security guard, sighed and jumped up to join him.

Matt waited until morning, when he and Derry were having breakfast, to ask him about the phone call. He'd lain in bed for the remainder of the night, wide awake. But since Derry had gone right back to sleep, he figured it was best to wait. He'd decided not to run away last night while the guy was sleeping. Not that he trusted Derry or anything, but he thought he would know if the man were getting close to making the decision to kill him. He was pretty sure he was still safe—for now, anyway. Besides, with Derry's bed pulled right across the doorway, it would have been impossible to get out without waking him.

And the lure of the promise that Derry could help him get back to his mother was too much to resist.

Derry seemed better in the morning. Didn't seem so stiff when he came out of the shower, walked a little straighter, his stride a little stronger. And beyond all that, Matt could sense it.

"You're feeling better today," he said.

Derry was pulling on his shirt. It was sweat-stained, even though he'd washed it in the sink the night before and hung it from the shower curtain rod to dry. "Yeah, quite a bit."

"The medicine is helping. That's good. So who is Reaper?"

"A friend."

"Vampire friend or a regular one?"

Derry slanted him a speculative look. "Vampire. But one of the good ones."

"There are good ones?"

The way the man looked at him made Matt think he'd just asked a pretty stupid question. But eventually the guy smiled a little, and tousled his hair as if he were a little kid. "Vampires are just like everybody else, Matt. There are good ones, and there are bad ones. And there are some who fall somewhere in between. Reaper's a good one."

"And my dad's a bad one," Matt said softly. When

Derry didn't answer, he nodded. "It's okay, I know. It's just, I thought they were all like him. He's the only one I ever really knew."

"He's had others with him. Didn't you ever meet any of them?"

"None of the real ones, no. Dad kept me away from them. I don't think they even knew I was around." He shrugged. "I saw those big dumb ones now and then. They scared me."

"They scare everyone."

"So your friend is coming to see you?"

"Yeah."

"And who's Crisa?"

Derrick's eyes narrowed. "You really *were* payin' attention to that phone call, weren't you?"

Matt shrugged and averted his eyes, afraid he was giving too much away.

"Truth is, Matt, I've been meanin' to talk to you about Crisa. I don't get the feelin' your dad has taught you a lot about…about what you are."

"One of the Chosen."

"And do you know what that means?"

"It means I'm better than ordinary people. Like a god or something."

Derry lowered his eyes. "No. It just means you can become a vampire if you want to."

"Yeah, but vampires are stronger and faster than everybody else. And they live forever. How is that not better?"

"Elephants are stronger than people. Tigers are faster. Tortoises live longer. Doesn't make them gods, pal."

Matt sighed. "Guess not." He could sense that Derry was thinking other things. He was thinking about telling him that he wouldn't live as long as ordinary humans did if he didn't become a vampire. And he was thinking about telling him that vampires didn't necessarily live forever, either, that they could die like anyone else. Then he decided to let someone else handle all that. And it crossed his mind that maybe Matt's mom should be the one to have that discussion with him.

The subjects—about dying and stuff—made Matt uneasy, but he forgot all that when he heard that one final thought cross Derry's mind: about his mom. It was the first time he felt sure Derry hadn't been lying to him. His mom really must be alive.

His heart felt like it was swelling up in his chest, and he had to blink fast to keep his eyes dry. "So tell me about Crisa, then," he said, his voice tight and soft, because somehow it was too hard to make it very loud.

"Okay. Well, first you need to know how vampires feel about the Chosen. People like you, who have a certain blood antigen in them."

"They can tell who we are?"

"Oh, yeah. They sense you very strongly. And there's some kind of instinctive urge they have to protect you, kind of watch out for you. Folklore says they couldn't hurt you if they wanted to, though I've seen a few vamps who made me doubt that. But mostly, they're like guardian angels to you guys."

"Cool."

"They usually have a more powerful connection to one of you than they do to any other. And I think the one with the most powerful connection to you is Crisa."

That brought Matt's head up fast. "But I don't even know her."

"Doesn't matter. The thing is, she's not…normal."

Matt lifted his brows. "Is she gonna hurt me?"

"No. She's a grown-up, but she's kind of like a little girl in a grown-up body. You know what I mean?"

"You mean she's mental?"

"Maybe. A little. She thinks you're in trouble, and she's on her way here to try to help you. But you should know that you're a lot safer with me. Like I said, she's not normal, and she's not as sharp as most. Heck, I think you have a firmer grasp on things than she does. So if she shows up here, you can't go with her, okay?"

And now Derry was, Matt sensed, looking out for his own best interests. Even Derry thought Matt might be better off with this Crisa. Deep down. But he wasn't saying so.

"How does she know where I am?" Matt asked.

"I don't know. Senses it, I guess."

"Why does she think I'm in trouble?" *Because I am,* Matt thought, answering his own question and knowing Derry wouldn't tell the truth.

"I don't know. Like I said, she's not quite right."

"But vampires sense when the Chosen are in trouble. You just said so. So she must be sensing it, right?"

He met Matt's eyes. "You're safe with me."

"Yeah, unless my dad doesn't do what you want him to." Matt lowered his head and shook it. "Does my dad know about her?"

"I think so, yeah."

"And your friend, Reaper? Does he know about her?"

"Yeah He's comin' up here because of her. She's his friend. He wants to help her."

"Why? Is she in trouble, too?"

Derry looked at the kid. "She's kind of...sick right now."

"Oh." Matt nodded slowly. He'd heard enough of the phone call to put the rest together on his own. Derry was using Crisa to get this Reaper to come to him. Just like he was using Matt to get his father to turn himself in to the authorities. Derry was a user. He hadn't deserved what Matt's dad had done to him, and he seemed like a decent guy, but Matt thought he was reading the man fairly well. He was pretty sure Derry would do anything, hurt anybody, to get what he wanted.

The only difference between Derry and his dad was that his dad's goals were bad—money and power and stuff like that. And Derry's were good, supposedly, because he worked for the government, after all, and he was mostly trying to bring a bad guy—his dad—to justice. Make him stop killing people all the time. That was probably a pretty good goal.

But aside from that, the two of them weren't much different.

Matt wondered briefly what Derry wanted with this Reaper guy. And then he wondered what Crisa was like.

His protector. He hadn't even known he had one, besides his mom, and he'd thought he'd lost her a long time ago. It was kind of cool to think there was someone else who wanted to look out for him. Crazy or not, Matt had a gut feeling that he would be safer with Crisa than he would be with his father *or* with Derry. And he knew Derry thought so, too.

"When do you think they'll get here?" he asked, suddenly eager.

"Tonight," Derry said. Then he clapped a hand to the back of Matt's shoulder. "Let's go out to breakfast, huh?"

"Yeah. Okay." Matt nodded, as, deep inside his head, he thought about what he was going to do.

By nightfall, Roxy and Ilyana had driven Shirley and her unconscious passengers five hundred miles closer to home. They'd been taking turns behind the wheel. Ilyana was driving at the moment, with Roxy resting in the passenger seat.

When the sun fully set and she sensed movement from the back, Roxy straightened up and hit the button that would lower the sunproof barrier behind the front set of seats, then turned to eye her cohorts as they roused from their deathlike slumber. She hit another button to open the bottom compartment, where Mirabella was already awake and waiting to be let out.

"Well, well, well," Roxy said, as they sat up, one after the other. "You have anything you'd like to say to us?"

"What the hell?" Jack looked around, then faced her

again with a grin that made him more handsome than
he was already, the devil. "Roxy! You rescued us!"

"Of course I did. I mean, *we* did." She looked at her
fingernails and shrugged. "Imagine that, just a couple
of mortals, mostly useless, saving your sorry asses from
an army of drones. Who'd have guessed it?"

Jack leaned over the seat, gripped her head and kissed
her right on the mouth. "You kick ass, Roxy." And with
a glance at Ilyana he added, "Both of you. How the hell
did you do it?"

"We went in by day, figuring the drones would be as
comatose as you guys were. Used the body bags to haul
you and Topaz out to the van, then repeated the whole
process when we got to where Seth and Vixen were. And
then, after patting each other on the back a few times,
we headed east."

"That was dangerous, Roxy," Seth said softly. "Gregor could have had people, mortals, watching, or—"

"Yeah, yeah. You'd have done the same for us."

"Yes," Vixen said. "We would have."

"Thank you, Roxy," Topaz told her. "And you, too,
Ilyana. I couldn't have taken another night sitting there,
surrounded by those oversized gorillas." She sighed and
smoothed her long mink-colored hair with one hand.
"How long before we'll be home?"

"Oh, we're not going home. We're cutting north,
heading for Connecticut."

"Why Connecticut?" Jack asked. "Is that where
Reaper is?"

"Yeah. And Briar—and Crisa, as far as we know.

Also on hand, apparently, is Raphael's former CIA boss, a guy named Dwyer. And according to him, Gregor is there, as well."

Frowning, exchanging glances with the others before returning his gaze to her, Jack asked, "What's going on, Roxy?"

"We're still not sure. But we think Dwyer is somehow behind Crisa's symptoms, and that he's luring her up there as a means to get to Raphael, knowing he would follow. Raphael and Briar are supposed to meet with him tonight."

"Are they nuts?" Seth asked, his voice rising. "Doesn't Reaper realize it's probably a trap? This guy wants to get him back so they can do some more tinkering with his brain, bring him back into the fold, make him their own personal freaking WMD."

"He knows that, Seth," Roxy said. "But it's the only way Dwyer will tell him what's going on with Crisa. He told Raphael he was expecting her to show up tonight, too."

"How could he possibly be controlling Crisa like that?" Vixen asked.

"We don't know," Roxy said. "But she's getting worse. At least, she is if Briar's symptoms are anything to go by."

"She's bad?" Jack asked.

Roxy nodded, meeting his eyes and seeing the worry there. He was more fond of the she-devil than any of them were, except, perhaps, for Reaper himself. Then she shifted her eyes, glancing at Topaz. "She was driving when the worst episode yet hit her. Blinding pain, Reaper said. I'm afraid your Land Rover is totaled."

"But they're okay?" Topaz asked.

Roxy nodded. "They're okay."

"That's what matters. The car's insured, anyway."

"What's our ETA, Roxy?" Jack asked.

Roxy glanced at the GPS system mounted on the dashboard. "If we drive all night and all day tomorrow, we can make it by tomorrow night. I think Ilyana and I are ready to take a turn napping in the back, though. You guys can take over the driving for a while."

"Amen to that," Ilyana said. "There's a rest stop five miles ahead. I'll pull off and we can switch. Roxy and I need a restroom and some food, anyway."

"I'll drive next," Seth offered. He eyed them both. "You two are something else, you know that?"

"Of course we do," Roxy said.

"Does Reaper know we're coming?"

Ilyana met his eyes. "We're under strict orders to keep our distance from him, in case this is a trap. But I think deep down he must know we won't listen. He can't possibly imagine I'd stay away, knowing Gregor is there." She flipped on the signal and moved smoothly into the right lane, spying the rest stop's lights in the distance. "That bastard has my son."

The vampires in the back nodded. Jack said, "We're going to get him back, Ilyana. Safely."

She frowned, glancing back at him and then at the others, who were all nodding, and something in her face softened. "Thank you."

"No," Topaz said. "Thank *you*."

* * *

Crisa had two desires driving her through the night, on foot, in the pouring rain. The boy, she had to get to the boy. And beyond that need was the evil voice in her head, commanding her to come to him. But the two were not in the same place.

Whenever she tried to resist the voice in her head, the commanding one that ordered her to come to him, the pain grew worse. When she headed toward him, it eased. And yet, the boy needed her. He *needed* her. She was compelled by everything in her—everything except that voice in her head—to go to him.

So despite the pain that seemed to increase with every step she took, that was what she did.

She was getting weak. The pain was wearing her down. She could feel Briar coming for her, getting closer all the time. And the man, the boss man, shouting at her, *Come to me. Now!*

She'd been ignoring him, refusing to reply as she emerged from the brush onto a busy street in the village of Byram. She peered through the rain at the lighted neon sign of a motel, and she *knew* that was where the boy was.

What are you doing, Crisa? That's not where I am. You have to come to me. The words were accompanied by excruciating pain that made tears spring to her eyes.

"I have to go to him. I have to help the boy." She spoke aloud, knowing, somehow, that the voice in her head could hear her. And that he could see what she saw, as well, though she didn't understand how. Was he a demon? A ghost? Another vampire? Who was he, and why was he inside her head?

The boy? The boy is there?

"I think so."

There was a long moment of blessed silence. Then, *All right. Get the boy, then come to me. Bring him with you.*

She stopped halfway across the street. "Why? What do you want with him?"

A horn blasted, and she moved out of the way of the passing vehicle. "I won't do it," she said as she finished crossing and stood in the parking lot of the motel, honing her sense of the boy, finding the room, the door with the tin number tacked to its face. 16. The six hung crookedly, its bottom nail missing.

You don't have a choice.

She closed her eyes, knowing she *did* have a choice. She could suffer the pain, die from it, rather than do what this voice demanded.

He's not safe where he is, Crisa. The voice had softened and felt…almost kind now. *He's not safe. The man who has him will hurt him. You have to save him. Get him away from that man and bring him to me. He'll be safe here. So will you.*

She stared at the door with the numbers on it. "He's not safe?"

He needs you to save him. He's counting on you, Crisa.

"He's counting on me," she whispered, and then she walked up to the door.

Matt was sitting on the floor, watching TV when he felt something tickle its way up his spine and lift his head. It was involuntary, that movement. And the way his gaze speared the motel room door was involuntary, too.

Derry had been getting more nervous and jerky by the moment ever since the sun went down. He would sit still for five minutes, then get up and go from one window to another, peering outside.

Like if there was a vampire coming after him, his looking outside would do a darn thing to stop it.

And one *was* coming now, Matt thought. *His* was coming now. He felt her.

Crisa.

The door slammed open as if someone had pounded the other side with a sledgehammer. It hit the wall, and she stood there, kind of hunched up, like a cat with its back arched. She was dripping wet, pale, and she had dark circles around eyes that glowed with a reddish light. Her hair was wet, too and stuck up all over, like the feathers of a bird caught in a windstorm.

Matt was kind of surprised that he wasn't scared. He probably should have been. But he felt certain, right to his toes, that she wasn't dangerous. Not to him, anyway.

Derry had frozen in place in the doorway from the bathroom, where he'd gone to peer out the window again. He just stared at her.

Matt got up onto his feet. "Crisa?" he asked.

The glow in her eyes blinked out. They were big and brown in the room's pale light, and when she saw him, her lips trembled into a small smile, and she came inside.

"You're okay," she whispered.

"Yeah, I'm fine."

She sent a look toward Derry. "You're lucky, mister."

"Hey, I wasn't gonna hurt him."

"Not much," Matt muttered.

Derry sent him a frown but shifted his gaze quickly back to Crisa again. "Look," he said. "I know you've been having pain, odd symptoms, and I can help you with that."

"I don't know you." She held out a hand to Matt. "Come with me. No one can hurt you if you're with me. But we have to hurry."

He looked at her. Then he looked at Derry.

"Don't do it, kid. She's sick. If she doesn't let me help her, she's not long for the world."

"And I'm supposed to believe you?" Matt grabbed his coat. "You've only been using me to get to my father."

"Matt! I've been good to you."

"To keep me from bugging out, yeah. But you've been using me, and I know it. If you really wanted to take me back to my mom like you promised, then we wouldn't have been hiding out in some stupid motel all this time."

Shrugging into his coat, Matt moved toward the door.

Derry lunged at him and grabbed him by the shoulder, as if to pull him back. But Crisa, the drowned bird in the doorway, pounced so fast that Matt didn't even see her move. One minute he was walking toward her as she stood there in the rain, and the next she was straddling Derry, who was lying on his back on the floor, gasping for air. Matt wasn't sure, but he thought she might have punched him in the chest and knocked the wind out of him.

Or broken his ribs.

"Don't *touch* the boy!" she shouted.

"Uh, my name's Matt."

She rose slowly, her eyes pinning Derry where he lay, never wavering.

"Do you, um…do you think you could help me find my mom, Crisa?"

"I'll help you do whatever you want me to," she said as she backed toward the door. "Do you know where she is?"

"No. Her name's Ilyana, and my father told me she was dead, but this guy says she's not."

That brought her gaze off Derry and onto him in a hurry and she was smiling in a way that made him forget she was a dripping wet mess. "Ilyana? She's your mom?" Her smile got bigger as he nodded, and the look in her eyes seemed to beam a warm, wonderful feeling into him. It was like a big hug, only not one. "I *know* her," she said softly.

Matt felt his eyebrows go up.

"She's too skinny. And she has really short hair, so blond it's almost white, and her eyes—"

"That's her! That's my mom!"

Her smile became a soft laugh. "I know *right* where she is. I came from there." Then she frowned. "It wasn't an easy trip, though. It took me a long time and I had to take rides with strangers, and you're a kid, and kids aren't supposed to ride in cars with strangers." She frowned, working through it in her mind. "Maybe we need a car of our own."

"*He's* got a car," Matt said, looking at Derry.

Derry pushed himself backward, until he could brace himself in a sitting position against the wall.

"Give me your car keys, Derry," Matt said.

"No. No way in hell. You aren't—"

There was a half growl, half bark, and Crisa was holding him up in the air by the front of his shirt.

"Okay, okay!" He fished the keys from a pocket and tossed them to Matt.

"You shouldn't go with her, Matt. She's gonna take you right back to your father."

"Shut up," Crisa said, shaking him once.

"He's controllin' her mind, Matt. There's a chip in her head, and he has the remote. He can *make* her hand you over."

She slammed Derry into the wall—hard—and his neck snapped back. Then she just let go. He thudded to the floor, his head lolling to one side, eyes closed. There was a smear of blood down the wall, leading from where his head had made contact to where it was resting now.

Matt stared at him and blinked. "Is he…dead?"

Crisa knelt and looked at Derry. She tipped her head to one side, then all the way to the other. And then she stood up. "Nope. Why? Do you want him to be?"

"No. He was pretty good to me, even if he *was* lying to me and using me. So is it true, what he said? Is my father controlling you?"

She shrugged. "There's a mean guy talking to me inside me head, telling me what to do. When I disobey, it hurts, and sometimes it hurts for no reason at all. But he can't make me do anything. He can only hurt me if I don't." She frowned at Matt. "Do you think the mean guy in my head is your father?"

"Yeah, probably. Crisa, I don't want anyone to hurt you. And he will, if he can."

"I don't want anyone to hurt you, either," she told him. "And I won't take you back to your father…unless that's what you want. Is it?" She seemed a little bit afraid of his answer.

"No way."

Her smile returned. "Good. So let's go. We'll find your mom for you."

She held out a hand.

Matt nodded and handed her the keys.

She looked at them, then smiled widely. "This should be fun. I never drove a car before."

"Uh. Okay, maybe you should give those to me," Matt said. She looked heartbroken, but she handed over the keys.

Matt thought she was just like a little girl, not like a grown-up at all. And that made him trust her all the more. It even made him feel like maybe he was the one who ought to be taking care of her.

He walked into the bathroom, and grabbed a big towel and the oversize terry bathrobe Derry had been using. "Here. Tuck these under your shirt, and once we get in the car, you can dry off and put the bathrobe on to keep warm. Okay?"

"Okay."

Matt stood a little straighter when he saw the gratitude in her eyes and pulled up the hood of his coat so he could stay dry. "His car is over this way, Crisa. It's not far. Let's go."

She nodded and followed. But as she did, she spoke, and for a minute, Matt was startled. "No," she said. "No, he doesn't want to come to you, and I won't bring him!"

And then she cried out in pain. Matt spun around to see her kneeling in a puddle, clutching her head.

"Fine!" she cried. "Kill me, then. I still won't do it. I can't!"

"Crisa? What's going on?" Matt helped her to her feet, opened the car door and settled her into the passenger side. He put her seat belt around her and buckled it, and then he went to the driver's side, got in and pulled the seat as far forward as it would go.

He started the car, found the headlight switch and turned them on. Then he put the car into gear and drove—very slowly—forward. It wasn't as easy as he'd hoped it would be. Especially since he could barely see over the steering wheel.

"Where's my mom?" he asked.

Holding her head in her hands and rocking back and forth, she whispered, "North Carolina."

"Ahh, heck." He looked at the speedometer. He was going about fifteen, and he was scared to go much faster. "Maybe we'd better find a bus station and see if we can get a ticket. Do you have any money?"

"No." She squeezed her eyes tighter. He knew she was hurting. His dad was doing that to her.

He could probably rob somebody. God knew she

could, if the pain would let up long enough to let her.
And then they'd have money for the bus. But what if she
died before they got there? What if this pain didn't stop?

She'd made it all the way from North Carolina to get
to him, to take him away from Derry, all without a car
or any money, or even a decent coat. She was soaked
and exhausted. And now she was hurting really bad
rather than turn him over to his dad, just because he said
he didn't want to go.

He was right to trust her, he thought. She was probably the best person he'd ever met, besides his mom.
She told the truth when she talked to him and she cared
a whole lot, even though she'd never met him. He could
feel how much she cared just pouring out of her. It was
real. It made his chest feel kind of tight, and it made
him care back.

"Let's just go find a place to rest, Crisa. Let's see if
we can figure something out. You need a break. And
probably something to—uh—drink."

She nodded. "But we have to get away from here a
little. My friends are chasing me. And your dad is after
me, too. Plus I think that guy back at the motel will be
coming, too, pretty soon. We've gotta hide really good."

"We can do that," Matt promised.

She smiled at him through her pain. "I knew we'd
be friends."

He knew it, too. He didn't know how he knew it, but
he did. There was a warm feeling in his belly for her.
He guessed it was partly something to do with her being
a vampire and him being one of the Chosen, and maybe

that stuff Derry had told him about them having a special connection hadn't been totally bogus, either.

It felt good to have someone who cared about him more than anyone else. He hadn't felt this good since he'd been with his mom.

Maybe, when they got back together, his mom would let him keep her. Like a big sister.

He kept driving the car but took one hand off the wheel long enough to tug the towel from where it was sticking out from under her shirt. "You'd better dry off," he said. "And get warm."

She looked at him, huge brown eyes searching. "Thanks," she said. And then she smiled as she rubbed the towel over her hair. "Vampires don't really get cold, you know."

"Yeah, well, still…" He looked for the heater controls, figured them out and cranked it up for her as he continued driving, slowly, but a little faster than before, along the town's main road.

11

—➤◄—

It was nightfall. Briar and Reaper had entered the warehouse, where they'd spent the day, too near to dawn for there to be any opportunity for sex, or for the annoyingly deep and sickeningly emotional conversations he seemed to prefer to have beforehand. And afterward. He would probably try to analyze her *during* sex, too, if she stopped kissing him long enough, she thought.

But it hadn't mattered this morning. This morning, there had been no time. They'd leaped through the window and barely had time to search the place, find a comfortable, dark closet-sized room with a lock on the inside and settle onto the floor before the day sleep had claimed them.

She *hadn't* expected, however, to wake in his arms.

He was sitting semi-upright in a corner, his long legs stretched out in front of him, his back supported by two walls right in the very corner of the tiny room. She remembered sitting down beside him, but not close enough to touch, though. No point touching him if she wasn't going to fuck him, she thought. Anything else was just mush. At any rate, she'd sat down beside him, and she supposed she must have fallen asleep before he did, because she woke snuggled up close beside him, the big jerk. His arm was around her shoulders, cradling her so that her head rested in the crook of his neck.

When she came awake and found herself there, she didn't move right away. She stayed very still, taking stock, smelling him and feeling him. The way his arm tightened just a little bit as he came awake. The way his fingers moved, then stopped, as if he'd been sort of caressing her arm for a moment there, before he'd caught himself.

She lifted her head, looked him in the eyes. "Romantic bullshit doesn't work on me, you know."

"What romantic bullshit would that be?" he asked.

"The way you held me all day as I slept. The way I woke to find my head on your shoulder, and your hand stroking my arm and your lips close to my hair. *That* romantic bullshit."

"It wasn't a conscious effort to…work on you."

"No? What was it, then?"

He shrugged. "Instinct? I don't know. You felt good in my arms. Feeling good is a big deal to vampires."

She frowned at him, but he broke eye contact and got to his feet, then leaned close to the door to listen, before opening it and stepping quietly out of the tiny room. She followed suit, keeping quiet, being alert. But the place was pretty much empty.

He went straight to the window where they'd come in. "Let's go find Crisa," he said.

"I'm all for that." She didn't try, though, to home in

on the girl. Not just then. Best to get on the ground before she risked another episode of crippling pain.

Reaper jumped from the window, landed easily on the ground, and rose from a crouch to turn and await her.

She jumped, as well, landing a couple of feet away from him. As soon as she rose and got her balance, she closed her eyes and felt around in her mind in search of Crisa.

The pain came like a blade driving down through the center of her skull.

She didn't drop to her knees on purpose but that was where she found herself. On the ground, kneeling, head bowed, hands pressing against her temples. And then in his arms as he scooped her up and carried her against his chest, through the rain, to the car they'd abandoned the night before. She could only assume he'd scanned the area and found no hint of ambush.

He lowered her onto the front seat and smoothed her hair away from her rain-spattered face. "We'll get to her. We'll fix this, I swear."

She nodded. "I think we'd better hurry."

She didn't try to look at him. She couldn't open her eyes just then, and she was fairly certain she knew what he looked like, anyway. His eyes would be worried, searching her face, looking for all the world as if he cared.

It was tough to understand the way those eyes of his could look, sometimes, when they met hers. She knew damn well no one could feel about her the way those eyes seemed to be saying he felt. No way. Not about her. She wasn't the kind of woman to elicit a feeling that… deep. Tender. Powerful.

It couldn't be real. She was glad she hadn't opened her eyes to see it.

A moment later the car was moving. She fumbled for her seat belt, then said the hell with it and left it off.

"We meeting Dwyer now?" she asked.

"Yeah."

He sounded grim. No wonder, if he was as doubtful about this as she was. It was probably a trap. She needed to buck up and be ready.

"Is it far?" she asked.

"Five minutes. We should stop and give you time to get yourself together before we get there."

She lifted her head and opened her eyes to meet his, forcing herself to appear normal. But she knew the pain showed. She could see its reflection in his eyes.

He cupped her cheek.

"I'm fine. I'm ready. Let's go."

He nodded, and then he drove.

Five minutes later they were pulling into the parking lot of a motel that looked even cheaper than the last one she'd seen.

"I want you to wait here," he said. "In fact, it might be a good idea to take the car and drive a ways a—"

"Bullshit." She shoved her door open and pushed her hair off her forehead as she got out.

He got out, too, and they met in front of the car, and continued forward. "You're in pain."

She shrugged. "Doesn't mean I'm going to curl up and shiver while you get your ass killed. I'm a bitch-vampire, not a delicate flower, Reaper."

He watched her as they walked, but finally sighed and focused ahead.

"Room number?" she asked.

"Sixteen."

Nodding, she turned her throbbing head and spotted it. "There we go."

They walked up to the door together. Reaper lifted his hand to knock, but Briar jump-kicked the door right off its hinges before he could rap his knuckles even once. She sprang inside, moving as if she felt like a million bucks, despite the debilitating pain currently ripping her skull apart. She mentally congratulated herself—just before she spotted the mortal.

Reaper was beside her one second, then crouching close to the barely conscious CIA agent the next. "Briar, what did you—"

"Hey, it wasn't me. And it wasn't the door hitting him when I kicked it, either. He was like that when we got here." She sensed something, wrinkled her nose and turned slowly, no longer paying any attention to Reaper or his backstabbing friend.

"Dwyer, come on. Snap to attention. Tell me what happened," Reaper was saying. "Who did this to you?"

"Crisa did," Briar said.

Reaper's head swung around, eyes no longer focused solely on the confused and dazed man on the flood.

"I feel her. She's been here, and recently. And…and someone else." She lifted her brows. "One of the Chosen."

"The boy?" Reaper asked.

She'd been trying to shield her mind from Crisa's as

much as possible, to prevent the inevitable rush of pain, but she was going to have to open herself to the other woman in order to answer that question.

Or she thought she was, until Dwyer answered it for her.

He lifted his head weakly and said, "How do you know about the boy?"

Reaper's brows arched, and he slanted a quick look Briar's way before returning his attention to Dwyer. She could tell by the slight bend of his brows that he was concentrating hard, trying to read the man's thoughts, and while Dwyer was well-trained in blocking them, Briar rather hoped he would forget or waver, given his injuries and recent trauma.

"We've know about him all along," Reaper said. "Crisa thinks he needs her protection. Why do you think that is, Dwyer?"

"I wasn't goin' to hurt him. I swear. Yeah, I threatened to, unless Gregor turned himself in, but I would never have gone through with it."

"And did it work?" Reaper asked, thinking before speaking.

"No. He wouldn't surrender, not even for his own son." Reaper's eyes met Briar's quickly and briefly, but Dwyer kept right on talking. "He's huntin' me, I've got no doubt about that. And Crisa, too, now that she has him."

"Crisa has the boy?" Briar asked.

"Yeah. She took him from me."

"Where does she want to take him?" Briar went on.

Dwyer shrugged, then pushed himself up straighter

against the wall and glanced at Reaper. "Help me up, will you?"

Reaper gripped his forearm and pulled the man's full weight upright. Once Dwyer was standing, he braced an arm on the wall and rubbed the back of his head with the other hand. "The kid wants to go back to his mother. That's all he talks about. You know that bastard told him she was dead?"

His mother. Ilyana. Briar didn't guard her thoughts, and Reaper heard them clearly. He nodded in confirmation. "You say that as if you think Crisa wants something different."

"Crisa doesn't know what she wants," Dwyer said.

"Maybe it's time you told me exactly what's going on with her. I know you know. And I'm pretty sure you're behind it." Reaper's voice was low and calm, but vibrating with barely contained rage.

Briar wasn't even trying to contain her own, and she was sure Dwyer could read it in her eyes.

Dwyer nodded and made his way to a chair, then sank into it. He sighed. "It's a long and rather complicated story."

Briar stood over him, close, menacing, and leaned closer. "Give us the short, simplified version."

He looked up at her, then looked away quickly and nodded. "When you were in Mexico, you had a run-in with my agents. The agents took Topaz captive from that makeshift vampire clinic in order to force you to trade yourself for her."

"Your agents. Working under your orders," Reaper said.

Dwyer nodded once. "Look, Reaper, I've been under intense pressure to get you back into the fold. My life was on the line. It still is. If the agency finds out I'm helpin' you, I'm as good as dead."

"And if you keep stalling, you're *already* dead," Briar said. "Finish the damn story."

Dwyer lifted a hand to rub the back of his head. "Your people were tranquilized. So was Crisa. They implanted a microchip into her brain."

"There wasn't time—" Reaper began.

"It was a simple procedure. The chip is minuscule, the implantation accomplished with a small bore drill and an injection. It only took minutes. The idiots were supposed to put it into one of your people. Seth or Vixen. But they didn't know who was who. It was just dumb luck that you took Crisa with you when you left there."

"We didn't have a choice. She was bleeding out."

"She shouldn't have resisted," Dwyer muttered.

Briar had him by the front of his shirt before he could blink, then lifted him out of the chair and bared her teeth as she stared up at him, her eyes gleaming red.

"Briar," Reaper snapped.

She hated the CIA bastard with everything in her, but she let go. He landed hard in the chair, grunting in pain.

"Tell me about this chip," Reaper said. As he spoke, he moved closer to Dwyer, put a hand on Briar's shoulder and moved her a few steps away, effectively putting himself between her and his former boss, an act that irritated her no end.

"It feeds a signal that's picked up by satellite and

transmitted to a receiver that feeds into my computer. Through it, I'm able to literally see through her eyes. Hear what she hears. I can communicate with her, tell her what I want her to do. It's extremely difficult for her to refuse."

"Because pain results when she does?" Reaper asked.

Dwyer slid a quick glance at Briar. "Yes. But that's not the only reason for the pain. There are other things goin' on." He shook his head. "I didn't understand at first why I kept catchin' glimpses of Gregor's son in her mind. It was as if he was there, too, competin' for her attention. It's like they have a bond, and I think it might mean—"

"That part we understand," Reaper said. "And you don't need to know any more about it than you already do. Let's stay focused here. So you used this chip to command Crisa to come up here?"

"No. No, I didn't. The extent of my interest was to use her to find out where you were, to track you down. I was goin' to remove the chip just as soon as I caught up to you. I swear it, Reaper."

"Then what the hell is she doing up here?"

Dwyer lowered his head. "Gregor tricked me, captured me, then went to my place and stole the equipment, the notes, everything. He's in control of her now, and even though she's with Matt and probably wants to do whatever *he* asks of her, she's not goin' to be able to refuse Gregor. Not while he's on the other end of that chip."

"Then we'll just have to get to him first," Reaper said. "Where is he?"

Dwyer swallowed hard. "I'm goin' to need…protection."

Briar released a bark of disbelief. "Yeah. From me, you bastard."

He ignored her, staring up at Reaper. "I knew you were comin' here tonight. I didn't have an ambush waitin', I didn't even inform the agency you'd be here. I've told you things that are highly classified, Reaper. They'll kill me for this. And Gregor—"

"Gregor's my problem now. I'll deal with him. As for protecting you—"

"Don't you even think about it, Reaper," Briar whispered.

He glanced at her, held up a hand. "You've used and basically tortured one of my own, Dwyer. Crisa's an innocent. You nearly got Jack and Topaz killed in Mexico. Your men tortured Jack so badly I wasn't sure he would survive."

"I didn't sanction that."

"Your men. Your responsibility. You've gone too far to ask for my help now."

"It's more than that, Reaper," Briar said.

Reaper turned and met her eyes. "Don't—"

"We can't leave him alive, and you know it."

Reaper closed his eyes briefly, and Briar felt the tiniest stab of regret, knowing this man had been his friend once. But facts were facts, and she was too practical to ignore them. "His cronies will catch up with him before this night is out. He'll tell them where we've gone, what we're doing, and they'll be on us before we know it. Who the hell is going to save Crisa then? What's going to happen to Ilyana's kid if Gregor gets him back again?"

Reaper's eyes narrowed as he studied her.

"If you kill me, Crisa will die," Dwyer said.

Briar felt her eyes widen, and with a swing of her arm she shoved Reaper aside and gripped Dwyer by the nape of his neck, jerking him to his feet. "I'm getting really tired of listening to your bullshit, you know that?"

"It's the truth!" He didn't struggle, probably knew it was useless to try. His eyes were wide with fear, though. He knew he was staring death in the face. "The chip is beginning to deteriorate, releasing toxic metals into her brain, into her bloodstream. It has to be removed, and soon, or it'll kill her. And I'm the only one who knows how to do it."

"I'm sure we can find a qualified surgeon to take care of Crisa," Briar said, and she bared her fangs, tilted her head, opened her mouth.

Reaper's hand landed on her shoulder. "Are you willing to bet Crisa's life on it?" he asked her softly. She hesitated. He felt her wavering and went on. "Briar, we need him. At least until she's safe."

"If we leave him alive—"

"We'll take him with us," he said.

"He'll slow us down."

"It's…not that far. Honestly," Dwyer said. He was begging for his life, and Briar knew it.

She straightened her head and looked him dead in the eye. "I'm going to kill you for what you did to Crisa. And I'm going to enjoy it. Don't you even doubt that.

You're on borrowed time, Mr. Dwyer." She released her grip on his nape and his head snapped backward, he'd been pulling so hard against her hold.

Fear in his eyes, he rubbed his neck with one hand and said, "If you're going to kill me anyway, then what reason do I have to help Crisa at all?"

"You son of a bitch!" Reaper whirled on him, but it was Briar who stepped in front of him, preventing the assault.

"Because if you let her die, your death is going to be far less pleasant, my friend."

"I'm no friend of yours."

Pushing a hand through his hair, Reaper turned his back to them both. He was shaking with pent-up rage and frustration. And something else.

Briar started as she probed his mind and realized what it was. It was fear. He, Reaper, the lone hit man, the most fearless bastard she'd ever met in her life, was freaking afraid of this weak, wounded mortal.

And then it hit her why. Dwyer knew the trigger words. The one that would send Reaper into an uncontrollable rage, and the second one, the one that would pull him right back out of it again. He could control Reaper as surely as Gregor could control Crisa through that chip in her brain.

"Where is Gregor?" Reaper asked Dwyer, focusing again on the business at hand, pushing his own fear aside, though the awareness of it remained at the forefront of Briar's.

"He's staying out at the old Marquand Mansion, on the peninsula."

"The *Eric* Marquand Mansion?" Reaper asked.

"Yeah."

Reaper nodded slowly. "All right, then. Let's go."

"He'll probably be expecting you."

"Of course he'll be expecting me. That's been his plan the whole time, hasn't it? To get his hands on Crisa in order to lure me to him? Looks like it's worked. But he's not getting out of this alive. Not this time." Reaper slid a look at Briar. "I'm sorry, Briar, but that's the way this has to end. Gregor has to die."

She frowned and tipped her head to one side. And another revelation came clear to her. He really believed she cared about that bastard.

Well, hell, that was what she'd wanted him to think, wasn't it? It was a way to keep him at a distance, a way to convince him that his desire for her was never going anywhere. That she would never feel anything for him.

And that was still true. She couldn't feel anything…for him or for any other man. Men had taken that ability away from her. She'd given it up willingly, as her only defense against them. They could take her physically, yes, but nothing more. There would never be anything more.

Not for her.

Matt drove as best he could, but he wasn't doing great. He could barely see over the steering wheel, and even at his age, he knew thirty miles per hour wasn't going to get them very far very fast.

Crisa sat in the passenger seat, her head in her hands, moaning more loudly with every mile that passed.

She kept lifting her head every little while and staring into nothingness, saying the word *no*. Like she was having some kind of inner argument with herself.

At length he pulled the car over into a wide spot on the side of the road that looked as if it were meant for that purpose. Not a real rest stop, of course. No restrooms or maps or vending machines. Just a worn dirt semicircle off the side of the road and boasting a beat-up payphone.

When the car came to a stop, Crisa lifted her head. "Why are we stopping?"

"Because the highway is up ahead. And I don't know which way to go."

"South." She blinked slowly. "I said *no!*"

Matt frowned. "Crisa?"

"God, it hurts," she whimpered. Tears were streaming from her eyes, flowing like rivers down her face.

"Crisa, I'm sure my mom will be able to find someone who can help you. But we have to figure out how to get there. 'Cause if we take the highway, I think we're going to get pulled over pretty quick. I mean, I can't go faster than thirty or so, and the cops are bound to notice us crawling along when every other car is going seventy."

"North Carolina," she whispered.

"Okay, but where in North Carolina?"

She leaned her head back against the seat and closed her eyes. Matt grabbed the road atlas he'd found on the backseat and flipped to the first big map in the thing, a map of the entire United States. He found Connecticut, then looked for North Carolina. And then he blinked.

"Man, it's a long, long ways to North Carolina, Crisa. Farther than I thought."

"I know."

"I don't think I can drive that far."

"I can't drive at all," she said. "I can barely see. Every time I tell him no, the pain gets worse."

He frowned and reached out to touch her shoulder. "Maybe you should stop telling him no, then." He sighed. "Derry says that with vampires, there's always one person—one of the Chosen—that they feel closest to. Sort of connected to, you know? He thought I was that one for you."

She squeezed her eyes tighter. "That makes sense, I guess."

"Well, that explains why you knew I needed help. And why you're letting my dad hurt you like that, instead of just doing what he says."

"He's bad," she said. "I know he's bad. I can feel it."

"What's he telling you to do, Crisa?"

She grimaced and began to sob softly.

Matt rubbed her shoulder. "Come on, you can tell me. You have to tell me, right? We're in this together now."

She nodded, sniffled. "H-he says I have to bring you to him before morning."

Matt felt his heart trip over itself inside his chest.

"He says he'll make the pain worse until it kills me if I don't. He says he can. He says we're going the wrong way. He says we have to turn around. But I won't. I won't, Matt. I won't take you to the bad man. No matter what he does, I won't."

Matt's eyes got hot, as he watched her there, suffering. No one had ever cared about him that much, at least no one besides his mom. God, he wished she were there to tell him what to do.

"Maybe we should just do what he says," he said softly.

"He'll hurt you."

"No, he won't. He won't hurt me. He'll hurt *you*, though. Maybe you should take me back. Just…not all the way. Just partway, and then you can hide out someplace, and I'll go the rest of the way alone, and maybe—"

"No."

"But, Crisa, you're sick. You're getting worse."

She shook her head from side to side, very slowly. "We can't even be sure it *is* your father. What if Derry was lying? What if it's someone else? Someone who *would* hurt you?"

He drew a deep breath, sighed, and decided to share his secret for the first time ever. "Crisa, I'm kind of…special."

She opened her eyes wider and gazed at him as if she were looking at the baby Jesus lying in the manger or something. "I know you are," she said, and she ran a hand over his hair.

"I mean, more than you know. I can kind of…read people's thoughts sometimes."

She frowned at him. "I thought only vampires could do that."

"No, there are regular people who can do it, too. I've always known how. As long as I can remember, anyway. Mom knew about it, but no one else. She told me to keep it to myself. So I never told anyone. Not my dad, even."

"It's probably smart not to tell. People can be… awful…when you're different."

"Have people been awful to you?" he asked.

She nodded. "Yeah. Before. You know, before I was a vampire, and before I found Rey-Rey. He took care of me. But then he died, and I went with Briar."

"Briar?" He frowned. He'd only known of one woman named Briar. A vampire, part of his father's gang. And he'd only glimpsed her from a distance, but from what he'd seen, she was dangerous. Evil.

"I was dying, and she saved me," Crisa said.

"Huh. Must be a different Briar than the one I was thinking of."

"She and the others took me with them. They looked out for me, the way Rey-Rey used to do. But then all this started, and…I left them." She lifted her head. "Your mom is with them, too."

"And they're vampires?"

"All but your mom and Roxy. Roxy and your mom are pretty close."

"So these vampires…they've got my mom and this other woman? Roxy?"

She frowned at him. "Oh, it's not like that. They're friends. They're all friends."

He narrowed his eyes, trying to picture friendly vampires and failing miserably. Dwyer had said there were good vampires, but Dwyer had said a lot of things, and he had trouble imagining any such thing could exist. Except for Crisa. But she was different.

"Crisa, since we have this…connection and I can

read thoughts, maybe I could listen in when this guy is talking to you. Then we can tell for sure if it's my father. Do you think that would work?"

She blinked at him. "Maybe. Only he's stopped talking now." She frowned hard. "And the pain has stopped, too."

"Ever since we stopped the car, I'll bet."

"Yes! How did you know?"

"He must know where we are, where we're going." Eyes widening, he asked, "Can he hear what we're saying?"

"Only when I'm talking to him—thinking at him, really."

"You stopped heading away from him, so he must think you're changing your mind, thinking about taking me to him, doing what he says."

"Oh." She thought for a minute. "So if we start driving again, he'll talk to me again. And make it hurt again."

"Yeah, but I don't know if I can listen in while I'm driving."

"What if we were walking?" she asked.

He swallowed hard. "I kind of want to stay right here. As long as you're not in pain, it seems silly to make it come back."

She blinked and nodded. "I don't like the pain, either, Matt. But we can't stay here forever."

He sighed, nodded. "Okay. Let's try it. Are you strong enough to walk?"

In answer, she nodded and opened her car door. She got out, so he did, too, taking the keys and putting them in a pocket. Then he walked to her side of the car and took hold of her hand. "Just think about me, and I'll focus on you and see what happens. Okay?"

"Okay." She tightened her hand around his, and together, they began walking.

They'd gone about ten steps when Matt felt it. A pain like nothing he could imagine shot through his head, and with it, his father's voice, booming and angry.

I told you to bring the boy to me. Do as I say, Crisa. Do it now. Or die!

Matt clapped his hands to his eyes, and his attention was driven right out of Crisa's mind. It curled up in a corner of his own brain like a puppy that had been booted across a room.

The pain and the voice vanished immediately. He lowered his hands, lifted his head and opened his eyes.

Crisa was lying on the ground. Her eyes were closed, her face was wet, and her body was shaking visibly, but other than that, she didn't move at all. The pain must have been too much.

Matt knew he had a choice to make, and it wasn't one he liked, but right now, he didn't have to think very hard to make it.

He could put her in the car and try to drive all the way to North Carolina, but if he tried that, he knew two things. He would never be able to drive that far, and she would never survive long enough to get there, even if he could.

He could take her back to Derry. But Derry had been thinking about killing him. And he knew that was still a possibility.

Or he could call his father.

He knew his father would come for him. He didn't know if he would help Crisa or not, though. He also didn't know if he would punish him for leaving in the first place, or believe him when he said he hadn't been given a choice. But he did know his father wouldn't kill him. And he also know his father *could* help Crisa, if he wanted to. He knew that because there really wasn't anything his father couldn't do.

It might mean losing his only chance to see his mom again. But the alternative was to let Crisa die, and he sure as heck couldn't do that.

Sighing, Matt left her lying there in the rain and slogged over to the payphone. He called his father's cell—collect.

On the other end, he heard the tinny sound of a ringing phone, followed by the operator's question.

And then he heard that hateful voice that made him shiver just a little. "Well, it's about time."

12

"He's not there."

Reaper crouched in the bushes outside the mansion. It was a stunning place, or had been once. Time had contributed to its gradual decay, but shadows of its long ago glory remained. The tall wrought-iron fence that surrounded the place was punctuated by stone pillars topped with gargoyles that seemed nearly alive. And the gate at the front was locked, though its electronics had probably long since rusted and been rendered useless by wind and rain. The fence marched along both sides of the property, all the way to the cliff at the back, a cliff that overlooked the pounding sea far below.

It was a fortress. Defensible, private, secure.

He couldn't even get close enough to look through the windows without first getting over the fence. And he had no idea whether there were sensors or other methods that might alert Gregor to his presence once he did.

"You can't be sure he's gone," Dwyer said.

He and Briar were hiding just behind Reaper in the bushes alongside the curving drive, just beyond the gate. Briar said nothing. Reaper sensed that her entire focus was on the house, though whether she was seeking Gregor or Crisa, he couldn't tell.

"Reaper, the CIA—"

"Meaning *you*," Reaper said.

"Meaning me. Us. We taught Gregor some…techniques to help him in his mission."

"Having nearly lost my life to him twice now, not to mention the lives of several of my—"

"Puppies," Briar put in.

Reaper slanted her a stern look but went on without acknowledging her interruption. "Given my experience with him, yes, I know he's latched on to some methods not widely known among our kind. Like how to create that army of drones he uses. They have the strength of vampires, the minds of morons. They obey without question."

"It's a top secret program. I can't discuss it with you. And that's not what I was talking about, anyway. He can seal off a room or an entire building using advanced electronics, so that mental communication is impossible between vampires inside the room and those outside it. He can turn the force field on and off with a single switch."

"Yeah. I know about that, too," Reaper said. "I also know he's not using it now. I can sense the drones, a dozen or so of them, lurking around in there. But there's no sense of Gregor."

"Could he be in his own quarters, Reaper?" Briar asked. "A place within the house that he's sealed off against mental communication?"

"It feels like he left." Reaper stared at the road, the path from the house in the distance to the old rusting gates in front of him. Then he laid his palm on the worn dirt driveway. "Just recently. He drove. And he was alone."

"If you say it, I believe it. I don't pick up any sense of Crisa at all," she said.

"Anything on the kid?" Dwyer asked.

Reaper and Briar glanced at each other, the exchange so brief, so quick, it went unnoted by Dwyer. But along with it went the mental question *Why the hell is he so worried about the kid?*

"No. No hint of the boy." Reaper frowned at Dwyer. "You *do* realize he's one of the Chosen, right?"

"Of course I do."

"So you know he's under our protection."

Dwyer met Reaper's eyes, held them for a second, then looked away. "He's under mine, too. I like Matt. I don't want to see anything happen to him."

Reaper noted Briar's frown and the wheels he could see turning behind her eyes. He wanted to pick her brain and was rather surprised by that, then wondered *why* he was surprised. She was smart. Insightful. Wary and cautious and cunning. He valued her opinion, particularly about men who were not to be trusted. God knew she'd seen enough of those to be familiar with the type.

And from the vibe he was picking up right now, he thought she trusted Derrick Dwyer even less than he did. And yet he thought there was a chance Dwyer might actually be concerned about the child.

"It would be a good time to get a look inside, check the place out," Briar suggested.

"He would know we had been there," Reaper replied.

"Yeah, but not until he was there, too. And by then it would be too late."

"And we still won't know where Crisa and the boy are," Reaper said. "You know damn well he'll never tell us. Not even under torture. He'd rather die."

"How do we know he even knows where they are?" she demanded.

Reaper sighed, glanced at Dwyer. "All we know for sure is that none of them are there right now. Let's withdraw. I have an idea how we can learn all there is to know about this place without setting foot inside. It'll give us an advantage."

He rose slightly, turned and started back along the path. Then Briar's hand closed on one shoulder and spun him around so fast he nearly lost his balance. "Crisa is *dying*, you cold son of a bitch. We don't have *time* to worry about research and recon and planning. We need to find her. *Now!*"

He studied her face. "You care for her, don't you? You might even love her."

"Don't be an idiot, Reaper."

"It's a phone call." Reaper watched her hand fall from his shoulder down to her side when he said that, so he gripped her shoulders instead. He pulled her a step closer, so there was very little space between them, and he didn't give a damn that Dwyer was watching them with a speculative look in his eyes. He had to make her listen.

"It's nothing more than a phone call, Briar. We get a safe distance away and I make a call. And while I do, you can open your mind and try to get a sense of Crisa.

If you can feel her, anywhere, we'll head that way. I promise. I'm not trying to delay this, I'm just trying to make sure we do it right. That's all."

She closed her eyes, as if searching inwardly for patience. "Okay. All right."

"She's more important to you than he is, isn't she?" Reaper asked.

"Crisa? More important to me than who?"

"Than Gregor."

She looked at him and licked her lips. "Look, my wanting to find Gregor is *not* based on my *wanting* Gregor. It's not like that. Never was."

"But you led me to believe—"

"I didn't lead you anywhere. I just didn't correct your misconceptions."

He blinked as she kept walking right past him and back along the winding road toward where they had left the car. And after the revelation sank in, he caught up to her again. "So why is it you're so determined to get to him again?"

"None of your damned business."

"I think it is."

She stopped walking, the car only a few yards away now, sitting in the shadows beneath a nearly leafless maple tree. Skeletal twigs clacked against each other as the wind picked up.

"I'm not going to discuss it. Not with you, and not with anyone else. So forget it. All right?"

He held her gaze for a long moment, then finally, seeing the determination and—more than that, the pain—in her nearly black eyes, he gave in. "All right."

He moved past her to the car, opened the passenger door and held it for her. "Get in, relax, and try to pick up on Crisa. I'll drive us just far enough to get out of Gregor's range, in case he gets back here. And then I'll make that call."

She got in. He went around to the driver's side and got in, and then they both sat there waiting for Dwyer to catch up. She glanced at Reaper while they waited and said, "That call. It's to Eric Marquand, isn't it?"

"How'd you know?"

She shrugged. "Who better to help us know this place's secrets? Hell, he might know things about it that even Gregor hasn't managed to figure out yet."

"That's pretty much what I'm hoping for."

She nodded and leaned back against the headrest as Dwyer finally plunked himself down in the backseat. "Let's go," she said. "The night's waning."

The car pulled into the rest area, and the headlights went immediately dark. It was low slung and black, and it had the look of evil about it, if a car could look evil. To Matt, it did.

His father opened the door and got out, then stood there with his hands in his pockets, looking at Matt and the woman who lay close to where he was kneeling in the rain.

"Hello, Dad." Matt got to his feet, though he was tired and frozen clean to the bone, not to mention soaked. "I'm really glad to see you." And that, he knew, was a lie. But maybe his shielding technique was good enough to fool even his father.

"Matthias." His father came forward, his pace measured and deliberate. Not fast, but not slow. Sure. It was sure, if it was anything. It spoke of confidence, impatience and a hint of anger. When he got close enough, he put his hands on Matt's shoulders and stared down into his face. "Did that Dwyer bastard hurt you?"

"No. But I'm pretty sure he was planning to. That's why I ran away from him just as soon as I could."

"You did, huh?"

Matt widened his eyes. "Of *course* I did. That guy *kidnapped* me. It's not like I *wanted* to go with him!"

"Mmm-hmm." His father glanced at the soaking wet woman in the mud and nodded in her direction. "And this drowned kitten?"

"Her name's Crisa. She's a vampire, like you, Dad. She saved me from Derr—er…Dwyer."

"But she didn't bring you home. I wonder why?"

"She was going to. She was like…" He paused for a moment, remembering the words he'd rehearsed in his mind over and over again while he'd awaited his father's arrival. "She was all into making sure you weren't being watched, that there wasn't some kind of ambush waiting. She said with Dwyer being CIA and all, we couldn't be too careful. But then before we could come up with a way to make sure, she just…she got really sick. She passed out."

"I see." Gregor hunkered down and tipped his head as he studied her.

"She saved me, Dad. And she's been really good to me. Can you help her?"

"I don't know. I don't know for sure what's wrong with her."

It was a lie. Matt was sure of it.

"Well...will you try?"

His father met his eyes, and then he nodded twice. "Yeah. I'll try. If you'll make me a promise, son."

"Anything."

Gregor studied him, grim-faced, for a long moment. "Next time someone tries to take you from me... kill them."

Matthias felt his eyes go wider and his throat go bone-dry. He tried to swallow and damn near choked. "K-kill them?"

"Yeah. I'll teach you how. There are plenty of ways to kill someone without even needing a weapon. Even when they're big and you're small. I should have taught you a long time ago, Matthias. I'm sorry I didn't. But it's an oversight I intend to remedy."

"That's okay. I didn't need it. Till now."

"Yeah. Well, you could have." Gregor sighed, then slid his arms underneath Crisa and picked her up as he straightened. "Come on, let's get you two into the warm car. We'll get home, and I'll see what I can do for her. All right?"

"You'll really try to help her?"

Pausing, Gregor turned and stared at his son, a deepening frown etched in his brow. "I said I would."

"Sometimes...you lie."

"I never—"

"You told me my mother was dead. That was a lie. I

could hate you for that. I could. But I won't, because I know you only did it because you were afraid I'd leave you, that I'd run away to go to her."

Stunned, Gregor shook his head and opened his mouth as if to speak but couldn't seem to find the words.

"If you let Crisa die, I *will* hate you. I'll try to run away every chance I get, until eventually, I'll pull it off. Or if I never do, I'll wait until I grow up and you make me into what you are, and then I'll kill you myself and go find my mother. But I'll hate you, and I'll never stop hating you, if you let her die."

"What if I can't—"

"I *know* you can. There's nothing you can't do. I know that, because you told me so yourself." A big sob choked him, and tears welled up in his eyes. He swiped at them with the back of his hand and tried to take a big breath around the lump in his throat, but his voice was tight as he went on. "You save her and let her stay with us, and I'll never leave you again. I'll stay. I'll even try to forgive you for lying about Mom."

As he stared into Matt's eyes, Gregor seemed to be searching for an answer he couldn't find. It was odd to see realization dawn on his face as he lifted it skyward, and when he lowered his head again, he looked at Matt with a funny kind of admiration and a sort of surrender in his eyes.

"It wasn't really a lie, about your mother. She turned against us. What we are. To me, that was the same thing."

"She turned against what you are, you mean," Matt said. "I'm not the same—not yet."

"But you will be. And you'll be one of the strongest, most highly trained, most godlike creatures the immortal world has ever known. Because I'll have taught you. I'll have prepared you. You'll be like—"

"A prince. I know."

"You will. I love you, son, I want the best for you. I swear it."

"Then save her, Dad. I've never asked you for anything. But I really want this. Please…save her."

Gregor licked his lips, and then he nodded. "Yes. You're my son, and you want this. So you'll have it. It's only fitting. I'll take care of it, Matthias. You have my word."

Reaper hung up the phone and turned to Briar. They were sitting together in the motel suite's living room, while Dwyer had gone to the bedroom to take a nap. They, too, would have to sleep before long. It had taken time to reach Marquand. He'd been on the road, already on his way to join them at Rhiannon's request, and the conversation had been a long one. The night was growing short.

"Eric will be joining us here shortly after sundown," Reaper said. "He says the mansion has an underground entrance Gregor may not know about. It was installed as an emergency escape route, and if it hasn't caved in by now, it should still be accessible."

"That's great." Frustrated, Briar glanced toward the bedroom. "What are you going to do with *him?*"

"Do?"

"We can't just leave him free to run off while we

sleep. Either he'll be long gone by the time we wake, or we'll find ourselves in a CIA dungeon somewhere."

"I don't think he'll betray us."

"How can you *possibly* be sure of that?"

He thinned his lips. "I can't. That's why we're going to spend the day elsewhere."

"Yeah? And are we going to knock that Fed bastard out and hog-tie him before we leave?"

He shook his head slowly. "He'll be here when we come back at sundown. He's not going anywhere."

"What makes you think so?"

"He wants something." Reaper lifted his head and gazed into Briar's eyes. "I feel it. I don't have anything else to base it on. Haven't read any errant thoughts or picked up any dark vibes from him. I just feel it. There's something in this that he's after, and he's as determined to get it as we are to get Crisa back. I just don't know what it is."

"Or who," Briar said softly. And she looked at him then, as if she were worried about him. As if she were concerned. For him. Imagine that.

Yeah, he thought. That was exactly what he *was* doing. Imagining it.

He sighed, shaking his head, doubting his own intuitions about Dwyer, as much as he doubted them about this woman. From the beginning he'd believed there was something deeper in her, something more. Something real. He still did. But he was all too aware that he could be wrong.

She put a hand on his shoulder. "Don't," she said.

"You're right, I've sensed it, too. But what can he be after, Reaper? What...besides you?"

"I don't think that's it. He'd have tried to take me in by now. Could have had a team waiting in ambush when we first showed up. Why wouldn't he, if that were his goal? No, it's something else."

She glanced at the bedroom door. "Let's get out of here, okay?"

He nodded, gripped her elbow and thought about asking her to tell him what she wanted with Gregor, but then thought better of it. She'd asked him not to. She'd refused to discuss it. Maybe he needed to respect that.

Besides, he would find out soon enough. They would be face-to-face with that bastard as soon as night fell.

He nodded, opened the door and led the way. He didn't bother waking Dwyer to tell him they were leaving. He would figure it out on his own when he woke.

Reaper drove them to a pretty, if garishly painted, little house, white with pink shutters and trim, and a lavender door. It looked like a place where Strawberry Shortcake would want to live.

He slowed the car down as he cruised slowly past the tiny paved driveway. "Will that do for the day?"

She looked at it as they cruised past. At the flower boxes in the windows, where orange and yellow marigolds were about the only things still in bloom. She looked at the heart-shaped cutouts in those pink shutters and grimaced. "Fortunately, someone lives there."

"They're on vacation."

She lifted one brow higher than the other.

"Feel around for yourself," he said.

Sighing, vowing she wouldn't spend the day in that cute little peppermint candy cottage if her name were Gretel, she focused on the place, opened her mind and let the sensations rush through her.

Nothing. Not even an animal's energy emanated from inside.

"There's a doghouse." Reaper pointed. "And a doggy door. But no dog. It feels like it's been awhile since anyone's been here. Three, maybe four days."

"Okay. But how do you know when they're coming back?"

"Who goes on a four-day vacation?" he asked. "Look, we'll find verification before we settle in for the day, all right? Let's just go inside and look."

She narrowed her eyes on him. He was pulling the car to a stop a block and a half away from the little house, in a lay-by where it wouldn't attract undo notice. "Why that place?" she asked.

He shrugged. "It's homey. Cozy."

"Two words I wouldn't have expected to exist in your vocabulary."

"They haven't," he said. "Not in a long time."

She sighed and decided to humor him. "All right, what the hell."

They got out of the car and started walking back toward the house. It was one of three on the block, but there wasn't a lot of space between it and its nearest neighbor, so they kept to the shadows. Briar looked skyward. There was at least an hour until dawn. Maybe an hour and a half.

Damn.

They cut through the backyard, senses alert. If a human noticed them, they would have felt it, but no one did. At the back door, Reaper reached for the knob, crinkled his brow and stared at the lock as if trying to make it burst into flames.

Briar laughed. She couldn't help it.

He glanced over his shoulder at her, brows lifted. "What's so funny back there?"

"You. Are you trying to melt it or just scare it to death?"

"I'm…concentrating."

She laughed again.

"*What?*"

"Uh, would you mind if I just…"

He moved aside, flipping a hand, palm up, toward the door, as if to say, *All yours*. Then he stood there, arms crossed over his chest, watching her.

Briar held her palm an inch from the door, just beneath the knob, then moved it quickly upward about two feet. Then she gripped the knob and turned it.

"Oh, come on, you can't possibly have—" Reaper began. But he shut up when the door swung open.

"I can't possibly have…what?" she asked, sending an innocent look at him as she stepped inside.

"How did you…?"

She grinned. "Jack taught me. He's even better at it than I am. Don't feel bad, though. It takes months of practice."

"I've *had* plenty of practice."

"At telekinesis—moving objects with your mind. But with locks you have to go beyond just pushing the tumblers around. You skip the details and just command it to open."

"And it just does?"

"Yeah. Eventually, when you get good enough to make it."

He closed the door behind him, smiling back at her as his eyes roamed her face, and she felt an odd little hitch in her breathing. Then her smile died, and she averted her eyes.

"It's good to see you smiling, Briar."

"Yeah, well…"

"Everything's going to be fine, you know. We'll get Crisa, we'll get that damn chip out of her, and she'll be fine. Even if Dwyer can't do a lot, you can bet Marquand can. He's a genius, you know."

She shook her head. "No. I don't. I'd never even heard of him before I met you."

"Guess you'll have to take my word for it, then."

"Okay."

She looked around the house. They'd entered a neat-as-a-pin kitchen with sunny yellow walls, white wooden cupboards, a sunflower-patterned wallpaper border and matching curtains, dish towels and pot holders.

"It's almost puke-worthy."

"No, it's really not. Feel the energy. The people who live here are happy. They love this place."

She could feel that without even trying. "Which

makes it even more puke-worthy," she observed. Then she crossed the room and looked at the calendar that hung on the wall. The photo for October featured a pumpkin-faced scarecrow reclining on a bale of hay amid russet leaves under a harvest moon.

"Looks like you were right," she said, and she pointed to where one word was written across seven days' worth of spaces. BAHAMAS. "They won't be back until the day after tomorrow."

"Then we're safe here for the day."

She moved through the place. "I could use a snack."

"We probably shouldn't hunt too close to where we're going to rest, though," he said.

She agreed. "It can wait until nightfall. Maybe I'll eat your friend Dwyer. He's got it coming."

"There are things we need from him first," he said.

She nodded. "More than you know." He looked at her oddly, but she just shifted to a new topic. "So is this the kind of place where you lived with Miss Sunnybrook Farm?"

"Sunny…?"

"Rebecca," she clarified.

"Oh. Uh, no. We had an apartment in D.C. Huge, modern, expensive. Nothing like this."

"That shoots one theory out of the water," she muttered.

He shifted his feet. "I think I'll find a shower, get cleaned up before bed."

"Okay."

He walked away, and Briar took the backpack from her shoulder, opened it up and took out her notebook. She had a list of items that were her priorities. She'd been adding to it, altering it, changing the order, daily since they'd left on this mission. Sometimes more than daily.

Right now it read:

Save Crisa
Kill Gregor
~~Kill Daddy Dearest~~
Leave the Scooby Gang
Forget him

She studied the list, licking her lips. She'd crossed out the part about killing her father, because it no longer applied. Killing him would have been a mercy, so it was no longer on the list. Saving Crisa was still first. But now she had so many other things on her mind, essential things. Vital ones.

She tore the page from the notebook, crumpled it and started a new list on a fresh page.

Save Crisa
Return the kid to his mother
Torture secrets out of Dwyer & give them to Reaper
Kill Dwyer
Kill Gregor... slow.
Leave the Scooby Gang
Forget about him

She tapped the pen on the final line numerous times, so there were dots all over the space after the final word.

Forget about him.

She was no longer sure that was possible. And she didn't like what she was seeing in the way she'd rearranged her list. All of a sudden her own needs: vengeance against Gregor, getting the hell away from the white-hats, erasing her feelings about Reaper from her mind forever—which shouldn't be hard, because those feelings were purely physical—had been pushed off the top of the list in favor of things that had to do with other people.

With helping Crisa and the kid and Ilyana—a woman she didn't even *like* for God's sake—and Reaper.

Helping Reaper. Yeah. And if she were being really honest with herself here, she would move that one right up to the top of the list. Right underneath saving Crisa's life, or maybe even side by side with it.

Because in spite of herself, and in spite of what she had always thought she knew about men, he was a good one. He'd dropped everything to try to help her save Crisa. He'd left his precious pups on their own, even when they got themselves into trouble— which was, she figured, inevitable—and stuck with her. He'd kept his promise. She had no reason to think he wouldn't keep it right to the end.

He wasn't like her stepfather. Or Gregor. Or the pimps who'd tried to own her and sell her. Or the johns who'd thrown handfuls of money at her and treated her like a piece of garbage. Or those who'd raped her and refused to pay her at all. Or the ones who'd humiliated her and denigrated her in ways she'd vowed never to forget.

He wasn't like them. As much as she'd convinced herself that all men were, he'd been steadily, consistently, proving her wrong.

And because of that, it was even more important that she get away from him once all this was done. Because of that—the fact that he'd convinced her, that she believed it now—it was vital.

He'd told her once that he thought the reason he was attracted to her was because he didn't believe he could hurt her.

Tough as she was, Briar knew better. Though she would rather die under slow torture than admit it to anyone in the world, she couldn't deny the truth that had made itself so clear to her over the last few days.

She believed in him. More than she had in her stepfather. More than she had in Gregor. More than she ever had in anyone. Ever.

That gave him the power to hurt her more than she'd ever been hurt before. And that was a risk she just wasn't willing to take, a situation she wasn't willing to accept, wasn't capable of living with.

She had to leave him.

But the least she could do, she thought, was try to give him a little recompense before she did, a little reward for all he'd done to help her out, no matter how bitchy and vicious she'd been.

So she would get information from Dwyer. Two pieces of it. One that would free him from the condition that made him live in constant fear, and the other that would free him from the self-loathing he'd been living with for too long.

Dwyer would talk. She didn't have any doubt about that.

13

━━━ ◆ ━━━

Gregor pulled through the gates, and headed along the drive and up to the mansion, not stopping until he was all the way to the front door. His son was shivering—despite the fact that the car's heater was blasting full force—and still soaking wet. And yet the boy's attention was fully on the pathetic bundle of flesh and blood in the backseat.

Crisa hadn't regained consciousness. Gregor wasn't sure she ever would. He glanced at his son and honestly hoped he could save the girl. Sure, she might present a problem later on. Matthias's loyalties would obviously be divided, and she might undermine Gregor's authority. But he was fairly certain he could bring her under control, with or without a toxin-seeping chip in her brain. And if not, he would simply kill her.

Hell, given the childlike mind of the girl, he could probably make her into his most devoted worshipper. The way he'd tried to do with Briar.

Too damaged, that one. Too deeply hurt and furiously seeking vengeance. Too angry. She would destroy any-one who got too close to her, turn against them all one by one. Reaper would soon find that out. She would betray him. She hated men, all men, and it was too late to turn that around.

The damage was done.

Gregor opened his door and got out, moving quickly to the rear door to fetch Crisa. He gathered her up into his arms as carefully as he could, and, with Matthias running ahead to open the mansion's doors, he carried her inside.

Matt headed for the stairs. "The bedroom next to mine?" he asked.

"No, we need to go downstairs, not up."

Matthias stopped in his tracks and turned, and the look he sent his father was one of such maturity and such raw fury that Gregor wondered if he'd made a severe mistake.

He glanced down at the woman in his arms. Was she going to cause problems between him and his son?

"You can't put her in a cell, Dad. She's not one of your prisoners, okay? She's my friend."

"I'm clear on that. And we haven't been in this place long enough for you to know all its quirks, so I'll forgive your misjudgment of me. Once, Matthias. Once and only once. And I won't have you forgetting who is in charge here."

Matthias pursed his lips hard, as if he had to press them tight to keep from speaking his mind, or worse.

At least he was showing some restraint. He clearly meant to do what he thought was right, though his motives might be in error. Gregor carried the woman toward the doorway that led to the basement stairs, leaving his son with no choice but to rush along in his wake. Once he reached the door he stopped and nodded once, firmly, ordering Matthias without a word to open it.

"Why the basement?"

"If you get the door, I'll show you. But I have no intention of justifying or defending or explaining my decisions to you prior to making them. It's decided. I speak, you obey. I told you I'd save her if I could. Unless you want me to withdraw that promise, I suggest you fall into line, young man, and obey without question, the way you've been taught to do."

The rebellion that gleamed in the boy's eyes made Gregor swell with pride at the same time that it troubled him. He had a feeling that if he did toss Crisa into a cell, his son would do everything in his power to get her out. He just might manage it, too.

He was becoming a man. It would be harder and harder to keep him in line. Maybe keeping Crisa would turn out to be more useful than he'd imagined. He could use her to keep his son loyal. Threaten her, hold her safety over the boy's head. Yes, this could work to his benefit in the long run.

But first he had to save her.

He reached the bottom of the stairs and went through another door there, leading the way through parts of the basement the boy had never seen before, he knew. Pausing outside a large steel door, he turned slightly. "Take the key from my back pocket and unlock this door. Then you'll see why I want her down here."

Matthias obeyed, finding the key and then unlocking the door. He pushed it open and stepped inside, quickly finding the light switches and throwing them.

The entire room lit up, fluorescent tubes flickering to life in the ceiling, one after the other, illuminating the fully equipped laboratory in all its glory. Glass-fronted cases filled with chemicals, liquids and powders, lined one wall. The other three were filled by counters, one of which held a stainless steel sink with oversized faucets. The rest held microscopes, burners, test tubes and vials. In the center was a semicircular desk, the entire surface taken up by computers and monitors, and stacks upon stacks of files—those he'd taken from Dwyer's place. He'd only found this room recently, and even he couldn't work fast enough to have identified most of the equipment in here, much less have learned to use it all.

Marquand had left most of it. The rest was what he'd confiscated from Dwyer's place.

Gregor looked around for a suitable place to put Crisa. There was no bed, but there was a gurney, off in a corner, near a doorway to a smaller room he hadn't even checked out yet. So he carried her to it and laid her down.

Then he turned to Matthias. "I'll have some of the drones dismantle a bed from upstairs, bring it down here and put it back together for her. You can supervise, if you want. If she's down here where the equipment is, and the notes, it'll be easier to figure out what to do for her and how to do it in time."

Matthias frowned, tipping his head to one side. "Do you know what's wrong with her, Dad?"

Licking his lips and glancing at the unconscious vampiress, pale and twitching, Gregor nodded. "Let's check this room out while we talk, hmm?"

Matthias buckled Crisa safely onto the gurney, so she wouldn't roll off. Then he joined his father in entering the second room.

Gregor found the lights and turned them on. The room was white and stark, but it contained a perfectly usable hospital bed, an IV pole and a functional nightstand. "I guess we won't need the drones after all, will we?"

"Maybe just some clean sheets and blankets," Matthias said.

"You can take care of that while I start going over Dwyer's notes."

"Yeah. Right after you tell me what you know. I know you know something."

Gregor narrowed his eyes and wondered, not for the first time, if his son were more than just intuitive. "Matthias, Crisa has a chip in her brain. It feeds a signal via satellite into a remote computer. The person on the other end can tune in to her and see what she's seeing, hear what's hearing, and also speak to her. They can control her, more or less."

"And cause pain when she doesn't do what he says?"

Gregor nodded.

"Why would you do that to her? I mean, before she even met me. Why would you—"

"You're jumping to conclusions. I'm not the one who put it there. The CIA did that. Derrick Dwyer ordered it. He was the one controlling her, right up until the day

I captured him. I went back and got his computers and all his notes. Until I actually fired up the machine and saw it working, I had no idea about any of this."

"But you used it. You used it to hurt her."

"And I'd do it again to get my son back where he belongs, Matthias. But what I did to her isn't what's wrong with her now. Dwyer's own notes told me the chip would begin to decompose, and as it did, it would release toxins into her brain and bloodstream. That's what's killing her."

"K-killing her?" Matthias's eyes grew damp.

"People die, Matt. Vampires die. It's a perfectly common event, not one to get emotional over. Buck up."

Matt swallowed hard, his Adam's apple swelling and receding.

"We're going to need to get the chip out, then get some kind of medication into her to clean out those toxins. I just need to review the notes. I'm sure there are some kind of instructions somewhere."

"You need to…you're gonna…cut into her brain?"

"Well, someone has to."

"But you're not a doctor!"

"Well, no. I'm not sure we have time to find a doctor we can trust, though I'd certainly prefer that, if it's possible." He sighed. "We'll make do with what we have, all right? And in the meantime, you go up and get the clean sheets and bedding, bring them here, make up this bed and get her moved into it. I have—" He glanced at his watch. "I have just over an hour before daylight, and I need to spend every minute of it poring over those notes if I'm going to have any chance at all of saving her. And on top of all that, I've got to be sure we're prepared for her friends. They'll be coming after her. And I doubt they'll believe I'm trying to help her."

Matt looked up sharply. "Her friends?"

"If they were coming tonight, they'd have been here by now," Gregor said. "They'll attack us tomorrow night, though, Matthias. I'm sure of it. And there's no way to know if they'll arrive before we fix her up, after, or even during the procedure." He sent a mournful look Crisa's way. "Their well-intentioned rescue efforts could end up killing her." Then he shook his head and sighed deeply. "We'll do what we can. Go on now, get that bedding down here."

Reaper showered quickly, and when he exited the bathroom, wearing a borrowed Turkish robe that felt like heaven, he found Briar on the bed. She was lying on top of the covers, her back against the headboard, her face in a fashion magazine.

She wrinkled her nose and said, "Stilettos. God, I hate the things. Who would wear them, anyway?"

"Topaz, I imagine."

She lifted her head. "Nice robe," she said.

"There's a matching one hanging in the bathroom. Help yourself."

"Oh, I intend to." She tossed the magazine on the bed and got up, then headed into the bathroom.

"Any interesting articles?" he asked as she passed him.

"Oh, hell yes, if you want to know what little black

pumps are in and which ones you might as well be shot as to be seen wearing. I found it was kind of a fun game to try to pick out the differences. So far, I only found one."

"And what was that?"

"The *in* shoes cost five times what the *out* ones do." She rolled her eyes. "What I don't get is how you can be smart enough to make that kind of money, yet dumb enough to believe that kind of garbage and blow it on such baloney."

He smiled to himself as the bathroom door closed behind her; then he went through the house, locking all the doors and windows, lowering all the shades, drawing all the drapes. He returned to the bedroom, and spent extra time and attention on those windows. He took several heavy blankets he found in a trunk at the foot of the bed and tucked them around the drapery rods. He located duct tape and used it to affix the edges of the blankets to the walls, so no light would spill through. And the whole time he listened to the shower running and imagined Briar standing naked beneath its spray. Her smooth skin all pebbled with droplets. Tiny rivers of water running down her body. Over her spine, trickling over her thighs, spilling over her breasts. Dripping, maybe, from a taut nipple.

He closed his eyes and suppressed a groan, then pulled back the covers and got into the bed.

The shower stopped. He wondered what was going to happen between them, if anything. She opened the door and stood there, staring at him.

She hadn't bothered with the robe.

He stared at her. She was naked, completely naked, and her hair, black and curly and wild and wet, dropped and tangled over her shoulders like the untamed thorny vines of a wild rose. And the water beaded on her skin just like he'd been imagining. She'd barely dried off.

She kept her eyes on his, though his were everywhere *but* on hers, as she walked slowly closer. She stopped beside the bed, yanked back the covers, stared down at him, hard as hell already, and then she licked her lips.

"I didn't think—" he began.

"Don't think. Just fuck." She put one leg over him, straddled him and lowered herself until she could rub herself over his erection. She was sitting upright, and he wanted her closer. He wanted her against him. He wanted to kiss her.

He put his hands on the small of her back, but when he tried to pull her forward, she held herself stiff. She didn't like intimacy. Kissing. Embraces. Foreplay, even. Just the act. Just that and nothing more.

But this time he wanted it his way. Because he had a feeling it might very well be the last time for them.

She would leave once Crisa was safe. He knew it right to his gut.

So he clasped her hips in his hands and held her, and then he drove into her so hard and so fast and so incredibly deep that it knocked her for a loop. A cry was driven from her lungs, and the sensation, so sudden and unexpected, weakened her, so that her body went lax.

He tightened his arms around her instantly, yanking her forward until her chest lay atop his, and then he kissed her. He took her mouth with his, and he kissed her as if he could never get enough. He put his tongue inside her, tasted everything she was, and then he tasted more.

He tasted the salt of her tears as they rolled down her cheeks to her lips. And he didn't ask why, because he knew she wouldn't answer. He just kept kissing her, kept driving into her, kept holding her flush against him, kept taking all she had to give, until there was no more.

They climaxed together, swallowing each other's screams of pleasure, their mouths still melded.

And when the sun rose, that was the way they slept. Locked together. Him inside her, buried deep. Her utterly relaxed on top of him. His arms holding her tight.

He felt the day sleep stealing over him, and he kept running his fingers through her hair until he lost the ability to move them at all. He thought about telling her that he just might love her. And then he decided that would be the surest way to send her running away.

And even though he was certain she was going to leave him anyway, he thought there might be a chance, if he were very careful with her. There might be a chance she would stay.

Night fell. Briar woke in Reaper's arms and experienced a rush of emotions so intense they overwhelmed her. She lifted her head to look at him, startled and frightened by the power of them, and then, as he stared back at her, a tender smile taking shape, she rolled away from him and got to her feet.

"Briar?" He sat up in the bed, even as she began to put her clothes on. "Are you okay?"

"Why wouldn't I be?"

He was frowning, watching her dress, working up to saying something. He probably wanted to talk about... last night. This morning. Them. Feelings and sex and all that sappy bullshit. But before he could begin, she turned, buttoning her blouse, and said, "We need to get going, Reaper. Time is short. And your friend Eric will be here soon."

"So will the others, if I know them," he said. "I might as well call them on the way back to the motel and give them instructions." He hesitated, sighing deeply, then got up and got dressed, and the two of them drove back to the motel. They entered the room without a key and found Dwyer sipping whiskey from a short fat glass.

He hadn't shaved, and Briar didn't think he'd showered, either. He wasn't ripe, but it was obvious to her heightened senses.

"Nervous, are we?" she asked.

He glanced at her, said nothing and took another swig. There was a knock at the door that made him jump. The ice cubes clattered against the glass.

Reaper opened the door, and a vampire walked in, dressed all in black. He took in the room with a single glance, then focused on Reaper and extended a hand. "Eric Marquand," he said.

"I'm Reaper."

"Rhiannon speaks very highly of you." And then, to Briar's surprise, he shot her a warm smile. "And even more highly of you, if you're Briar."

"I am. But I'm surprised Rhiannon had anything nice to say about me."

Eric lifted his brows. He had an aristocratic face, and he was shorter than Reaper, handsome in a more traditional way. He seemed…sophisticated, with an old-world sort of style. He felt old, very old. Not as ancient as Rhiannon, but very old. The power that exuded from him was almost palpable.

"Rhiannon sees in you a reflection of herself," Eric Marquand said. "And believe me when I tell you, there is no one she thinks more highly of than herself." Then he glanced at the unshaven mortal, who sat trembling and drinking. "And this would be…?"

"This is Derrick Dwyer," Reaper said. "I worked for him during my CIA days. He's been trying to get me back, and Gregor was one of his projects. As is the chip in Crisa's brain that's slowly killing her. "

Eric's pleasant expression turned dark. "And he is here with us and still breathing, why?"

"Because he knows how to remove the chip."

"And you trust him to do that?"

Dwyer lifted his head. His voice low, he said, "I never intended to leave it in place long enough to do the girl any lastin' harm. I don't enjoy hurtin' people."

"Just doing your job, I imagine." Eric barely glanced at him, his attention returning to Reaper. "I ask you again, do you trust him?"

"No," Reaper said. "But if there's even the smallest chance he can help us save Crisa…"

"Understood. Well, let's get to it, then. I'll tell you

about the place as we go. You said something about others joining us here?"

"Yes," Reaper said. "They'll be here within the hour. But I've instructed them to wait for us elsewhere."

Briar frowned at him. "Did you tell them that Ilyana's son is with Crisa?"

Reaper met her eyes, shook his head. "We'd never be able to keep her from going there if she knew. Though I'm sure she's already speculating that Matt is with his father. I just…I don't want the others at risk if we can avoid it."

"Just as well," Eric said. "If we get into trouble, it will be good to have someone on the outside who can help." He glanced again at Dwyer. "Is he coming with us?"

"I'd rather wait here," Dwyer said. "If Gregor gets his hands on me agai—"

"He's coming with us. I don't know how far gone Crisa is, and if she needs immediate action, he'll be of help."

"We'll need to get her to a surgeon," Dwyer said. "Insertin' the chip was far simpler than removin' it is goin' to be. And I'm no brain surgeon."

"I can do the surgery, if necessary," Eric said.

Everyone looked at him then, surprised. He shrugged off their awe and opened the door. "I've been studying science and medicine for more than two centuries, after all. Let's get going."

"One thing you need to know before we leave," Reaper said. He reached into his jacket and pulled out a small tranquilizer gun, then handed it to Eric, who looked at it oddly. "You may need to use this. On…me."

. Eric glanced up at him, then nodded slowly. "In case someone uses your trigger word to send you into a murderous rage, you mean?" When Reaper seemed startled, he went on. "Rhiannon warned me about your…condition. She wouldn't have sent me to you without telling me." He looked around the room. "How many know the trigger word, Reaper?"

"Everyone here except you. And Gregor knows it, as well."

Eric frowned. "Perhaps you're the one who ought to stay behind, my friend. It seems as if you're putting yourself at greater risk than any of us by going there."

"Not me. But anyone within my reach. Don't hesitate to use that gun if you need to. Don't…let me hurt anyone."

Briar looked at Dwyer, her eyes narrow. "I don't think you would *ever* hurt anyone you truly cared about, Reaper. Not even in that state. Do you agree, Dwyer?"

Dwyer looked at her with a puzzled frown.

"We both know that's not true," Reaper said.

"Do we?" She looked at him, but her eyes went right back to Dwyer again. "Do we *really*?"

Roxy was driving, with Ilyana on the passenger side, when she hung up from Reaper's call. "We have some specific and challenging instructions from Reaper. And not a hell of a lot of time to carry them out."

"Has he seen my Matt?" Ilyana asked, her tone hopeful bordering on desperate.

"No. Not yet. But if your son is with Gregor, as you suspect, you should be seeing him before this night is

out." Roxy licked her lips. "As long as all goes accord-.
ing to plan."

"What's the situation, Roxy?" Topaz asked from the
back of the van.

"Gregor has Crisa. Rhiannon's friend, the vampire
scientist Eric Marquand, is with Reaper and Briar. So
is Reaper's former CIA boss, Derrick Dwyer. They plan
to go into Gregor's hideout tonight."

"Why the hell is he taking a CIA agent in with him?"
Seth demanded. "He knows the guy can't be trusted."

"Dwyer knows about Crisa's condition. The bastards
implanted some kind of chip in her brain when we were
in Mexico. It was supposed to go into one of you. They
got the wrong vampire, then lucked out when we took
her in. They tracked us through the chip. I don't know
all the details, but apparently, if the thing isn't removed
soon, it'll kill her."

"Those animals," Jack muttered.

"They're going to try to get her out of there and bring
her to us. Marquand can do the surgery. Dwyer knows
the details. Between the two of them, they might be able
to save her. But we're going to need a safe place with
medical equipment to pull it off."

"And how the hell are we supposed to get that?"
Topaz snapped. "Pull it out of our—"

"Jack's going to help us out there."

"I am?" Jack asked.

"Yes. And here we are." Roxy pulled the van into a
driveway of a one-story brick structure with a sign on
the front that read Byram Health & Wellness. She drove

all the way around to the rear of the building and shut the engine off.

"Jack, we need to disable the locks and any alarms so we can get inside undetected. The rest of you need to be on constant alert, scanning the minds of anyone who comes near, so you'll know if anyone figures out what we're up to."

"And if they do?" Topaz asked.

"We don't have to hurt anyone, do we, Roxy?" Vixen slid closer to Seth and clasped his hand.

"I hope not," Roxy said. "Anyone catches on, we're just going to have to bring them inside and keep them quiet until this thing is over."

"Police included?" Seth asked. He sounded alarmed at the notion. Roxy simply nodded.

Jack rubbed his hands together and smiled. Then he looked at the worry on the faces of his comrades and lifted his brows. "What?" he said. "This is going to be fun."

"Let's do it, then." Roxy opened her door and started to get out.

Jack put a hand on her shoulder to stop her.

"Just a sec." And he pointed. She looked and saw the video surveillance camera mounted above the entrance. It would catch anyone entering or leaving by the main door. "Better let me handle that first. We won't show up on tape, of course, but you and Ilyana will."

"Let's do as little damage as possible, Jack," Roxy told him.

"If you insist." He was whistling as he got out of the van and walked up to the camera. One little jump, to reach it, and he easily tilted its lens upward, so it was focused on the night sky and nothing more.

Then he turned his attention to the door.

14

The four of them walked stealthily through the woods outside the former Marquand mansion, well beyond the guardian fence that surrounded the place. Eric moved some brush and, a moment later, lifted a hidden door camouflaged by branches and twigs. Stairs inside led downward into the dark.

"This is our way in," Eric said. "This tunnel leads directly into the basement lab. Or at least it used to. If it hasn't caved in or been sealed off, we should still be able use it. The only problem is, Gregor is probably going to sense us coming. We can shield to some extent, of course, but he's sure to sense the mortal."

"I can shield, too," Dwyer said, sounding defensive. He lowered his head at Eric's quick look. "I've worked with vampires for a long time. It was an essential skill to master."

"He can't block entirely," Reaper said.

"I'm not picking up on Crisa." Briar sent Reaper a desperate look. "But I can sense others inside. Gregor is in there. So is the boy. And I feel that heavy energy the drones put out—a lot of it. But no Crisa."

"She might be unconscious, or maybe he's got her locked up in a room that he's sealed off," Reaper said.

"Or she's already dead," Dwyer added softly.

Briar swung her head toward him, her eyes blazing. "You had better hope to God that's not the case, because if she is, you'll be joining her soon, I promise you that."

Dwyer swallowed—hard.

"We still haven't solved the problem of him sensing our approach," Eric said.

"We'll have to leave Dwyer here. If he gets any closer, he'll be detected," Reaper said. "Eric, you and Briar go in through the tunnel. I'll go right up to the front door. With any luck, I can distract him, giving you time to locate Crisa and get her out."

"If she's there at all, she's probably under guard," Briar said. "And you can't go in alone, not against Gregor and his goons. You wouldn't stand a chance, Reaper."

"We can worry about that once Crisa's safe."

She searched his face. "He'll kill you on sight, Reaper."

"I'll negotiate with him."

"What the hell have you got to negotiate with?"

"Dwyer, for starters. And you. Don't forget how badly he wants to get you back, Briar. That's a lot of motivation for a man, believe me."

She averted her eyes and fought the warmth that suffused her at that adamant statement.

"It'll buy me some time," he went on. "Enough time for you to get Crisa safe. The boy, too, if you can locate him. Then you can bring the others back to mount a rescue, if necessary."

"It's too big a risk." She gripped his arm and dragged him a few steps from the others, though she was under no illusion that Eric couldn't listen in if he wanted to.

Staring up into Reaper's eyes, she asked him, "Why are you doing this? Why are you risking your life?"

"We need to get Cri—"

"Bullshit. You do this for a living, Reaper. You've been putting your life on the line over and over again since before you even became one of us. I think you've been doing it ever since your wife—"

"Don't. Don't go there, Briar. Please."

"You have a death wish? Or maybe it's not that cut and dried. Maybe you're not suicidal, you just don't particularly care if you live or die. There's part of you that thinks you deserve to die."

He closed his eyes. "If that's true, then it's what makes me good at what I do. If I've got nothing to lose, it gives me an edge."

"Maybe that used to be true," she told him. "But not anymore. You've got an entire freaking litter of vampy-pups who worship the ground you walk on. They'd traipse barefoot over hot coals for you, Reaper. And they need you. They'd be devastated if you died, and I think you know it."

He searched her eyes, waiting for her to say more. When she didn't, he asked what she'd been hoping he wouldn't. "What about you, Briar? Would you be devastated if I died?"

She licked her lips. "Look, I'm not…I don't…" Then she lowered her head. "I'm not capable of…"

"It's okay. I get it."

"I'd be really pissed if you died. I've known a lot of men in my life, Reaper, and you're not like any of them. You're different. And I…I'd like to hang around a while, figure out just how different. You know?"

"You…you're not leaving when this is over?"

"I'm…having second thoughts about leaving when this is over," she admitted. "So?"

He lifted a hand and pushed her hair behind one ear. "So I guess I'd better not die. Now let's get on with this."

She closed her eyes, wishing there was a way to talk him out of his hare-brained plan and knowing there wasn't. Sighing, she leaned forward and kissed him hard on the mouth. "You're an idiot."

Then she stomped back to where the others were. "Dwyer, if you're not here when we get back, I'll hunt you down if it takes me the rest of my life," she said. "Let's get on with this, Eric." And with that she jumped into the opening in the ground and vanished from their sight.

"Dwyer," Eric instructed. "Close this hatch after we leave. Cover it so it's invisible again, and then get yourself into hiding, but stay close."

"All right. Listen, Gregor has all my files in there. If you can get them, they'll be helpful later on."

Eric nodded. "I'll try."

Reaper was already walking away from them, circling back to the road, to approach the mansion's front gate.

* * *

Crisa was lying in the bed in the hidden room off the basement lab. Matt had located clean sheets in one of the closets upstairs. It had taken him three tries to find a set that actually fit. By the time he did, his father had gone to bed for the day, locking himself up in his private bedrooms upstairs.

At their old place, in the very beginning, Matt used to spend the days at a private school not far from where they lived. His dad had arranged it and hired a limo driver to drive him both ways. When he wasn't in school, he was on his own, knocking around the house, except for the days when the housekeeper used to come. He'd liked the housekeeper. Her name was May, and she was cheerful, with silvery hair and a large round shape that shook when she laughed. And she laughed a lot.

Matt knew his dad had messed with her mind somehow. Vampires could do that sort of thing to humans, at least to the weak-willed ones. She knew, without being told, which rooms she was to stay clear of. She knew never to arrive before full light and to always be gone before nightfall. She knew not to mention anything that might seem unusual to her.

But more importantly to Matt, she knew how to make the best cookies, and how to make the day interesting for him.

He missed May and the old place. And even the private school, though none of that had lasted long. His father had decided it was too big a risk to have other people in his son's life. There was no one to keep him company in this new place, and they hadn't been there long enough for his dad to get anything set up, if he ever even intended to. So there was no housekeeper, no limo driver, no private school. Nothing for him to do during the day.

He guessed, or at least hoped, his dad would get onto all that in time. But for now it was boring as hell here. At least he would have Crisa now.

Matt stood beside the bed, watching her sleep, wondering if it really was just sleep, or if she would ever wake up. Before dawn, she had been shaking every once in a while. Moaning a little now and then. But once the sun came up, she went into that deep, deathlike sleep just like every other vampire did. And he wouldn't know if she was alive or dead until sundown.

He'd managed to change the sheets on the bed by himself. Then he'd located some pillows from other rooms in the house, put clean cases on them and brought them down. He'd stacked them on the bed and then gone back up in search of blankets, while the entire time she lay on the gurney in the lab, motionless.

Once he had the blankets ready, he plumped up the pillows, and then he wheeled the gurney into the room, right up beside the hospital bed. He locked the wheels so the thing wouldn't move, and then he carefully rolled Crisa's body from the gurney onto the bed. It wasn't too difficult. She didn't weigh much. And he wasn't worried about hurting her, because she couldn't feel anything in this state. More than that, he knew this was the time when vampires healed from any wounds they'd gotten during the previous night.

And that made him wonder if the day sleep was powerful enough to heal Crisa from the problems that chip in her brain was causing her. Or if it could at least reverse the damage a little bit, so she would be stronger when she woke up tonight than she had been when she'd fallen asleep this morning.

He took his time arranging her head on the pillows, and tucking the top sheet and the warm blankets around her, even though he knew vampires didn't tend to get cold. Especially not while they slept. But he didn't have anything else to do.

After that, he read to kill the time. He would have played videogames, but his system was up in his room, and he didn't dare get that far away from Crisa. He stayed right by her side. When he got hungry, he went up to the kitchen and made himself a sandwich, then brought it back down with him. When he got tired, he pushed the gurney over to one side of the room, climbed up on it and took a long nap.

When he'd gotten up from his nap, just a few minutes ago, he'd known it was dark outside. But he couldn't hear anything yet from his father, and Crisa didn't seem any different than she had been all day. Pale. Absolutely still. Cold to the touch.

He waited a few minutes, hoping his father would show up, so he could ask when they were going to try to fix her, and when his father didn't appear, Matt got antsy. He was just getting ready to go upstairs and search for his father when he heard a door opening in the lab.

Assuming it was his father, hopefully with a surgeon

in tow, Matt jogged into the lab. But it wasn't the door swinging open, as he'd expected to see. It was a part of the wall, shelves and all.

He stood there, too stunned to move, as a woman and a man—vampires, both of them— stepped through the wall and into the lab.

The woman looked around, her eyes nervous. He knew her. He'd glimpsed her before. She was Briar. She'd been part of his father's gang, and one of the mean ones, or so he'd always thought.

But Crisa said she had saved her life.

"You must be Matt," she said.

He nodded, taking a step backward. "You're Briar. I know you. You used to run with my father's gang. He told me you were one of the meanest vampires he ever met. He warned me to stay away from you. Said you were dangerous."

"You must have done a really good job, since I hardly ever set eyes on you," she said, not denying anything else he'd said. "But I did glimpse you once or twice, in passing."

"Father doesn't like me being around other vampires." As he said it, he looked at the strange man.

"This is Eric Marquand," Briar said. "This used to be his house—that's how we knew the way to get in. I brought him here to help me save Crisa."

Matt blinked when Briar said her name, trying to look puzzled. "Who?"

"Don't try to fool me, kid. I know she's here."

"No one's here but me. And my father, but he's upstairs." As he spoke, he moved himself slightly to one side, putting himself directly between Briar and Eric and the doorway that led to where Crisa lay.

"Yeah, I know. My friend Reaper went to the front door to try to keep him busy long enough for us to get Crisa out of here. You, too, if you want to come."

"I told you, she's not here. And even if she was, I wouldn't let you take her. She's sick. My dad's gonna help her."

"He tell you that?" Briar asked. And when Matt nodded, she said, "And you *believed* him?"

Matt wasn't sure what he believed. He thought Briar was evil, but Crisa said she'd saved her life. Crisa was *so sick*. If he made the wrong choice, he knew she might die. He swallowed hard. "I'd be pretty stupid to take off with a couple of strange vampires."

"Except that the rest of our group is waiting in town. And that includes your mother, Matt. Ilyana. She's your mom, right?"

He nodded, but he didn't know if he believed her. He narrowed his eyes on her. "How do I know you're not just lying to me?"

"She's a beanpole. Platinum-blond hair she keeps cut kind of short and spiky, like the top-knot feathers of some exotic chicken. Really unusual eyes, kind of violet, like Liz Taylor's—only I guess you wouldn't know who that is, would you? And she really doesn't like vampires at all, much less trust them. But she's starting to trust us."

Matt tipped his head to one side just as a sense of ten-sion from above made Briar tilt her own head. Then she pushed the boy aside and moved past him, through the door and into the room where Crisa lay.

"Hey, there, my crazy little loon," she said. She leaned over Crisa, pushing her hair off her forehead with one hand. "Baby, hey. Come on, wake up, it's your favorite hell-bitch."

Her brows drew together, and she shot a look toward Matt. "How long has she been like this?"

"Since yesterday," Matt said. "Is she—I can't tell, I'm not a vamp. Is she even alive?" He felt tears in his eyes and tried to blink them away.

"Oh, hell, yeah." Briar dropped down to one knee, putting herself at eye level with him. "Yeah, she's alive. She is. You poor kid. You've been sitting here not even sure of that much, haven't you?" He nodded. "For how long?" she asked.

He shrugged. "All day. And for a little while before that."

Eric lifted his head, glancing upward without any real focus. "We need to get her out of here before we're unable to. Matthias, you can come with us or stay behind. It's up to you. But I'd far prefer you come with us."

Briar glared at the man. *What do you mean, it's up to him?* She thought the words urgently, unaware, Matt knew, that he could hear them, too. *We're not leaving it up to him whether or not he stays with a killer like Gregor. We show up without him and Ilyana will never forgive me. Neither would Roxy, and God knows I'd never hear the end of it from her. Besides, the kid could end up dead if we leave him here.*

Eric shrugged and looked again at Matt. "What do you say, son?"

Matt looked from one of them to the other, and then he nodded. "I'll come with you." Then he looked toward the desk in the lab. "Those are the files Derry, uh, Mr. Dwyer had on her. You might need them."

"Good man," Eric said, clapping the boy on the shoulder. "Let's gather them up and go."

Raphael Rivera, Gregor said mentally. *It's about time.*

It's long past time, Gregor. Reaper had allowed Gregor to sense him as he approached the front door. He hadn't made it too obvious, but not too challenging, either. And apparently it had worked.

Gregor flung the front door open wide even as Reaper jogged along the walkway toward it. Reaper had a tranquilizer gun loaded, drawn and clutched in his hand, ready to fire. So, he noted, did Gregor. "I've been expecting you," Gregor called.

"Oh, I have no doubt. But I'm not here for you, Gregor. Not this time. This is about Crisa. She's an innocent in all this. Let me take her out of here, and then you and I will settle what's between us."

"Who's Crisa?" Gregor asked, feigning innocence.

Reaper poured on vampiric speed, staring into Gregor's face in an instant, gripping his shirt front in a fist. "Don't play games with me, Gregor. She's dying. She needs help immediately." He held his gun to Gregor's head, but Gregor did the same. If Reaper fired, Gregor would, too. Stalemate.

"I know." Gregor jerked himself free of the other man's grip, then smoothed his shirt front down, still holding the gun steady. "That's why I've sent the drones to bring me a surgeon."

Reaper's brows drew together. The man's words didn't make any sense to him. "Why would you do that?"

"Because Crisa needs that chip removed from her brain or she'll die. And because I have decided to keep her alive if I can. And if I can keep her alive, then I've decided to keep her."

"*What*?" Reaper asked, his eyes narrowing.

Gregor shrugged. "I don't have to explain myself to you. However, you should know that I'm not going to let you leave, even though I'm not going to be able to deal with you until after I do what needs to be done for Crisa."

"It's because of your son, isn't it? It's because of the boy."

Gregor's eyes narrowed. "What the hell do you know about my son?"

"I had a conversation with Dwyer," Reaper said, debating how much to give away and still unsure whether Gregor knew that Ilyana was with Reaper and his gang. "He told me he had the boy. He told me about the chip, the mind control power it provides, the fact that you had taken those controls from him and had them here. It wasn't much of a leap from there to guessing that you would have forced Crisa to bring Matthias back here to you. So where are they, Gregor? Where are you keeping them?"

"You're good. Very good. But I wouldn't tell you where they were even if you shot me." Gregor walked over to the fireplace, where a fire was burning, though the flame was extremely low.

"Interesting that you put it that way, since those are your precisely your options," Reaper said, following him, not wanting to let him get too far away. He was constantly sensing for drones, constantly monitoring for a signal from Briar that she and Eric and Crisa had made it clear.

But he heard nothing.

And then he did.

He heard the grating of metal hinges beneath him, and he felt the floor giving away. Before he could react, he was plummeting downward, a long way downward. Finally he landed hard on what felt like a cold concrete floor in a room of utter darkness. The single square of light from above quickly vanished, as Gregor swung the trapdoor closed again.

"Enjoy your stay, Reaper," Gregor called just before he extinguished the last bit of light. "As soon as I've granted my son's request to save your friend Crisa, I'll be coming down to drain you of every ounce of blood— and of power—you possess."

"Damn you, Gregor!"

Reaper whirled in a circle, arms reaching outward, eyes adjusting rapidly. And soon he could see and feel the situation. He was in a small room. Windowless concrete walls on all four sides of him, and the chute through which he had plummeted above. Nothing else.

* * *

Gregor trekked down into the basement. The cell where he'd sealed Reaper was in a sublevel below this one. The chute through which he'd fallen was wide and completely enclosed. From here, it looked like an over-sized chimney, a square pillar that reached from floor to ceiling. No one would guess that it opened into the living room floor above and ended in a tomblike pit below.

He'd expected to hear Reaper shouting at him, cursing him, demanding to be released. But he heard nothing. The man had gone silent. Probably plotting his escape. Gregor wondered how long it would take him to figure out that there was none.

But that was for later contemplation. And enjoyment. For now, he needed to shift his focus to Matthias and his pathetic newfound companion. He hoped the drones could find a surgeon and bring him here before this night was through. Even then, there was still no guarantee the woman would survive. But he had promised to try, and he intended to.

Gregor's thoughts ground to a halt as he realized that there was no sense of Matthias anywhere nearby. He frowned and sharpened his focus, but he felt the emptiness of the room even before he reached it. He opened the door to the basement lab, then moved through it and into the room beyond.

Crisa's hospital bed lay empty. Clean sheets, and mounds of blankets and pillows, were rumpled, as if they had been used. But no one was using them now. One small blanket and a pillow lay on the gurney on the far side of the room, and he guessed that must have been where his son had napped today. Close to Crisa's side. Watching over her as if he were a man grown, and her protector, rather than a young boy. Gregor's chest swelled with a feeling of pride in his son, even as his stomach lurched in worry.

Someone else had been here.

Briar!

He could smell her, almost taste her on the air. She'd been here, and so had someone else. Another vampire, a male, and one Gregor did not know. Gone now. Though how the two could have come and gone unseen was beyond him.

He followed his sense of them, knowing they had taken his son and Crisa away. As he moved back through the lab, he noted that the stack of files was also missing. The ones he'd taken from Dwyer, the ones that had all the information on Crisa.

And then he searched the main part of the basement lab, again following his senses. One wall had a freestanding rack of shelves against it, only he realized now that it wasn't freestanding at all. The bricks behind it were actually attached to it. The marks on the dusty floor showed him the truth. It was a secret door. He ran his hands over the books, touching only where *they* had touched, until the shelf sprang free. He pulled it open.

Whirling back toward the room, he howled in rage.

What's the matter, Gregor? Reaper's mind reached out to his, adding to his fury. *Your kid run away again?*

I'll kill you for this, Reaper. Make no mistake. I'll get

them back. All of them—Briar included. But you, my
friend, you are not going to be around to see it.

Gregor started for the hidden entrance to that subter-
ranean cell, then stopped himself.

He called out to his drones, most of whom were pa-
trolling the woods or standing on guard duty. *There are*
intruders on or around the grounds. They have taken my
prisoner and my son. Find them. Kill the man, and bring
the others to me. And do not hurt the boy.

That done, he hauled open a trapdoor in the basement
floor, climbed down the ladder to the bottom and stood
in the small open area, facing the solid door to Reaper's
cell. He was going to kill the bastard, and he was going
to do it now. No more waiting.

He reached for the door, unfastened the bolt, gripped
the large handle and shoved it inward.

But the door didn't budge.

He shoved again, but still there was no movement.

From the other side, Reaper laughed softly. "Did you
expect that I'd make it easy for you? I suppose you can
always come in the way I did. Though I'll be waiting to
tear you apart when you land, so you'd have a hell of a
time getting out again."

The bastard was blocking the door with no more than
the force of his mind! Telekinesis, of a sort, fueled by
the power of his bloodline, perhaps. Gregor tried to bat-
tle it with the force of his own powers, but he knew already that he was no match for the vampiric powers of
someone descended from Rhiannon, and from Vlad the
Impaler before her.

Gregor gave up trying after a moment, knowing he couldn't open the door that way. "I don't have to resort to coming in that way," he said. "You *will* die, Reaper. Even if I can never get inside that cell, you'll die. Either slowly, of starvation, or more quickly."

"Either way, you don't get to drain me. My power dies with me."

Gregor narrowed his eyes. "Honestly, as long as you're dead, I no longer care."

"Bull."

Gregor shrugged, never admitting that he really did care, that he craved Reaper's power. The man would be just as dead, either way. He climbed the ladder and crossed the basement, then headed back up the stairs to the main part of the house. In the living room, he went to the mantel and picked up the remote control he'd left there. He'd been preparing this place for months before he'd actually taken up residence, and this particular feature was his greatest innovation. With a thumb to a button, the trapdoor dropped open again. Then he thumbed another button and watched the floor as a solid, impenetrable, glasslike panel slid silently across in its place.

Do me a favor, Reaper. Look up.

He knew full well what his nemesis would see when he did. He would see the long chute through which he had plummeted. He would see that the trapdoor in the living room floor was open, a window in its place, and directly above that, in the towering ceiling above Gregor, he would see the skylight, as its electronic shades drew back.

Right now that skylight would show Reaper only a distant glimpse of the night sky, the twinkling stars, perhaps even a corner of the crescent moon. A tantalizing, teasing bit of the freedom he would never again know…and the slowly dawning realization that in the morning, that window onto the world would reveal a far different view. A view of the daylight—and of the sun. As it rose, its rays would flow down into the chute, and by the time the sun reached its zenith, Reaper's tiny cell would be flooded in light.

And he would go up in flames.

Briar followed Eric into the tunnel, then turned to pull the section of wall closed behind them, as the boy stood trembling beside her. With the door closed, the passageway was black as pitch, and the child's fear was palpable. She could see as well in the darkness as by full light, but she knew he couldn't, so when he groped blindly, his eyes wide, his lips trembling, Briar caught his hand and closed hers around it. "It's okay, Matt," she said.

Ahead of her, Eric was carrying Crisa, who hung limp in his arms. She was so still that Briar wondered if she had any chance of survival.

"Is Crisa going to be all right?" Matt asked. He shuffled his feet when he walked, unsure of his footing, slowing Briar's pace. She held on to his hand even more tightly, pulling him along.

"Honestly, I don't know," she told him. "I want her to be."

"My father is going to know I'm gone. He's going to try to stop us, and he's going to be *really* mad."

She nodded, though he couldn't see her. "Does he know about this passageway?"

"I don't think so. If he did, he never said anything."

"Then we should be fine. We're almost to the end. Hang in there, Matt, okay?"

"I'm trying." His hand tightened on her fingers. "You must have changed, I guess."

She frowned down at him. "Just keep moving."

"You used to be one of the bad guys. But now you're not."

"I'm no different than I ever was," she told him. God, the kid was as bad as Reaper, searching for noble motives for everything she did. There were none. She hadn't changed.

"Yes, you are. You're different. You care now."

"You're nuts, Matt. I don't care about anyone."

"You do. You care about Crisa…a *lot*. And even about me a little. And your friend—Reaper? You're worrying about him even more than you're worrying about whether we're gonna get out of here or not."

She stopped walking. "What are you, some kind of mind reader or something?"

He clamped his lips tight and picked up his pace a little. She'd hit on something there, she thought. For a mortal, the boy was sharp, insightful. More than that, maybe, but he didn't want anyone to know.

She watched his face as he battled his fears and marched onward. "I don't want to see anything bad happen to Crisa," she admitted. "Or to Reaper. Or to you, either. Doesn't mean I care."

"What *does* it mean, then?"

Hell, she was damned if she knew. And she didn't have time to analyze it, then explain it to a kid, right now, anyway. "We're at the end. There's a trapdoor in the top. We need to climb up to it. It comes out in the woods, a few hundred yards away from the house. We're going to have to be very quiet now."

"I know. The drones are probably out there."

Eric stopped, and, bending down, he laid Crisa gently on the packed earth floor. Then he climbed upward, pausing to listen and sense. Eventually he whispered, "Dwyer? Are you there?"

"Here," a hoarse voice whispered. And then the trapdoor in the forest floor opened and Dwyer peered in from above. "God, what took you so long? There've been drones passing by on all sides every little while. It's a miracle they haven't found me."

"We'll be out of their reach soon," Eric assured him, then climbed back down.

"I don't think anyone's near. We move fast from here, all right? You'll need to carry the boy, Briar, or he'll never keep up."

Carry the boy? Hell.

"All right?" Eric asked.

"Yeah, whatever, though how you expect Dwyer to keep up with us is beyond me."

"I've got that covered."

She didn't even ask how, just sighed. "Let's get on

with this, then. I don't have all night. And I'm not getting any younger."

To her surprise, the kid laughed, just a little. She shot him a look, and he said, "That's funny. Not getting any younger. Not getting any older, either."

"Kid's a freakin' comedian," she muttered.

Eric Marquand picked Crisa up again, and, anchoring her over his shoulder, he climbed up the steps and emerged into the forest. Briar crouched down in front of Matt. "Wrap your arms around my neck and your legs around my waist."

"Like piggyback?" the kid asked, even as he complied.

"Yeah, just like piggyback." She rose, with the child clinging and rising with her, and then she climbed upward quickly.

As soon as they were out, Eric bent to lower the trapdoor. "This way," he said. And as he spoke, he clapped an arm around the cowering mortal's waist, and yanked the man up and over his other shoulder.

Briar felt something—someone approaching. Many of them. "The drones are closing in. Go!"

Eric burst into a run, though his speed was hampered by the need to carry two others as he went. Briar didn't hesitate to do the same. But the drones could move at preternatural speeds, too, and there was no way to be sure they wouldn't be cut off or ambushed, or simply caught, before they got clear.

15

━◆━

Everything was ready. Roxy paced the small clinic, moving from window to window, constantly looking outside in search of Reaper and Briar and poor, wounded little Crisa.

"Roxy, you need to stay away from the windows," Jack said for about the tenth time. "If we get spotted in here, our entire plan goes up in smoke without passing go."

She shot him a scowl. "We should have heard from them by now. Shouldn't we?"

"Yeah, well, *we'll* hear from them long before *you'll* see them. We'll get a mental shout-out as soon as they can send one."

She nodded, knowing Jack was right, even as Vixen came over to lay a hand on her shoulder and nodded toward the rear corner of the waiting room. Ilyana was sitting in a chair there, her eyes riveted to the door. She was so still she seemed to be holding her breath.

Roxy met Vixen's eyes and got the message. She pulled her nervousness under control and went over to Ilyana, pulled a chair up beside hers and joined her there.

"They won't bring Matt. I know they won't," Ilyana said softly.

"What makes you so sure?"

Ilyana met Roxy's eyes. "Gregor is expecting an attack. He'll have Matt hidden. And even if he doesn't, Crisa is the main goal here. She's one of them. They'll make her the priority."

"Over an innocent child?" Roxy shook her head. "You don't know these people very well, if you really believe that."

"I know Briar well enough. She wouldn't lift a finger to help anyone but herself. Hell, she's said it often enough. I doubt she'd even be helping Crisa if not for the power of that blood bond they share. And *that* was against Briar's will."

Roxy shook her head. "Briar had a choice. Let Crisa die, or share blood with her. None of us could have forced her. There's more to that one than you know, I think."

"Humph."

Clearly Ilyana didn't believe that.

"But there's more than just Briar," Roxy went on. "Reaper is with her, and so is Eric Marquand."

"Marquand is a stranger. We don't know anything about him."

"I'll tell you what I *do* know, Ilyana," Roxy said softly. "I know Raphael. He's a good man."

"He's a former CIA assassin," Ilyana corrected.

"He's a *good man*. And if there's a way to save your son for you, he'll do it."

"Someone's coming!"

They both looked up sharply as Mirabella turned toward the door. Seth and Vixen flanked her. Topaz drew a weapon, one of the tiny tranquilizer guns they all carried to protect themselves from Reaper's rage. She checked to be sure it was loaded, then tucked it into the back of her designer jeans.

"It's a mortal," Jack said. "A cop."

"Hell." Roxy lowered her head and massaged her brow with one hand. "Don't kill him, guys. Please? Not unless you really have to."

Jack sent her a playful look. "You're ruining all our fun, you know that, don't you?"

"I've got this," Topaz said. "The rest of you, get out of sight."

And with that, she went to the door, just as the knob began to turn. The officer was testing the lock. When he found it engaged, he punched in the code that would open it. Drawing his weapon, he cautiously pushed the door wider and stepped inside.

Topaz was standing right in front of him when he did. He started when he saw her. His hand tightened on his gun, but something kept him from raising it. Something in Topaz's eyes, Roxy thought, as she watched from the next room, through a tiny crack in the door.

"Who are you? What are you doing here?" the cop demanded. "This is private property."

"I know. What made you come?" she asked.

"Just put your hands up and turn around."

She shook her head slowly. "Oh, come on. I'm no

threat to you. You *want* to talk to me. You can see there's nothing wrong here. Just tell me, what made you come?"

"Dispatch got a call," he said, speaking slowly. "Neighbor reported someone moving around in here after hours and got suspicious."

"They must have been imagining things," she said. "There's no one here. Everything here is fine."

"What do you mean no one's here?" he asked, looking at her as if he thought she might have mental problems. "*You're* here."

In the next room, Roxy shot a worried look at Jack. Jack whispered, "He must be exceptionally strong-willed."

"We're not going to be able to let him leave, are we?" Roxy looked at the man. He was handsome. His soft brown hair was cut short and neat, and his body was strong and lean. He had kind eyes. Sharp, knowing, kind eyes. She looked again at Jack, listening as Topaz made another attempt to gain control of the man's mind.

"There's no one here," she said again, her voice taking on a soft, hypnotic cadence. "Everything here is fine, you can see that clearly. You've found nothing amiss here. You need to be on your way and report back that there's nothing wrong here."

He frowned until his brows touched. "You're *standing* right in *front* of me, lady." And still he couldn't quite lift the gun. "I'm going to have to take you with me. Is there anyone else here?"

"*No one's* here." She was beginning to sound a bit impatient. No doubt it ticked her off to be unable to enchant a man with her looks and the combined power of her mind and will.

The cop reached for the radio mike that was clipped to the front of his uniform shirt. Topaz's hand closed over his so fast that he couldn't have detected the movement. She clamped hold of his wrist. "Don't do that."

He met her eyes, and she quickly gripped his other hand, the one holding the gun.

"No, Roxy," Jack said softly. "I'm afraid we're not going to be able to let him leave."

Just as Briar, Eric and their "passengers" were about to emerge from the woods onto the road where they'd left the car, they sensed a solid wall of drones at the forest's edge. Briar dropped to the ground behind a tangle of brush, gripping Eric's arm and yanking him down with her. She lowered Matt to the ground, telling him to stay low. The poor child was petrified.

Then again, so was she. But oddly, not for herself.

Wide-eyed, she looked around them, and while she couldn't see any others nearby, she could *feel* them. They were approaching from both sides, and more were coming up from behind.

"We're surrounded," she whispered.

Eric released his hold on Dwyer, who crouched beside him, trembling with fear. Then he laid Crisa gently on the ground.

"How is she doing?" Briar asked him.

Eric met her eyes, and his were grim. "Not well. We

need to get that chip out of her brain, and we need to do it soon."

"All right." Briar moved Matt, pushing him closer to Eric. "You're going to stay with Eric and Crisa. All right?"

"Stay? Here?" B-but...the drones..."

"I'm going to take care of them." She dug in her pocket for the keys to the car that waited by the road side. It was Seth's Mustang, and it was faster than hell. She handed the keys to Eric.

"What are you thinking?" Eric asked. "Briar, you can't—"

"Look, I was going back anyway. Reaper's still in there. This just speeds up my plan a bit."

"What plan?" Eric demanded.

She lowered her eyes, because she had no plan. Not much of one, anyway. "I'm going to go out in the open, make sure the lugheads see me, and then make a run for it. It'll lead the damn drones away from here. They're not too bright. They'll come after me, and by the time it occurs to them that Matt and Crisa aren't with me, it'll be too late. Because the *second* they come after me and give you a clear path, Eric, I want you to take Matt and Crisa and make a break for that car. Get in, take off and don't look back. Do you know where the clinic is, where the rest of the A team is waiting?"

"Yes. But I'm not going to leave you to fight off those creatures alone." He peered out of the brush at them. "What the hell are they?"

"They start out as the Chosen, I think. Humans with

the belladonna antigen and certain other physical char-
acteristics in common. That protruding forehead, the
oversized bodies, the strength. I've heard that they're lo-
botomized before they're transformed, but I think
there's more to it than that. What you see is the result."
She sent a look at Dwyer. "What I don't know is where
you find such a steady supply of them."

Dwyer swallowed hard and lowered his head. "I can't
tell you that."

"Oh, you'll tell me everything I want to know,
Dwyer." She gripped his shirt front and jerked him
closer to her. "Or are you not *getting* that your life is in
my hands right now?"

He met her eyes and swallowed hard.

Eric clapped her shoulder. "There's no time, not now.
The drones are closing in. Have no fear, Briar. I'll make
him tell us what he knows once we get clear of this place
and the innocents are safe."

"Oh, he's not going with you," Briar said.

Dwyer's eyes widened, and his head snapped up.

"You and I have unfinished business, Dwyer. More
than a little. You're coming with me."

"I can't go back there. I *can't!* Gregor will kill me."

"He'll probably kill me, too, if the drones don't do
it first. Buck up, pal. It's for the greater good and all
that bullshit."

Matt shook his head. "Wait. If you take me with you,
they won't hurt you. Dad will have told them not to hurt
me. And sometimes they listen to me. I can make sure
they don't hurt you."

Briar smiled slightly as she looked at the boy, feeling a little awed. "You're a brave little shit, you know that?" Then she tousled his hair, an act so unlike her that she surprised herself by doing it. "Tell your mom I said she'd better take good care of you, pal. And tell her…for a human, she's not so bad." She glanced toward Eric. "Do everything you can for Crisa."

"You have my word on that, Briar." Then he thinned his lips and pierced her eyes with his. "Rhiannon was right about you."

"Oh, hell, that arrogant bitch doesn't need to be told that. It'll just swell her head more than it already is."

"Be careful, Briar," Eric said. "Reaper will never forgive me for leaving you, if anything bad should befall you."

She frowned at him.

"He loves you, you know. And I don't blame him. You're quite remarkable."

"God save me from sappy men. You're as bad as he is." And with that she rose from her hiding place, gripping Dwyer by the back of his neck, so he was forced to rise with her.

"Leave me with them!" Dwyer pleaded. He pulled free, dropping to his knees again. "I'll tell you how the drones are made. I'll tell you *everythin'*."

"Too late." She crouched beside him, ready to yank him upright and make him run.

"I'll tell Eric, once we get clear, and I'll tell the rest of them, too. I promise I will."

"No."

She jerked at him. He had tears forming in his eyes now. "They can't save Crisa without my help. I know how to get at the chip."

She looked to Eric for confirmation. He shook his head. "I think I can manage just as well without him. I have the files." He patted the satchel over his shoulder.

She nodded and tugged at Dwyer again. He tried one more tactic. "I'll tell you Reaper's trigger word. The one you still don't know, the one that will break the rage after the first trigger word activates it. The word that will end it."

Briar hesitated, because that was precisely the information she'd been hoping for and planned to demand. She looked at him. "If I find out you lied to me…"

"I won't lie. And I can give you more. There's a hypnotist—the one who programmed Reaper in the first place. I'll give Eric his name, and if Reaper survives this, he can track him down, make him deprogram his mind. But in the meantime, the trigger word…"

"What is it?" she demanded.

"You'll let me go with Eric?"

"Yes, just tell me. What is it?"

"Mongoose."

"Mongoose?" She rolled her eyes. "You guys sure don't use much imagination for this shit, do you?" She looked at the man. "There's just one more thing. I need to know what really happened to Reaper's wife."

The man's face turned to stone. "He killed her. It was—"

"Uh-uh. I mean what *really* happened."

"I don't know what you're talking about."

"Yes, you do, and you're too good at blocking your thoughts. So I'm left with no choice but to find out in my own way. Besides, I could use a boost of strength." Without taking her eyes from him, she said, "Can you carry them both to the car, Eric?"

"I've done fine so far. I don't know what this is about, Briar, but I trust your judgment. Do what you think is necessary, but do it fast."

She nodded, and gripped Dwyer by the front of his shirt. "Reaper's wife," she said. "Remember." And then she jerked him forward and sank her fangs into his throat. He struggled as she drank him into her. He fought to block his mind from thinking of the thing she'd commanded him to think about, but she drank deeply, and kept taking, and told him mentally, *I'll take it all, if you make me. And then I'll know anyway.*

And then it came. Images. Memories. The truth.

She jerked free of him, her eyes still glowing, bolstered by the fresh blood, and full of energy and raw fury. When she let go of the man's shirt, he slumped to the ground.

"You make sure he talks, Eric, once Crisa and the kid are safe. We need to know how those drones are made."

"And the rest?"

"I've got all I need."

"You have my word," Eric said. "He'll tell us about the drones. And I'll get the contact information on that hypnotist he mentioned, as well. Good luck, Briar."

"Thanks."

Swiping her hand across her mouth, she sprang from the brush and began to run. She didn't intend to use her top preternatural speed. She knew she couldn't hope to outrun the drones, not when they surrounded her on all sides. Besides, she needed to be sure they saw her and followed. Her goal was only to lead them as far from the others as possible, to give them the best possible chance for escape.

As soon as she'd put a hundred yards between herself and her cohorts, she stopped, put two fingers to her lips and cut loose with an ear-splitting whistle.

She felt the attention of every drone in the forest turn toward her. And then she turned and ran.

Even as she raced through the forest, running at a high speed that was still a nearly mortal pace, she felt something swelling in her chest. A feeling she could barely believe existed in her. It was, she thought, the realization that what she had been denying for so long was nothing more than the truth. Okay, she cared about them—about Crisa, about Matt, about all those sappy white-hats in Reaper's gang—more than she cared about her own safety.

More than any of them, though, she cared about Reaper, and it was him she imagined herself running toward as she moved through the night.

And even though she was facing death right then, the feeling that suffused her wasn't a bad one. It actually felt good to care. As if a long dormant part of her heart had suddenly been reactivated. Jump-started. Electro shocked into life.

* * *

"Here they come!"

Ilyana heard Topaz's shout and spun to face the clinic door even as it burst open.

The first man who came through, shoved from behind, was a mortal. It surprised Ilyana that she could tell the difference now with no more than a swift glance, but she could. She'd spent enough time around the undead to have learned the subtle differences. This man was haggard, exhausted, afraid, as he stumbled into the room.

Behind him was Eric Marquand, with Crisa in his arms. She was limp and still dead, by all appearances, but Ilyana knew that looks could be deceiving in Crisa's kind. They all looked dead when they rested.

As she watched, the other vamps crowded the doorway. Jack took hold of the mortal by one arm. "You're Dwyer?"

"He is," Marquand said. "See to it he's unable to run away."

"Got it." As Jack pulled away from the throng with Dwyer in a firm grip, Marquand handed Crisa off to Seth. "Get her onto a table and get some blood into her. We need to operate immediately."

Seth nodded, taking Crisa, turning away and heading into the treatment room. Vixen, Topaz and Mirabella followed. And then Marquand lowered his head and turned slightly, extending a hand. "Come on, son. It's all right now."

As he spoke, Eric stepped aside.

Matt came in slowly, his eyes huge as he looked around the room. Ilyana sucked in a gasp, and his eyes flew straight to her. And then he ran to her, crossing the room in a heartbeat and flinging himself into her arms.

She hugged him hard as tears flooded down her face. She ran her hands through his hair over and over, and she held on as if she would never let go. When she finally did, it was only to kneel in front of him and kiss his damp cheeks.

"Dad told me you were dead," Matt said, his words broken, his voice hoarse. "But then I found out you weren't."

"No, I'm not. I'm fine, and now you're with me. Everything's going to be okay now, baby, I promise. We'll never be apart again."

"If he finds us—"

She clutched him tighter. "We have friends now, Matt. Powerful friends." As she said it, she lifted her head to find Roxy smiling down at her, standing very close by. Beyond her, the others were watching through a doorway, and Eric was there, as well. "They'll protect us," Ilyana said. "He'll never get you again, not with them helping us."

Matt sniffled and frowned, pulling away far enough to stare into her face. "But I thought you *hated* vampires."

"I thought so, too." She wiped a tear from her cheek. "But they brought you back to me. I can't hate anyone who would give me something so precious, now can I?"

"They're good," Matt said. "They really are. I can tell, you know."

"I know you can," she said.

"Even Briar," he added very softly, almost whispering.

And as soon as he said it, Ilyana frowned and looked around the room again, her gaze settling at last on Eric.

"Where *is* Briar? And what about Reaper? Why aren't they with you?"

"There's not much time, so I'll explain as I work." Eric marched into the treatment room, unloading the files from the satchel over his shoulder as he did. He spread them on a table, noting, as he did, an open door to a closet, where Dwyer sat on the floor, bound and gagged, beside another man, a mortal, dressed only in a T-shirt and boxer shorts.

Eric frowned.

"Cop," Jack said, closing the door on the two captives. "Came to check out a neighbor's report of movement in here after hours. Guy was too strong-willed for mind control, but we managed to force him to radio in that all was clear. Then I put on his uniform to drive his car out of here, in case the neighbor who called in was watching for that."

"Where's the car now?" Eric asked.

"Hidden. Safe. But you can bet his absence won't go unnoticed long. There will be more of them."

Eric nodded. "Go through these files. I need anything that looks like an X ray or a diagram of Crisa's skull, so I can see where the chip is."

One of the captives thumped on the closet door. Eric ignored the sound and turned to the cabinets, opening them, and removing items and instruments one after the other. "Did you get some blood into her?"

"Tried," Vixen said softly. "She can't seem to swallow."

Nodding, Eric went to the table, where two units of blood rested. He hung one bag on an IV pole and quickly ripped a needle free of its plastic protection, inserted it into one of Crisa's veins, taped it in place and finally connected the long tube that ran from the bag. He made some adjustments and watched as the blood began to flow into her body.

"We don't know for sure what happened to Reaper," he said as he worked. "He went to the front door to distract Gregor, giving Briar and me time to access the basement lab through a hidden passage—one I knew about but was fairly certain Gregor didn't. We found Matthias and Crisa there, and carried them out. We never heard anything from Reaper, though. And we should have, so my best bet is that Gregor has him."

"Or has killed him," Jack muttered.

Again one of the captives thumped on the closet door. Probably with a foot, since their hands were bound. "Shut up in there!" Jack ordered. Then he turned his attention to Eric again. "What about Briar?"

"That one," Eric said, and he shook his head. "We were surrounded by drones as we made our way through the woods. There was no way out. So she went off on her own, led them on a chase, to give us time to get to the car and get away." He looked at them each in turn, his gaze lingering on Ilyana. "I tried to talk her out of it, but she was having none of that. Said it was more important that Matthias and Crisa get to safety, said she was going back anyway, for Reaper."

Ilyana blinked. "*Briar* said that?"

"I tried to make her take me with her, Mom," Matt said. "I told her the drones wouldn't hurt her if I was with her, but she wouldn't let me go. She said to tell you…" He sniffed and closed his eyes.

Ilyana knelt and clasped his shoulders. "What did she say to tell me, hon?"

"To take good care of me. And that for a human, you're not so bad."

Ilyana stared at him, dumbfounded. And then she rose slowly, and looked at Jack. "We have to get her out of there."

Again one of the captives thumped the closet door. Jack grimaced, stomped to the door and yanked it open, glaring down at Dwyer. "What the hell is it?"

Dwyer made muffled sounds behind his gag, so Jack knelt and yanked it downward. The man licked his lips and said, "You won't find any X rays in those files. But you don't need them. The chip's on the right side, toward the front of her head. If you shave the hair away there, you'll see the spot marked by an X-shaped scar."

Eric came toward him. "I'll need a drill to get through the skull, correct?"

"No," Dwyer said. "We used a small bore to remove a circle of the bone, and we didn't replace it."

Eric frowned. "Pull him out of the closet and untie him. Clearly he can assist in this procedure." He nodded at the officer, who looked confused and terrified. "Sir, you have my assurances that you'll be out of here just as soon as possible, unharmed. Be patient just a bit longer." Then he looked at the others. "Is it really necessary to put the poor man to so much discomfort?"

"I'll see to him, Eric," Mirabella said. "I quite agree

with you." The others frowned at her, and she pursed her lips. "Really, there's simply no excuse for bad manners."

As Jack hauled Dwyer out of the closet and untied him, Seth spoke up. "We need to go after Briar and Reaper. How many of us do you need here to help you with Crisa and our two unwilling guests, Eric?"

Eric considered the question for a moment. "Leave me Roxy and Ilyana. Matthias, of course, needs to stay here for his own safety. One other vampire should be enough to ensure we keep our captives in line and get through this undiscovered." He looked around the room. "Mirabella, will you stay?"

"Of course," she told him.

"Good." He glanced at Seth. "Take the others and go. You know where the mansion is?"

"Yes."

"Be careful. There are around two dozen of those... creatures guarding the place, and I have no doubt Gregor will be expecting you."

"Got it. Let's go."

"One other thing, Seth. You all know the word that launches Reaper into an uncontrolled murderous rage, correct?"

"Nightingale," Seth said.

"The word to return him to normal is mongoose."

Seth's brows went up. "How—"

"Briar traded the CIA man his life for it, just before she went off to put her own on the line," Eric said. "I figured you all ought to know, just in case. Using the word is a better option than darting the poor man, after all."

"Thanks." Seth frowned. "Though I have to admit, I'm going to miss having an excuse to shoot the son of a gun from time to time." He looked at the clock on the clinic's wall. "We only have a few hours until sunrise. Let's move."

"Seth, I parked around the block, to avoid having the car seen here." Eric tossed him the keys. Then he eyed the instruments on the tray, completely focused now on the task before him: Crisa, and removing that chip from her brain.

Seth and the others trooped out the door, closing it behind them. The remaining group gathered around Crisa, who lay draped in sheets on the stainless steel table. "Roxy," Eric said. "I need something to clip her hair, and a razor to shave it once I find the spot."

Roxy rattled through some drawers and brought the required items to him. Eric bent over Crisa's head, moving her hair with his fingers. When he found the spot he was looking for, he turned on the electric clippers Roxy had located and they began to buzz softly.

And then, suddenly, Crisa's body began to tremble and shake on the table. Frowning, Eric set the clippers down and reached for her, even as the shaking became a full body convulsion.

"Hold her down!" he shouted. "Now!"

He didn't need to tell them. Roxy and Ilyana were already there, grasping Crisa's legs, shoulders and waist to keep her from shaking herself right off the table.

As the spasm eased, Roxy pushed her hair out of her eyes. "What the hell was that?" she whispered.

"Death throes, I imagine," Eric said softly. "We have to do this now." He reached for the clippers again, as Matthias crowded his way up beside the table and closed his hand around Crisa's.

"Be okay," he told her. "Crisa, you have to be okay."

16

— ► ◄ —

The drones dragged Briar right up to the front door of the mansion. They hadn't needed to rough her up as much as they had, she thought angrily. The bastards. She hadn't even fought them all that hard. Just enough to make it convincing. They'd pummeled her anyway, and she was pretty sure it wasn't based on their own love of inflicting pain. She was pretty sure they didn't do *anything* based on their own preferences. Hell, she wasn't even sure they *had* preferences. Their treatment of her was far more likely based on orders from their commander. Gregor.

The door of the impressive Marquand mansion opened even before the drones had dragged her all the way up to it. One drone held each of her arms, and she thought her shoulders had been damn near torn from their sockets. But she managed to lift her head and saw Gregor standing there, smiling.

"This has been a long time coming," he told her.

"Too long," she replied. "I'd say it's nice to see you, Gregor, but it would be a lie."

"Bring her inside," Gregor snapped. "You can deposit her over there, by the fireplace."

The two drones dragged her inside, while the others who'd trooped along behind them as if Briar were a bigger threat than, oh, say, Attila the Hun, stayed behind.

"The rest of you, patrol the property," Gregor commanded. "Their friends will make an attempt to rescue them soon. Don't let anyone past you. Kill anyone who tries." He slammed the door as the drones lumbered away, then turned slowly to face Briar.

The two big lugs stood on either side of the chair into which they'd thrown her, quietly awaiting further instructions. She wondered a little evilly what would happen if Gregor told them to go fuck themselves. As mindlessly obedient as they were, it would almost certainly be good for a laugh.

"She belongs on the floor, not in a chair," Gregor said.

One drone grunted and reached down, grabbing her by the neck, lifting her bodily and then shoving her hard to the floor, where she lay facedown.

"That's better. Now get out. Guard the entrances. No one gets in or out. Understood?"

They muttered their acquiescence and lumbered away. When the door swung closed, Gregor locked it and turned once again to face her.

Briar pushed herself up on her hands, lifting her head to look at him. "You're not what I thought you were," she said.

"That's a lie, Briar. You came to me thinking all men would do nothing but use you for their own gain, be it sexual gratification, as an ego boost or as a punching bag to relieve their stress. You never really thought I would turn out differently. Not deep down. You've never believed in any man. At least not since your birth father walked out on you."

He was right, she realized. She hadn't. At least, not until now. Until Reaper.

"He's no different, you know. Your heroic Reaper. Oh, you think he is. I can see you do, or you wouldn't be here now. He *is* why you came back, isn't he?"

She lowered her eyes. She would *not* talk about Reaper with this animal.

Gregor crossed the room and sank into the chair she'd been seated in only moments before. "You got away with my son, Matthias. With your friend, the mental invalid. You got away. But you came back. I can't think of any other reason. Or are you going to try to tell me you came back for me?"

"Where is Reaper?" she asked.

"Oh, he's nearby. Alive, though I'm sure he's blocking to prevent you from realizing it. He wouldn't want you to sacrifice yourself for him. I can understand that. He's suffering under the same misguided notions about you that I once harbored myself, after all."

"What notions would those be, Gregor? That I would be your willing slave forever?"

He shrugged. "I saved your life. I took you in. I gave you immortality. I expected gratitude. I expected loyalty."

"You *expected* sex."

"Well, yes, that, too." He smiled slowly. "Are you in love with him?"

She turned away, closed her eyes.

"What would you do to save him, I wonder?"

Tears burned in her eyes, because she knew what was coming. She knew what he would ask. But she swallowed hard and lifted her gaze to meet his straight on. "I'd do anything," she whispered. "So stop beating around the bush and let's just get on with this, shall we? Tell me what you want, as if I don't already know."

Gregor smiled slowly. "I'm glad you're being so reasonable. Because you owe me, after all." He rose slowly from his chair and stood over her. "Get up, Briar."

She did, though she had to cling to the arm of the chair to pull herself up onto her feet. But she tried to hide her weakness. She would do this with her head up and her dignity intact. She'd sold her body for far less worthwhile payment, after all. She could do this. For Reaper.

"Go upstairs," Gregor said. His tone was flat, but there was a new, excited gleam beginning to show in his eyes. "There's a bathroom down the hall on the right. In it, you'll find clean clothes, toiletries, hairbrushes. I want you to take a shower. Brush your hair. Put on the pretty little things I bought for you. And some of the perfume, too. And the shoes. Be fast. And don't even *think* of trying to escape. If you do, he dies."

Don't do it, Briar.

Her head snapped up, eyes widening, as she heard Reaper's voice in her mind and realized he was alive and nearby, and that he'd been privy to the entire conversation.

For God's sake, don't do it. I'd rather die.

Gregor snapped his fingers, drawing her attention. "Trying to contact him? It's no use, you know. He's at my mercy now, and so are you. If you want him to live through this night, you'll do exactly as I say." He turned his wrist and looked at his watch. "You have fifteen minutes, Briar. I need to finish up with you before your little army of do-gooders shows up in a futile attempt to rescue you, which we both know is inevitable. Upstairs. *Now.*

Briar!

She closed her mind against Reaper's voice and went up the stairs. And yet he broke through her resistance. She should have known he would. The bond between them was more powerful than she had ever admitted.

He'll kill you anyway. And me, too, you know that. Just get out while you have the chance. I'm dead either way, and dammit, I can't stand to have another woman's blood on my hands. Not yours, Briar. Especially not yours.

She found the bathroom, opened the door and stared in at the black bustier and matching thong panties that hung from a peg on the wall. Thigh-high stockings were draped over the peg, as well. A pair of open-toed stilettos stood on the floor below them.

Shit, she thought. *I hate stilettos.*

She'd sworn that no man would ever take her against her will again. But this wasn't exactly against her will. This was her choice.

There's a chance you can escape while he's distracted with me, Reaper. She sent the thought to him, praying he would listen to her. *You need to take it. And there's something you need to know before you do. You didn't kill your wife.*

She reached into the shower and cranked on the taps, then began stripping off her clothes. In a moment she stepped into the spray.

What are you talking about? I was there. I know I—

You didn't kill your wife. I know it for a fact. Trust me enough to believe it, Reaper. If I don't make it through this, I need to know you believe me.

But...if I didn't kill her, then who did?

Briar closed her eyes, standing beneath the pounding water, soaping her body from head to toe, pain bursting inside her chest.

No one did.

What?

Rebecca is still alive. She never died. It was all a setup, both to establish her cover for the agency and to control you through your guilt. But she's alive. It's a fact. Hold on to that knowledge. Use it to keep you alive, to get the hell out of here, so you can go find her and be happy again.

Reaper collapsed to the floor of his cell, holding his head in his hands, eyes closed. It couldn't be true. God, it couldn't be true. Rebecca wouldn't have deceived him that way. Not that way, not to take part in something that had ripped his soul from him and left a bloody, gaping wound that would never heal.

She couldn't have.

He remembered the night when he'd awakened to find her battered, broken body on the floor of their apartment. He remembered rushing to check on her, only to

be interrupted by the door banging open, revealing
Dwyer, with a crew of men. Dwyer had gripped him in
a crushing embrace, told him it would be all right.

"But...but Rebecca—"

One of the men was already bending over her. "She's
dead," he said as he straightened.

And Reaper had known exactly what had happened.
He remembered her speaking—they'd been arguing.
And she'd said the word, though he didn't remember
what it was. He never did.

He only knew that his world had dissolved into a red
haze, and he'd shouted at her to run before it had taken
over completely. He'd told her to get away.

They'd been alone in the apartment. They still were
when he'd worn himself out and collapsed, unconscious, which was the only way the rages ever ended,
without someone using the second trigger word. And
they were still alone when he'd awakened to see the de-
struction of what had been his home. His life. His love.
All at his own cursed hands.

Dwyer had led him away, promising to take care of
everything. The agency had concocted a masterful cover
story. A car accident that had never happened. A quick
cremation. A funeral where he'd been forced to play the
grieving spouse—and he hadn't been acting. He *had*
been grieving. And yet, he had also been guilty of murdering the woman he loved.

And now Briar wanted him to believe it had never
happened?

I never got that close to her body.

But he would have known, he told himself. He would have known if it had been a scam. He would have sensed her, or sensed the lie in Dwyer.

The man's good. He can block. He can lie. And I wasn't a vampire yet, not then.

Dwyer wasn't that good, he told himself. Even as a mortal, Reaper had possessed excellent instincts and an uncanny ability to spot a liar.

How did he know to come? How is it he showed up just as I came to and found her?

It was a question he'd asked himself before. He'd even asked Dwyer. Derrick had told him that he'd phoned the apartment to speak to Reaper, and that Rebecca had managed to pick up the phone and cry out for help in the midst of her husband's attack.

But that didn't make a lot of sense. If she could get to the phone, she could get to the door. She could get out. She could get away from him. Couldn't she?

What were the odds of her saying his trigger word? Briar had asked him the same question. She'd said it wasn't the sort of word that would come up in casual conversation, particularly not in an argument. What would have possessed her to say it? Unless it was all part of the bigger plan?

Alive. Rebecca is alive.

The knowledge was overwhelming. And it *was* knowledge now. He believed Briar, because he knew better than to think that she would lie to him about something like this. Given what she was about to do, in a last-ditch effort to save his life, he couldn't doubt her.

Not anymore.

Maybe not ever again.

He had to get the hell out of this hole. He had to save her.

Bending his legs, standing right beneath the open chute above him, he pushed off, leaping with all his might. And yet he didn't have enough power to reach the top. He landed hard, took a moment to recuperate and then tried again, and again fell short of his goal.

The third time, he mustered a strength he hadn't known he possessed. This time he reached the top—and his head smashed into the impenetrable clear barrier that sealed the top of his prison. Light flashed before his eyes, and pain exploded behind them. When he hit the floor this time, he was hurting, bleeding from a cut in his skull, and dizzy to boot.

As he opened his eyes, he saw, far in the distance, Gregor's leering face far above him. The man was peering down through the clear barrier, smiling at him.

"I'm going to take her in every imaginable way, Reaper. And I'm going to make you watch."

"You'll have to let me out of here to do that."

"No, not really. Look." He held up a small remote control, and the glasslike screen turned opaque, and then a picture came to life on its face. Like a television screen, the thing showed him Briar. She was standing in the shower, naked, washing her hair and crying.

"I've got the place rigged with cameras," Gregor said from somewhere beyond the screen. "I'll make sure we have our long overdue sexual adventures right in front of one of them just for your benefit, Reaper. Don't worry. You can thank me later."

He left the thing on, probably as a form of torture. And it was effective. Reaper couldn't look away, though he tried, as Briar toweled off. He noticed every inch of her, winced at every bruise marring her beautiful skin, her face. Her neck. All of it.

She took a garment from the wall and put it on. A bustier, black, with a pair of tiny thong panties that barely covered her. And then she sat on the john and pulled on the stockings, followed by the pointy-heeled shoes that Reaper knew she detested.

This is not going to happen, Gregor. I promise you right now, if it kills me, you are not going to have her. Not ever.

Yes, I am. She owes me. And despite all your fury, Reaper, there's not a damn thing you can do about it.

Eric pulled the fragment of metal from Crisa's skull and dropped it onto the surgical tray beside the bed. Then he irrigated the wound with saline solution, hoping to rinse away any toxins that hadn't yet been absorbed by her body. And finally he closed up the tiny wound in her head and wrapped it tightly, to keep the pressure on until dawn, so she wouldn't bleed out.

After he was done, he straightened away from the table and closed his eyes. "That's all I can do. There's no way to tell if she'll recover. Or if she'll be…the same, if and when she does."

"Let's hope for the best," Roxy said. "You're done

in, Eric. Give yourself a rest. Ilyana and I will do some Reiki healing to help things along."

Eric nodded, crossed the room and slumped into a chair. Then he looked up to see Mirabella sitting beside the police officer. She'd unbound his hands and returned his clothing to him, promising to leave him free as long as he cooperated. Her unrivaled beauty probably had as much effect as her natural charm. She'd located a small kitchen off the clinic's reception room, and made the man a sandwich and a pot of coffee, then sat beside him, keeping him company while he ate.

The cop's sharp gaze went to Crisa, then shifted suspiciously to Eric. He didn't seem to miss a thing, but he didn't ask many questions. Nor did he seem overly eager to get away.

Now, for the first time, he spoke directly to Eric. "I don't pretend to know what's going on here, but I can see that you're trying to save that girl's life. What I don't get, is why you didn't just take her to a hospital?"

Eric nodded. "She's not like you or Roxy or Ilyana, or even the boy over there. She's like us. We're…different. A hospital wouldn't know that, and their efforts to save her could have ended up killing her instead. And while you've been remarkably cooperative, that's all I can really tell you. And more than I probably should have."

The officer nodded, clearly still curious, but not demanding more. "I should have reported in again by now," he said. "They'll be sending another car to my last known location to check on me soon." He looked at the clock on the wall. "In fact, it may well be on its way already."

Eric raised his brows, surprised at the man's honesty. Then he turned to the others. "We need to move her. And there are only two hours left before the dawn."

"But we haven't heard from the others yet. What if Gregor has all of them?" Roxy asked.

"Look," the cop said, "if this Gregor guy is trouble, I can get you some help."

Mirabella smiled at him, and Eric was rather surprised that the man didn't melt into a puddle at her feet. "You would do that, after we held you here this way? All bound up in a closet?"

He met her eyes—seemed lost in them, in fact. "I've seen a kid reunited with his mother. I've seen a woman's life saved. I've seen a bunch of people go out to try to rescue their friends from this Gregor character. And I've got good instincts. My gut tells me you're the good guys in all this, even if your methods are a little bit over the line."

"Your gut is right." Mirabella held his gaze a moment longer, then took his plate and cup from him. "More coffee?"

Before he could answer, his radio crackled.

"Charlie-five, Charlie-five, report in."

He reached for the mike, which was once again clipped to his chest where it belonged, and when Eric started to protest, he held up one hand. "It's okay. I'm not going to give you away."

Then he answered the call. "This is Charlie-five. Everything's fine. I had a radio malfunction. Didn't realize it until just a few minutes ago."

"Charlie-five, what's your location?"

"I'm cruising Main Street. Everything's quiet."

"Charlie-five, we have a second report of activity at the clinic. Can you take another look?"

"Affirmative. I'm on it. Charlie-five out."

He looked up at the others. "That should buy you enough time to get out of here."

"Thank you," Eric said.

"Yes," Mirabella echoed. "Thank you…Charlie, is it?"

His smile was quick and genuine. "It's Marcus Jones. You know, you look like Mirabella DuFrane. The actress. Who died years ago."

"I know. But I'm not." She tilted her head to one side, watching him decide whether or not to believe her. In the end, he let it go.

"I'm not going anywhere," he said. "Not in the fore-seeable future, anyway. So if you ever get back in town…"

"Oh, Charlie. That's so sweet. I'll remember you."

He smiled again, and let her calling him Charlie slide. Maybe he would think of it as an endearment someday.

That Mirabella, Eric thought with a slight shake of his head. She could charm the spots off a leopard. Provided it was a male leopard.

"I'll go get the van," Roxy said. "We need to find shelter before daylight, and then we need to find out what the hell's happened to the others."

"Take *Charlie* here with you," Eric said, with a wink in the officer's direction. "You can show him where Jack stashed his car, and then he can get out of here and resume his life unhindered."

"All right." Roxy held out a hand. "Come on... Charlie."

He nodded and gave Mirabella one last longing glance.

Then, impulsively, she kissed him on the cheek. "Thank you for your help."

"You're welcome. Maybe someday...you can look me up and tell me what all this was about."

"Maybe I will," she said.

Eric sighed, knowing Mirabella was never going to give the poor sap a call, as Roxy and the cop slipped out of the clinic. Then he turned to where Dwyer had collapsed in a chair, exhausted.

"Before I let you take a well-earned nap, friend, there's something you promised to tell us. About the drones?"

Dwyer lowered his head.

"It's not as if I'm giving you a choice here. I'm being pleasant, but I don't have to be."

Dwyer still didn't speak. Eric shook his head and turned to Ilyana. "You'd best take your son into the other room. Mirabella, you might want to leave, as well."

"Oh, no," she said. "I might just want to help. I'm not *all* sweetness and light, you know."

Eric lifted his brows in stark surprise.

She shrugged. "Don't let anyone ever tell you I wasn't a great actress."

"You still are," he said.

Ilyana took Matt by the hand. Matt looked back at Dwyer, then at Eric. "Don't hurt him, Mr. Marquand. I can tell you what you want to know."

Every eye in the place fixed on the boy.

"Go on," Eric said. "What do you know about this, son?"

"Well, you've all been calling them by the wrong name. Though you were pretty close." Eric frowned. Matt smiled a little, as if he thought it was funny. "They're not *drones*. They're *clones*."

Dwyer leapt to his feet. "How the hell do you—"

"Shut up, Dwyer," Mirabella said, and she shoved him in the chest, so he landed firmly back in the chair.

"The agency has been working on the...the project for more than twenty years," Matt said. "They managed to make the first few drones by taking some of the Chosen captive and doing that lobo—lobolomy thing on them."

"Lobotomy," his mother said.

"Yeah, that. And then they transformed them, and ended up with these really obedient and really strong Hulk guys. Then they tried it again with people who were just born big and strong and wound up with even stronger ones. And then they found some guys who'd used steroids—really big guys who made themselves even bigger—who also had that antigen thing but probably didn't know it. And they ended up with really big, really strong, really dumb guys. And those were the ones they cloned."

Eric hunkered down to the boy's eye level and clasped his shoulders. "How do you know all this, Matthias? Did you hear it from your father?"

"No. He doesn't know any of it."

"Then—"

"Eric," Ilyana interrupted. "I believe him. And we're

short on time, and to be honest, there are reasons this part of the discussion would be better set aside until later."

Eric eyed her. And then it hit him. The boy was psychic. Powerfully psychic, especially if he'd managed to read Dwyer, a man accustomed to blocking his thoughts. Then again, Dwyer probably wasn't as guarded around the boy as he would have been around the undead.

"All right," he said.

"They have hundreds of them, Eric," Matt said. "They keep them in some kind of military place. It looks like a cross between a prison and a hospital. They've got all ages of them there, even baby ones, and they just keep making more, all the time. And they keep them drugged until they need them. And then they transform them into vampires and send them off to whatever mission they have for them. Dad's drones are just an experiment. They've got way bigger plans in mind."

"I'll just bet they do," Mirabella said.

"Do you know where this military installation is?" Eric asked.

"No," Matt said. And then he looked at Dwyer. "But *he* does."

Headlights penetrated the windows as the van pulled to a stop outside. Eric nodded. "Let's go. We can deal with the rest of this later." He scooped Crisa up into his arms, then nodded to Mirabella. "Bring Dwyer. And don't let him get away from you."

"Oh, I won't. Don't you worry." She eyed Dwyer. "*Babies*," she said, disgusted.

"They're clones," Dwyer snapped, instantly defensive.

"They're human beings. You bastard." She jerked him up by one arm and took him with her out to the waiting van.

17

―◆―

"Gregor, I'm unblocking the door to this dungeon you have me in," Reaper said. "I won't keep you from coming in."

"Of course you won't," Gregor said. He'd turned off the closed-circuit television for the moment, so he could look down through the glass at Reaper.

"I'm serious. That's what you want, isn't it? To come in here and drain me? To take my power? It's yours. Come and get it."

"You're baiting me."

"I'm not. I give up."

"Why? What do you have to gain, Reaper? I'll take her, anyway, and kill her when I've finished. You know that, would know that even if I told you otherwise. So what do you gain by giving your power to me?"

Reaper stood just beneath the window to let Gregor see him, see the emotions on his face, and feel them emanating from his mind and his soul. "If you kill me first, at least I won't have to watch you…defile her. I can't go through that, Gregor. Show a little mercy."

Gregor opened his mouth, closed it again. "It would

be better, ravaging her while your blood is pounding through my veins. I'd be on a power high. Everything would be…intensified."

Reaper tried to block the image of Gregor forcing Briar to endure his attentions from his mind, but without much success.

And then Gregor said, "All right. I'm coming down. If you don't let me in instantly, Reaper, I'll go back upstairs and make sure I hurt her even more than I had already planned. Do you understand?"

"Yeah. I understand. Come on down. I'm waiting."

Reaper focused on the door and mentally made sure he was no longer blocking it from opening, not even a little. It had taken a supreme effort to keep the damn door closed before. And he hadn't even been certain he could make it work. Now he made sure his force was completely removed from it. Let Gregor come in. He would fight for his life, and for Briar's, and maybe he would lose. But he had to try.

Seth pulled the Mustang over to the side of the road a quarter mile from the former Marquand mansion, and killed the engine and headlights.

"We go in from separate directions," Jack said. "The only way to do this is slowly and patiently. We've got to find the drones and take them out one by one."

"While Reaper and Briar are in there going through God knows what?" Seth asked. "No way. It'll take too long. I say we just charge the place, take out as many as we can on the way and get inside fast."

"If we do that, we'll be trapped in that house, just like Reaper and Briar are," Topaz said softly. "We won't be any help to them if we get captured, as well, Seth."

"But they could be dead by the time we get in there!" Seth clenched his fists and looked out the window.

"They could be dead already, Seth," Jack said. "We need to take out the drones. The more the better. We can work quickly but carefully. We have to try not to miss any."

"I'm afraid he's right, Seth," Vixen said softly. "We have to find them, and then we can disable or…or kill them. And with every one we get rid of, we'll be that much closer to saving Reaper and Briar."

Seth closed his eyes. "I know it makes the most sense, I just…dammit, Reaper saved my life."

"He's saved all of our lives," Jack said. "Mine included. Believe me, I want to repay him for that as badly as you do. But we have to keep our heads about this."

"And we'll make better time if we split up," Topaz added.

"Oh, no. No way, I'm not agreeing to that." Seth clutched Vixen's hand and looked into her eyes. "We go in pairs. I'm damned if I'm going to risk losing you, too."

"On that we agree," Jack said, but he was looking at Topaz, not Seth, as he said it.

"Yeah," Topaz added. "I'm not letting Jack risk his pretty neck without me nearby to save it."

He made a face at her.

"What, you think you'll be the one saving *my* pretty neck?"

"Let's hope neither of our necks needs saving." Jack

kissed her quickly, then opened the car door to get out.
The others followed suit. Jack and Topaz, armed to the
teeth, moved to the west of the mansion's grounds, while
Seth and Vixen headed east. They blocked their thoughts,
guarding the essence of themselves to keep the drones
from sensing their presence, and began moving into the
woods in silence, ready and watching for the enemy.

Briar came back down the stairs to find herself alone
in the living room. Gregor was gone. Instantly, she
called out to Reaper.

Where are you?

*Distracting Gregor with an offer he couldn't refuse.
Get the hell out, Briar, before he comes back.*

I'm not leaving you. Tell me where you are.

Even as she sent out the thought, she began searching the room. She wasn't sure what for. Items she could
use as weapons? A clue to where Jack and Gregor might
be? A way out?

She went to the locked door and peered outside. A
drone was standing guard just beyond. Dammit. She left
the door lock engaged to keep him from coming inside,
then turned to scan the rest of the room more carefully.
And then she saw it. A glasslike window in the floor,
with darkness beyond it.

What is this? What is this glass panel in the floor?

Leave it alone and get the hell out, Briar.

She hurried to the panel and peered through it. At first
she saw nothing, and then her eyes adjusted. A cell, far
below. A darkened, concrete room that had to be even

beneath the basement. As she watched, Reaper came into view, walking backward, his eyes on something in front of him.

And then Gregor stepped into sight. "Well," he said, sounding surprised. "You kept your word and actually removed the power you'd exerted on the door to keep me from getting to you."

Briar blessed her heightened vampire senses for allowing her to hear the men's conversation, even if only faintly.

"I told you I would," Reaper replied

I can see you! And I'm not leaving, so tell me something, dammit. Anything that can help you!

Gregor lunged at Reaper, delivering a crushing blow to his jaw that sent him flying backward. But even though Reaper hit the wall, he refused to go down. He pushed off and went after Gregor, landing a punch to the side of his head, then another to his solar plexus. Gregor bent over double, clutching his middle.

"I knew you wouldn't keep your word. Fortunately, I came prepared." When Gregor straightened again, he had a weapon of some sort in his hands.

He jabbed it at Reaper, and Briar could sense the powerful shock it delivered. It made Reaper's body go rigid in pain.

He collapsed to the floor, quivering.

Get out, Briar, he thought at her. *Please…*

No. I'm going to find a way down there.

Gregor bent over him, gripped the front of his shirt.

There's a remote control. I think he keeps it on the mantle.

Briar scrambled for the device, located it and began pushing buttons. She was shocked when one of them caused the glass panel in the floor to slide slowly open.

Bending over Reaper, Gregor looked up, startled by the sound of the panel opening, but almost before he could have hoped to process what was happening, Briar tucked the remote down the front of the skimpy outfit she wore, and jumped into the chute, stilettos and all.

She hit Gregor hard, a full body impact that took him to the floor. "I'm done with you, you bastard," she growled, and then she kicked him in the chin. His head snapped back. He got his arms beneath him, scuttling backward like a crab, then lifting the stun gun he still held in one hand.

She kicked again and sent it flying. Then once more, the impact connecting with his jaw this time. And then she lowered her high-heeled shoe to his throat while he flailed beneath her.

"You deserve this. In fact, you deserve a hell of a lot more, but I want you to know I'm going to enjoy this, Gregor. I've been waiting a long time to kill you, you bastard." She lifted her foot, determined to slam it down again.

But he grabbed her ankle, flipping her off her feet. She landed on her back with an impact that stunned her. Gregor jumped up, even as Reaper got to his feet. The two men stood nose-to-nose. Then, quickly, Gregor looked upward, knowing he was outnumbered. Just as quickly, Briar read his intent in his eyes, yanked the remote from her breast, aimed upward and thumbed the button.

Even as Gregor leaped with every ounce of power he

possessed, the clear partition slid closed. He smashed into it and tumbled back down, landing hard.

Reaper went for him, but Briar gripped his shoulder, jerked him aside, raced forward and then lowered one pointy heel as hard as she could. It jabbed straight through Gregor's throat.

"Like I said," she told him, staring down at his gaping mouth and bugging eyes with a sense of power like nothing she'd ever felt before racing through her, "I'm done with you." She gave a twist before jerking the heel free.

He lay there, writhing and bleeding. He clutched at his neck in an effort to stop the flow, but it was no use. As the blood spread out across the concrete floor around her, Briar stepped lightly back, out of its way.

And then, as the light faded from Gregor's eyes for the last time ever, Briar turned to Reaper. He stared at her, and she at him. And when he opened his mouth to speak, she put her finger over his lips and shook her head.

"You're about to rub it in, aren't you? You're going to say you knew all along I was capable of caring about someone besides myself. You're going to say I've proven it by risking my ass to save Crisa and then the kid, and now you. You're going to say you were right all along. And then you're going to tell me that you have to leave. To go find Miss Sunnybrook Farm, who turned out not to be so sunny after all. That you have to finish that before you can—"

He clasped her hand and moved it away from his mouth. "You don't know shit about what I'm going to tell you, Briar."

320 *Maggie Shayne*

Then he jerked her close, and he kissed her. And she swore her heart melted right inside her chest then, because that was what it felt like. He fed from her mouth as if he were starving for her taste, and he held her so close to him that every curve and line of her body melded to his.

When he finally lifted his head, he said, "I'm going to say that I'm really glad you turned out to have a heart in there after all, because it would be hell if I were in love with a woman who didn't."

She blinked, almost dizzy, completely confused. "In love?"

"I love you. You crazy, vengeful, relentless, stubborn, badass bitch, I love you to hell and back."

Her lips widened into a smile. A huge smile, and then a laugh bubbled up from somewhere deep inside her. When she could finally speak again, she said, "You moping loner of a killing machine, I love you, too. At least, I guess that's what this feeling is that's damn near splitting my chest open trying to get out."

"Yeah, I think that's what it is."

"So shall we get out of here, then?"

"Good idea. Nice outfit, by the way."

"Thanks. It was a gift. I'm thinking of keeping it, actually." She stretched a leg, pointed her toe and looked at her foot thoughtfully. "I'm growing particularly fond of the shoes."

"Me, too."

She pointed the remote at the glass above them, ready to thumb the button to open it so they could leap to freedom.

"Briar," Reaper said. "Hon, the cell door is unlocked."

She met his eyes, relished the teasing light in them. "Oh." She linked arms with him, and they walked out the door, then climbed the ladder that led up into the basement.

As they emerged, Reaper looked around, and saw the lab and the empty gurney. "How is Crisa doing?" he asked, his tone no longer playful.

"I don't know. I got her the hell out of here, along with Eric and the kid. Dwyer, too, once I got the information I needed from him."

"About my—former wife?"

"Yeah. And about your trigger words. The second one. We know it now. We also know the name of the asshole who programmed you for the CIA, and once we track him down, he can damn well undo what he did to your head or suffer the consequences."

"Hell. You really are useful to have around, you know that?"

They located the stairs and headed up them, emerging into the main part of the house just as the front door crashed open and four of their heroic sidekicks burst in, looking as if they were expecting to face down a pack of rabid grizzlies.

They looked around the room, weapons drawn, spotted Reaper and Briar, and then relaxed visibly, though they kept their tranq guns aimed.

"Where's Gregor?" Jack demanded.

"Dead," Reaper said. "He had a painful run-in with a stiletto heel."

Jack looked at the shoes Briar was wearing, then let

his gaze slide slowly upward until he met her eyes, brows raised.

"How is Crisa?" she asked.

"Uh...they were operating on her head when we left. Eric just contacted us mentally to say they got the chip out, but she hasn't regained consciousness. We still don't know anything for sure."

"Probably won't until sundown," Vixen said. "Maybe the day sleep will speed up the healing."

"We hope." Seth pocketed his gun.

"Won't you need that for the drones?" Reaper asked.

"What drones?" Seth sent him a wink. "Come on, daylight's not far off. Eric's found us a place to hole up for the day."

"Thank God for that," Briar said. "I'm beat."

"After you," Jack said, holding the door open. And as she and Reaper passed, he added, "Love the outfit, hon."

She shrugged. "It has its uses."

Reaper sent a scowl over his shoulder, and Jack quickly held up both hands. "Don't kill me, okay? I was just teasing her." Then he looked at Topaz. "*You* know that, right?"

She twisted his earlobe, even while she kissed his cheek. "Of course I do. Just don't let it happen again."

Reaper and Briar stepped outside, and the others followed, then took the lead. Briar watched them go. Seth, with his arm around Vixen's shoulders, holding her close to his side as they walked in lockstep. Jack and Topaz, arms linked around one another's waists, every part of them touching as they moved.

And then, like an answer to a prayer she'd never been aware of uttering, Reaper wrapped his arm around her shoulders. Smiling, she decided she liked it, and she slid her own arm around his waist and walked very close to his side.

"It's good, having somebody all your own, isn't it?" he asked.

"I could get used to it," she told him. In fact, she could hardly wait to get started on that little project. She lifted her head. "You did this, you know."

"Did what?"

She just smiled mysteriously, leaned against him and kept on walking.

Epilogue

─►──

They spent the night in an empty barn on the edge of town. It was one Eric had known about when he'd lived in Byram years ago, and he'd expressed relief to see it still standing.

Reaper spent the night with Briar in his arms, and he thought he had never felt such a sense of completion. Or of love.

They'd handcuffed Dwyer's right wrist to a beam, leaving food and water nearby just to be decent. They hadn't quite finished with him yet, and they didn't dare let him go, knowing he couldn't be trusted not to return with reinforcements to take them all out. Or take them in. No one was sure anymore whose side the man was on in all this.

As the sun went down, they stirred awake, one by one. And one by one, they gathered around Crisa where she lay, still unmoving.

Dwyer, tethered to a beam like a dog on a leash, thrust a slip of scrap paper into Reaper's hand.

"What's this?" Reaper asked.

"The name and last known address of the shrink who

tinkered with your mind. He always said he could reverse the process, the programming. How you choose to make him do it is your business. I gave it to Eric, and now I've given it to you." He glanced at the others around him. "And now that I've kept my promise, I would really appreciate it if you would let me go."

Reaper nodded. "I'd like to know one more thing before I do."

Dwyer sighed. "I told the others, I don't know the location of the installation where the cloning takes place. I did once. But it's been moved. They move it regularly, and no one who knows where it is one year is informed where it is the next. And that's the truth."

Reaper glanced at the others. "Cloning?"

"We'll fill you in later," Eric told him.

Reaper nodded and returned his attention to Dwyer.

"He wants to know about his wife," Briar said. "About Rebecca. I told him how she wasn't really dead. How it was a setup to establish her cover and load him down in enough guilt to keep him dancing to your fiddler for years to come. He probably wants to know where she is now."

Reaper looked down at her. She was standing close to him, so close, but not touching. He saw the fear in her beautiful dark eyes, and he understood it.

"I don't particularly care where she is right now," he said softly. "She let me think I had murdered her. What I was wondering was whether she was working for you all along. Whether our marriage was just the first step in the plan to recruit me."

Dwyer nodded. "It was. We knew you were one of the Chosen. We knew you had a powerful bloodline and few mortal connections. We wanted a vampire we could program and train as an assassin. She was already working for us, so she took on the job of bringing you in and helping us to keep you under control."

Reaper nodded slowly. "And now it all makes sense," he said. Then he turned to the others. "Is there anything else we need from him?"

Eric shook his head. The others concurred, so Reaper released Dwyer and waved an arm toward the barn door. "You're free to go. And, uh, just so you know, Gregor's dead, and so are all the drones who were on the premises."

Dwyer held Reaper's gaze for a long moment. Finally he lowered his head. "I'm sorry. I know it's not worth much, but you became more than a project to me over time. I've spent a lot of hours regretting what was done to you." He swallowed hard, then began again.

"I'm not asking your forgiveness. I just...I needed to tell you I'm sorry."

Reaper nodded. "Goodbye, Dwyer."

Nodding, Derrick Dwyer turned and walked slowly out of the barn.

Briar sidled up closer to Reaper, and slid her arm around his waist, which gave him an instant sense of ease and relief.

"Bri? Briar? Are you here?"

Crisa's soft voice brought them both around, and then Briar pulled free of Reaper and raced forward, dropping to her knees in the hay where Crisa lay. Her eyes were open, Reaper saw as he crouched down beside his woman. Crisa was blinking them all into focus and smiling a little crookedly.

"That's funny," she said. "My head doesn't hurt anymore."

Around her, every face split in a relieved smile. And then Matt crowded past them all and hugged her hard, even as she struggled to sit up. She hugged him back and ran a hand through his hair. "Hey, kiddo. I told you we'd all be okay." And then she looked past him, finding Ilyana with her eyes. "I really love your son," she said.

The others gathered around Crisa, helping her to her feet, all of them talking at once. As they did, Reaper tugged Briar just slightly away from the rest, folded her into his arms and hugged her close.

She rested her head on his chest.

"What did you mean before?" he asked her. "Just as we were leaving the Marquand Estate you said I did all this?"

She pressed even closer, held him even tighter. "You dragged me kicking and screaming into your little scout troop. You kept me around the bunch of them until they started getting under my skin. You treated me like I was…like I mattered. Like you cared. And you didn't lie, you didn't use me, not once. I was forced to watch you risking your neck for that crew of misfits until I started caring, too. You made me share blood with Crisa or watch her die, and then I loved the little nutcase."

She closed her eyes, swallowed hard. "And then I loved you. It's like you showed me how to be…real.

More than just the shell of a living thing I'd been before. And it feels good, Reaper. It feels really, really good."

She sniffled and lowered her head.

"Then why are you crying?" he asked.

She shrugged. "You brought me back to life, and I don't know how I'm ever going to thank you for that. I was dead inside, are you getting that? Dead inside. And you came along and you just—"

"It's mutual. You know that, right? I wasn't far from dead inside myself."

She lifted her head. He lowered his. And just before their lips met, he said, "But if you insist on sticking around and trying to repay me, I have to warn you, it's gonna take a long, long time."

"No problem. Because I plan to *be* around for a long, long time. So that works out perfectly."

"I love you, Briar."

She blinked away fresh tears. "You know, a lot of men have said that to me. But you're the very first one who wasn't lying. You mean it. And I know that, and I don't doubt it, despite how many times it's been untrue. And I love you for that as much as for anything else."

And then their lips met, and Reaper could feel what she felt just then. Briar felt true, pure happiness glowing from within her for the first time in her life.

It was a glow Reaper intended to nurture and keep alight for as long as he lived.

An enthralling new legal thriller by

JOSEPH TELLER

Criminal defense attorney Harrison J. Walker, aka Jaywalker,
has just been suspended for receiving "gratitude" in the
courtroom stairwell from a client charged with prostitution.
Convincing the judge that his other clients are counting on
him, Jaywalker is allowed to complete ten cases. But it's the
last case that truly tests his abilities....

Samara Moss stabbed her husband. Or so everyone believes.
Having married the billionaire when she was an 18-year-old
prostitute, Samara appears to be a gold digger. But Jaywalker
knows all too well that appearances can be deceiving.
Has Samara been framed? Or is Jaywalker just driven by
his need to win his clients' cases?

THE
TENTH
CASE

*Available the first week of October 2008
wherever paperbacks are sold!*

MIRA®

MJT2605

MIRA®

A spellbinding thriller
by international bestselling author

M.J. ROSE

A bomb in Rome, a flash of bluish-white light,
and photojournalist Josh Ryder's world exploded.
From that instant nothing would ever be the same.

As Josh recovers, his mind is increasingly invaded with thoughts
that have the emotion, the intensity, the *intimacy* of memories.
But they are not his memories. They are ancient...and violent.

Desperate for answers, Josh turns to the world-renowned Phoenix
Foundation—a research facility that documents cases of past life
experiences. His findings there lead him to an ancient tomb—a
tomb with a powerful secret that threatens to merge the past with
the present. Here, the dead call out to the living, and murders of
the past become murders of the present.

THE
REINCARNATIONIST

"A triumph!"
–David J. Montgomery, *Chicago Sun-Times*
& *Philadelphia Inquirer* reviewer

Available the first week of October 2008 wherever books are sold!

www.MIRABooks.com

MMJR2576

Silhouette

nocturne™

NEW YORK TIMES BESTSELLING AUTHOR

SHARON SALA

JANIS REAMES HUDSON
DEBRA COWAN

AFTERSHOCK

Three women are brought to the brink of death...
only to discover the aftershock of their trauma has
left them with unexpected and unwelcome gifts of
paranormal powers. Now each woman must learn to
accept her newfound abilities while fighting for life,
love and second chances....

Available October wherever books are sold.

www.eHarlequin.com
www.paranormalromanceblog.wordpress.com

SN61796

REQUEST YOUR FREE BOOKS!

2 FREE NOVELS
FROM THE ROMANCE/SUSPENSE
COLLECTION PLUS 2 FREE GIFTS!

YES! Please send me 2 FREE novels from the Romance/Suspense Collection and my 2 FREE gifts (gifts are worth about $10). After receiving them, if I don't wish to receive any more books, I can return the shipping statement marked "cancel." If I don't cancel, I will receive 4 brand new novels every month and be billed just $5.49 per book in the U.S. or $5.99 per book in Canada, plus 25¢ shipping and handling per book plus applicable taxes, if any*. That's a savings of at least 20% off the cover price! I understand that accepting the 2 free books and gifts places me under no obligation to buy anything. I can always return a shipment and cancel at any time. Even if I never buy another book from the Reader Service, the two free books and gifts are mine to keep forever

185 MDN EF5Y   385 MDN EF6C

Name _____ (PLEASE PRINT)

Address _____ Apt. #

City _____ State/Prov. _____ Zip/Postal Code

Signature (if under 18, a parent or guardian must sign)

Mail to The Reader Service:
IN U.S.A.: P.O. Box 1867, Buffalo, NY 14240-1867
IN CANADA: P.O. Box 609, Fort Erie, Ontario L2A 5X3

Not valid to current subscribers to the Romance Collection,
the Suspense Collection or the Romance/Suspense Collection.

Want to try two free books from another line?
Call 1-800-873-8635 or visit www.morefreebooks.com.

* Terms and prices subject to change without notice. N.Y. residents add applicable sales tax. Canadian residents will be charged applicable provincial taxes and GST. Offer not valid in Quebec. This offer is limited to one order per household. All orders subject to approval. Credit or debit balances in a customer's account(s) may be offset by any other outstanding balance owed by or to the customer. Please allow 4 to 6 weeks for delivery. Offer available while quantities last.

Your Privacy: Harlequin is committed to protecting your privacy. Our Privacy Policy is available online at www.eHarlequin.com or upon request from the Reader Service. From time to time we make our lists of customers available to reputable third parties who may have a product or service of interest to you. If you would prefer we not share your name and address, please check here. ☐

BOB08R

MAGGIE SHAYNE

32243	THICKER THAN WATER	___ $5.99 U.S.	___ $6.99 CAN.
32266	TWO BY TWILIGHT	___ $5.99 U.S.	___ $6.99 CAN.
32518	LOVER'S BITE	___ $7.99 U.S.	___ $7.99 CAN.
32497	DEMON'S KISS	___ $7.99 U.S.	___ $9.50 CAN.
32279	PRINCE OF TWILIGHT	___ $6.99 U.S.	___ $8.50 CAN.
20944	COLDER THAN ICE	___ $6.99 U.S.	___ $8.50 CAN.
32229	DARKER THAN MIDNIGHT	___ $6.99 U.S.	___ $8.50 CAN.

(limited quantities available)

TOTAL AMOUNT	$ _____
POSTAGE & HANDLING	$ _____
($1.00 FOR 1 BOOK, 50¢ for each additional)	
APPLICABLE TAXES*	$ _____
TOTAL PAYABLE	$ _____

(check or money order—please do not send cash)

To order, complete this form and send it, along with a check or money order for the total above, payable to MIRA Books, to: **In the U.S.:** 3010 Walden Avenue, P.O. Box 9077, Buffalo, NY 14269-9077; **In Canada:** P.O. Box 636, Fort Erie, Ontario, L2A 5X3.

Name: _____
Address: _____ City: _____
State/Prov.: _____ Zip/Postal Code: _____
Account Number (if applicable): _____

075 CSAS

*New York residents remit applicable sales taxes.
*Canadian residents remit applicable GST and provincial taxes.

MIRA®

www.MIRABooks.com

MMS1008BL